MAURA LAVERTY (1907–1966)

was born in Rathangan, County Kildare, the second of nine surviving children of Michael Kelly, a farmer and a gambler. Her mother, Mary Ann, took up dressmaking to support the family when they ran into financial difficulties. Maura Laverty went to the Brigidine Convent in Tullow, from where at seventeen she went to Spain as a governess. After four months, however, she taught herself a form of shorthand and typing and became private secretary to Prince Bibesco, husband of Princess Bibesco, the writer. Later she worked for the Banco de Bilbao and wrote for the Madrid newspaper *El Debate*.

She became engaged to a Hungarian and returned to Ireland to say goodbye to her family. Here she met James Laverty a journalist with whom she had corresponded when in Spain. Within three days they were married and she returned to Spain to tell her Hungarian fiancé. Afterwards she lived in Dublin with her two daughters and a son.

Maura Laverty had always written: articles, short stories, translations from Spanish etc., but her first novel *Never No More* was published to great acclaim in 1942. This was followed by *Alone We Embark* (1943); *No More Than Human* (1944); and *Lift Up Your Gates* (1946). Each of these novels was banned in Ireland until the 1960s. She also wrote two children's books, *Cottage in the Bog* (1945) and *Green Orchard* (1949), and two cookery books for which she was renowned in Ireland, *Kind Cooking* (1950) and *Feasting Galore* (1961). She continued to contribute to newspapers, including the *Sunday Empire News* (an English newspaper which was also banned in Ireland). In the 1950s Maura Laverty began writing plays, which were well-received. The first of these was a dramatisation of *Lift Up Your Gates*, called *Liffey Lane*, followed by *Tolka Row* and *The Tree in the Crescent*. During the 1960s she wrote a weekly TV programme called *Tolka Row*, which ran for some years, and she also contributed to a weekly radio programme.

Maura Laverty died of a heart attack at the age of 58.

Virago will publish the sequel to *Never No More*, *No More Than Human*, in 1986.

VIRAGO
MODERN
CLASSIC
NUMBER
169

To

THRUSH, MY BROTHER
who has always been the
buttermilk for my soda-bread

Published by VIRAGO PRESS Limited 1985
41 William IV Street, London WC2N 4DB

First published in Great Britain by Longmans 1942

Copyright © Maura Laverty 1942
Introduction Copyright © Maeve Binchy 1985

British Library Cataloguing in Publication Data

Laverty, Maura
    Never no more.
    I. Title
    813'.52[F]   PS3562.A84/
    ISBN   0-86068-484-9

Printed and bound in Great Britain
by Anchor Brendon Ltd at Tiptree, Essex

PREFACE

THIS is the story of a young girl's life in a little lost village on the edge of the great Bog of Allen. For me the book was a case of love at first sight, and I cannot imagine that it will not win the same immediate affection everywhere. May I tell how, first and last, it appealed to me? Three chapters of the book came to me quite casually as editor of a monthly magazine — a dismaying chunk in the middle of the usual weekly pile of manuscripts. I had not read three pages before I surrendered. A little later I read half the completed book and begged the author to publish. Then other things intervened, and though I never forgot the pleasure of that first reading, I began to get a little timid about my early enthusiasm. I was afraid that all I should be able to say in this preface would be that I had fallen for the book completely. "Afraid" — because a critic, like every mortal, must always be cautious when he falls in love as much as I with *Never No More*. Could the source of my pleasure really be as charming as all that? Perhaps my delight was the result of a mere association of ideas; because I, also, had spent some of the happiest days of my childhood beside this Liffey at Newbridge, and on that great Curragh of Kildare, or wandering on the same lonely, purpled Bog of Allen, and along the same silent fronded canal by Monasterevan? In short, was it all subjective and had I been deceived into thinking that it was described vividly merely because I was remembering vividly? I went so far as to dread that no other reader would feel the thing as I feel it and that there was no literary quality in the book at all. So, when the proofs

v

came along I promised myself to take them with a cold eye; this time there would be no willing suspension of disbelief, I would be cynical, I would watch every line, I would put myself into the position of the most casual reader from Timbuctoo.

It has made no difference. Be as critical as you like about this book, its charm is irresistible and lasting. In fact I believe that every reader will admit finally what must be a rare thing to admit about any book, that it is delightful even in its faults, and often delightful because of them. For *Never No More* is all of a piece; it is all the things that the romantic heart would wish a young girl to be and have. It has beauty, nostalgia, sentimentality (it drips with it); it has wisdom, folly, heartache, excess, generosity; and one need not even wish that this life were more fastidious, or without its rural crudities, or its rural gall — and how acid these countryfolk can be! — since the child gave to it all her innocence and lost none. It is charming even where it is priggish or minxish as when, after a whopping piece of hyperbole (no Irish fabrication of that order can ever be called a *lie* — she has merely said that a child ate the whole side of a wall!), she pronounces that "I fear I am sometimes given a little to exaggeration." When it is ingenuous, and it often is, one can only chuckle; though it is sometimes so artless and defenceless as to hurt unbearably, even as this child was hurt by her own bitter hatred for Sister Liguori who "wept when I went away," or by her unfortunate awkwardness with her mother, or by her too-great love for her Gran. It is even of a piece that the narrative should be as garrulous and as meandering as a village gossip so that any story is liable to be deflected by three intervening stories, or to begin in the best gossip style on such lines as: "Nellie's father Jim was married to Granny's only daughter and was often visited by her sister-in-law, a widow with a grown-up daughter over in Newbridge. When Nell died, etc. . . Now we had an old retired Excise officer who, etc. . ." Above all, its excessive feeling is right and true, one might almost say that it is in proportion for being in excess, because that life in that tiny village hidden away on the bogland was a superabundant life, and when if not in youth is the right time for tumbling heart over heels? But if some should find these things faults there is, in any case, the ample compensation of Maura Laverty's great natural gift of making things rise stereoscopically from the flat page, and — rare, very rare in a book of this kind — the gift of candour. In a sentence, Maura Laverty has a remembering eye keen enough and a heart warm enough to have plenty to tell that we enjoy hearing, and the skill to tell it well.

With an eye and a heart a writer has half the battle won. Give the happy subject and you may almost call it a day. The subject here is happy enough — a young, sensitive girl, delighted to be left all alone with a wise and kindly grandmother, in a comfortable ordered home in the most remote countryside, surrounded by a village life as stable and as lively as a tradition, as untouched by time as if we were back in the Dorsetshire of Hardy — though the date is the nineteen twenties! One may measure the strength of that isolation by remembering that only a few miles away were the two great adventures of Racing and War, on the Curragh racecourse and in the great red brick military camp across the plain, with their magnificent alluring jumble out of the modern world's Aladdin's cave, of lashing of money, endless rounds of parties, sport galore,

polo, tennis, golf, races, the hunt, servants, batmen, motor-
cars, silver, scandals by the ton, balls up in Dublin, foreign
fields of sport and bloodshed, and behind it all flags and
drums and glory and death and medals and kings . . . a
life linked by every sort of victory and disaster with the
great glittering world. Indifferent to it all, touched by it
only when somebody felt the lure of the gamble, or when
a recruiting sergeant walked hopefully into the village, or
when a raucous holiday crowd from Kildare offended by
their manners, this little life of Ballyderrig went its way.
A girl's first dance, her first kiss, an old maid's hopeless
love, a child's death, rouse here the swiftest pulse of life,
and — fortunate girl — offer it to this child at her most
impressionable age to touch intimately, to remember for
ever. She first felt life where it was without qualification,
and being without comparison, apparently incomparable
and absolute! What good fortune! What *fortune* since
what riches! How much richer than that glittering life
those few miles away where everything, as in every sophis-
ticated society, is pared away with friction with something
else. And did she lose anything? Learning? A library?
Fun? Culture? That amazingly elaborate cookery of
Gran was alone a compendium of rural civilisation. The
mere village nicknames are a string of saga, from the Long
Doherties whose immense strides made Granny say that
all those Doherties "are split to the shoulders," to Britches
Healy whose first garment was a one-piece suit made by
gathering a cast-off riding breeches about the child's neck
and cutting away the pockets for armholes. Every character was matter enough for a novel, certainly a short
story; such as Mrs. Timson-Ling who had her "late" husband prayed for in church to conceal the fact that he had

not died in London but deserted her. Oh, the subject is rich enough, and the fact that it was all so isolated suggests that they all subconsciously knew it and, like some rich recluse, were wise enough to remain independent.

The fact is, if Maura Laverty does not follow up this first book with a set of novels about the crowded world of her childhood she is simply throwing away a store of wealth that any writer will envy from the bottom of his heart. But if she does write these novels, and can make them as happy and as sad and as real as *Never No More* she may well make a fortune, and I dare predict for her that she will certainly make a name.

SEAN O'FAOLAIN

(From the first British edition, 1942)

AUTHOR'S NOTE

Some time ago, a copy of *Irish Country Recipes*,* compiled by Florence Irwin, fell into my hands. Brawn, white pudding, boxty-on-the-pan — as I read of these familiar dishes I found myself back in Derrymore again, standing in the buttery with Gran, helping her to prepare her lovely meals. These memories led to others: of dishes that belonged to Gran alone, ash cakes, mushrooms with clotted cream, baked hare and the rest, and, inevitably, to memories of the people associated with these things. Gradually, my memories grew into *Never No More*, and I offer my grateful thanks to Florence Irwin who, in bringing back so vividly the scenes and people and incidents recorded in this book, forced me to write it.

M. L.

* Published by The Northern Whig, Ltd., Belfast.

INTRODUCTION

Maura Laverty was a food pornographer, her pages are full of spicy vapours which would cajole a dying man to eat, luscious pools of butter on speckled surfaces of seed cake, potato apple cakes oozing with sugar and butter. She is sensual and specific and utterly convincing, and she is not even writing a cookery book.

Never No More is Maura Laverty's first and possibly most famous novel, it was published in 1942 and had an immediate success. Its acclaim was never literary. People were more or less bowled over by the force and strength of the country characters and incidents and cookery all thrown up with an astonishing exuberance. There was a huge over excitement about it that steamrollered people into approval. And it was only later when the characters and their amazingly intense village life remained always fresh in the memory that people began to realise Maura Laverty had much more than a girlish enthusiasm. She had the power to paint the stage and the scenery, put in the characters and make the whole thing stick. Delia Scully, the excitable thirteen year old, and her beloved Gran, "a withered little apple of a woman", are never forgotten. They have the dreamy quality of perfect love and total understanding, but they are so firmly rooted in their Irish landscape of the 1920s that they are much more than mere wish fulfilment. They are as real as the stony crooked roads they walked and the great monstrously sensual food that they cooked and ate.

Maura Laverty was the right one to get into big all-embracing novels like this one because she had all the qualifications. She knew what it was like to be very poor, then comfortably off, then very poor again. She knew small-town Ireland and yet she also knew the world, she worked on the Madrid newspaper *El Debate* and at another period of her life on the *Sunday Empire News*, an English newspaper which was often banned in her native Ireland. But then so was Maura Laverty banned at home, which is now considered to be a seal of approval and a badge of merit but then had undertones of Sin. In her own highly cluttered life she had time for adventurous periods, daredevil innocent romances, heart breaking, sensible settling down, and marriage, motherhood, and was an Agony Aunt on Irish radio. She had all the qualifications to write big rich novels crowded with character and incident, but punctuated with detail and pauses of recipes. She can never mention what they had for dinner without describing how it was made, lardy cakes or flummery made from oatenmeal, jelly and whipped cream. The story should carry a government health warning.

She wasn't born to great comfort even though her father was what was called a gentleman farmer. His name was Michael Kelly, he was aged fifty-seven when he married and began his role as family man, fathering thirteen children. Maura was the second child, born in 1907. The family lived on an estate of 200 acres, which should have been fine for Michael and Mary Ann Kelly and the nine of their thirteen who survived; but the elderly father was a gambler, and it wasn't long before the style to which they thought they might all be accustomed ran out. Mary Ann Kelly became a dressmaker to support the family, the old man died not hugely regretted and young Maura was sent off to a convent boarding school with the hope that they would make a teacher out of her. She didn't find the convent life to her liking, and never studied hard enough to make the great leap to teaching. Her heart was at home in her Co. Kildare village on the edge of the Bog of Allen, the wet central plain of Ireland, not nearly as dramatic as the Atlantic coast, not spectacular like the mountainous Kerry, not haunting like the lands that the River Shannon runs through, but greatly greatly loved by the bright young girl with the soft heart and the sharp eyes pining for the clustered confused hometown scene from the convent class-room. So far so good, *Never No More* must be a straight autobiography you will think. Delia Scully is young Maura Kelly as she was then, it's all the same except that with generosity of spirit she doesn't dwell on her gambling wastrel father. But in fact there is another huge difference. Delia Scully lives with Gran, she loves her Gran with a loyalty that is pugnacious, she will get her little fists up to defend her Gran's pot-pourri and claim that nobody in the world could equal it even though it has never been suggested otherwise. In real life there was no Gran. Well there WAS a Gran but she didn't live with her eager little granddaughter making boxty cakes and taking her by the hand to pick the early morning mushrooms. No, the real Gran had a dressmaking establishment in the town of Kildare and that was where her heart lay rather than in the eager little minds of the grandchildren who must have wanted more.

But the young Maura must have wanted a grandmother like that so much that she created her with the love and care she might have given to the very delicate embroidery that she did for a child's layette, embroidery never seen since it was put on the stillborn child for burial. Gran was carved out so well that she exists now anyway. She was given no real vices, an occasional hasty turn of speech, sometimes a little impatience based on her own excellence and a wish that others could be of like mind. But it's Gran who encourages the restless Delia to keep to her books, it's Gran who tells her in somewhat overblown symbolism the facts of life ... yet flowery or not Gran's explanation would have been streets ahead of anyone else's at that time or place. It's a bit of a disappointment to know that there wasn't a Gran like this, but maybe she was the one we all wanted, someone who could deliver the tinker's baby, look after the town tart and lend her candle-sticks and a crucifix when she had to bury her crippled child. A Gran who could supervise the killing of a pig and all the ritual that went with it, not to mention the unbearably attractive recipes that she knew for every part of the animal. A Gran who could wipe away your guilt about not loving your immediate family more, a Gran who told you that you looked like the Queen of Sheba as you were going to your first dance. No wonder that Gran's death is a howl of pain for the writer who created her and a sense of rage for the rest of us.

But the real Maura, who must have been very like the book's Delia, is no disappointment. As a child she struggled with little poems which she sent to religious magazines, and they won prizes. Even in the early 1950s we did that, there was an endless market in the various Missionary Annals and pious publications. Their editors were delighted to hear from the young Faithful and the nuns at school were always proud to see a pupil appearing so gloriously in print. For the young writer it was a confusing experience. I remember the combination of pride and shame when a religious poem I wrote at the age of ten was published in a magazine called *The Pylon*: bursting with pride that I was getting a lot of notice, wincing with shame seeing the looks of scorn from those who were more into rounders than religious mania.

And at an earlier time the young Maura saw the religious

press as her chance to get into print. She tells in *Never No More* of how Delia wrote a poem for the *Irish Monthly* and it was published. At her stern convent school this brought great credit on the rebellious pupil and when Mother Superior read it out the religious community were so delighted that they would come and shake her hand in congratulation. The young Delia said she got no money for the poem from the *Irish Monthly* and this made her think it mustn't be a very good poem. Because in earlier life while living back with Gran, Delia had earned the unbelievable sum of half a guinea, a whole ten shillings and sixpence for a poem printed in the Poets Corner of a Dublin newspaper. She gives the full and sentimental text of the Flight into Egypt, a sudden rush of pity for St Joseph having to leave all his unfinished carpentry behind him when he had to take Mary and the Child Jesus and flee from persecution. Why did she say she couldn't remember the other poem, the one that was read to the school? Was it so embarrassing that there would be more wincing than beaming with pride? Hardly. Maura Laverty's strength is her refusal to examine everything with a mental checklist, trying to spot sentimentality. In the text she talks of the honour of having the poem read to the whole school and adds "I forget now how it went."

Not long ago when *Never No More* was being read on RTE (the Irish Radio Service) the actress who was reading it suddenly remembered as a child copying out a poem from the *Irish Monthly*, a poem about what would happen if Jesus had the good fortune to be born in Kildare near the Bog of Allen instead of where He did arrive. This is the poem that the real-life Maura wrote.

> At times when I think of the place where you grew
> I think it a pity that you only knew
> Queer looking trees and the pathways of sand
> The dry hills and fields of that strange foreign land,'
> With never a bog hole to dabble your feet
> And never a taste of the blackberry sweet.
> The sport that we'd have were you with us again
> And choose for your birthplace a cottage in Clane!
>
> It's jumping a bog hole or fishing for eels,
> Or getting a ride on the top of the creels,
> Or out picking mushrooms together we'd be

> And eating the griddle bread hot for our tea!
> I'd show you the nest I found down by the mill
> Where the mother bird hatches so happy and still.
> I'd make you a whistle from tough greeny reeds
> And show you the hole where the water rat feeds.
>
> Ah little Lord Jesus, were you born again,
> Would you choose for your birthplace an acre of Clane?

It has a lot of the familiar themes of good food like blackberries, fresh gathered mushrooms and hot griddle bread, enough surely to woo the Lord to that part of the globe were He to come again.

Even though we know there will be no more Gran because *Never No More* ends at her funeral, there is a hope that young Delia Scully hasn't entirely disappeared, and indeed her story is taken up in *No More Than Human* which was published two years later in 1944. This takes up Delia's story and also the lifestory of Maura Laverty herself, and this time according to those who knew her, it's entirely true. There are no imaginary grandmothers but instead a whole world just as richly filled with Irish governesses drinking chocolate and eating *churros* on the Gran Via in Madrid. Maura followed a course quite familiar to Irish girls of her age and background—but almost unheard of in England, she went as a matter of course to be a governess in a Spanish family. The link was obvious. A young Irish girl might be allowed to Spain without overpowering danger of her losing her faith. After all Spain was dripping with cathedrals, and statues and saints and cardinals, it would be nearly BETTER than home. And as for the Spanish Señoras, also terrified that their young might rub up against some dangerous atheism or agnosticism, what better than to have an Irish governess who wouldn't let any of the wrong stuff into the schoolroom?

Maura was too spirited to put up with servitude for long, a governess in a Spanish home was rated in some kind of pecking order not by her own achievements but on the strength of the wealth or nobility of the family where she worked. If you worked for titled folk you got even more house points although your life and duties might be restricted and irrelevant. Anyway it was all far too constricting for the young Maura and she did a sort of secretarial training which got her a job as private secretary to Prince Bibesco and then allowed her to slide away from that role which still smacked of service towards the Banco de Bilbao and then even better the Madrid daily newspaper *El Debate*.

And her life was not only bounded by work: she fell in love with a Hungarian, called Peter, she got engaged to him and her life looked set to go in one direction, but she explained that she had to go back to Ireland first and say goodbye to everyone before they married. That's fine thought Peter, wrongly as it turned out. As soon as she was back in Ireland Maura Kelly met James Laverty a journalist who had been a pen friend during her time in Spain; his letters had meant a lot to her during her loneliest days, and when she met him those letters served as an excellent introduction, cemented their friendship and began their love. After a mere two days they decided to marry, and Maura had to turn round and go back to Spain to explain the new situation to Peter who was waiting eagerly for her return. It was no use Peter hoping that she would change her mind again. By the time she got back to Spain, Maura was now Mrs Laverty.

It was just as well that she had begun to earn her own living from writing because the fortunes of her husband were almost as varied as those of her father. He had his high financial period when he ran an agency for the Irish Sweepstake and therefore received a tiny percentage on each of the massive number of tickets he sold for the greatest lottery in the world. But the coming of the war changed all this and the Lavertys moved from comfortable Dublin middle-class living to housing that Maura considered slum accommodation.

She now had three children, two girls and a boy, and she began to support the family through her writings, but she did not know as yet where her real popularity lay. It was only when reading an old cookery book that she remembered the smells and ingredients of her young and carefree days, and she decided to write about them. She gave Delia some of the courage and attributes that she would LIKE to have had herself, and as we know she also changed radically the role of her grandmother. As a hankering for happier times, as a nostalgia and an exercise in describing the everyday life of a village already changing in the two decades since she had left it, she sat and wrote *Never No More* and nobody could have prepared her for the success it had. In

America it was fêted and she could hardly believe what she read in the *New York Times*: "This is a book written as only one of Irish blood could write it, breathing a civilisation that has never succumbed to industrial strain or to over exigencies of modernity." So the Americans liked it because it told of a dream Ireland in terms that they could see were real and far from the shamrockery they had been accustomed to when anyone described the Old Country. Then the great Sean O'Faolain, the prince of Irish storytellers, set his seal on it by a glowing preface where he said that he first feared he might be in love with the book because he was in love with that part of Ireland, the villages of Kildare, the purple Bog of Allen, the same canals and windy bits of the River Liffey where the story unfolds. But then he realised that this was not so: he had deliberately put himself in the position of a stranger to the neighbourhood and he felt that the book worked just as well. "Be as critical as you like about this book," he wrote, "Its charm is irresistible and lasting."

And there was more praise still from an even more unexpected quarter. Brendan Behan wrote to her from Cell 26 of Arbour Hill Military Prison in Dublin where he was serving a sentence in the Republican Prisoners Block. Apparently they were all enthusiastic readers, and subscribed to journals like the *New Statesman* and the Irish literary publication the *Bell*. In the *Bell* under Sean O'Faolain's editorship some extracts of *Never No More* appeared, and the prisoners were very eager to get the whole book...

With unanimous voice the cry was raised. "We got to get *Never No More*. How much is it? Fifteen bob. Good enough." So, one-and-a-tanner or two bob amongst us reading folk here and in she came. Mrs Laverty, ma'am, I give you my solemn word there was nearly bloodshed over it. Each of them started taking a peep here and a peep there, and having once pept ... they wanted to go on reading irrespective of the fact that there was a fellow waiting in his turn to have it. And in the heel of the reel, we got a bit of order into the reading of it. And, God help me, altho I was last, I had it longest ... We'd go out to exercise in the morning and the fellow that had it since the night before would start discussing it with the blokes who'd already read it ...
"Begod that was a good bit about the lads looking in at the oul wan and the young fellow and he tickling the soles of her feet."
"It was, all right. But did you come to the tinkers' baby yet?"
"Ah, the convent part is the great part."..

With thanks from myself and all in the Hill for the great enjoyment
you gave us.

Brendan Behan

It must have been very cheering at a time when Maura Laverty
needed a bit of cheer, but praise however warming and widely
spread does not pay the bills. She moved on and on, her
newspaper articles appearing regularly as she went on with
Alone We Embark (1943), and then almost by public demand more
of little Delia Scully in *No More Than Human* (1944). Then
children's books *Cottage in the Bog* (1945) and *Green Orchard* (1949),
and her cookery books which are still a legend in Ireland. Hardly
anyone I know grew up without a copy of Maura Laverty's
cookery book with its blue and yellow cover on the kitchen
window. We didn't know there was any other way to write a
cookery book except like that, full of incident, memory, advice,
harking back and story. Just as her stories are full of culinary
tips and recipes, she has never known how to draw any dividing
line between the two.

Then in the 1950s she turned to playwriting and based on her
own unlooked for experiences of living in a poor area of Dublin
she wrote *Liffey Lane* and *Tolka Row* from her last novel *Lift Up Your
Gates* (1946). She had intended to write a series of six plays about
the same street but viewed from six different social classes. She
started at the lowest end and the three moving towards the top
drawer were never written. The Irish television station came
into being in the 1960s and this was where Maura Laverty's
name reached a great number of Irish people who were either
too young for her writings in the 40s or who had forgotten
them. *Tolka Row*, a weekly series each of the episodes fifty
minutes long and all of them written by Maura Laverty herself,
had the kind of popularity that *Coronation Street* has in Britain.
And the fact that she also had a weekly radio programme where
she answered readers' letters as a sensible no nonsense yet
affectionate agony aunt made her even more widely known.

I met her once because my best friend had a flat in the
basement of her house. She had moved by then to Leinster
Road, Rathmines, up again in that strange up and down social
ladder that had been her lot. She was in her mid fifties then with
a strong handsome face, lined beyond her years maybe or
perhaps it was weatherbeaten, or again perhaps I was just

young and thought that the old were really old. There wasn't a great deal of the gaiety of the young Delia Scully about her I thought, but suddenly a flash of it returned. She said to me that people should be hanged for making cooking a school subject that you did in examinations and got marks for. Hanging she repeated was too good for anyone who took away the sheer PLEASURE of having your hands in the texture of flour and butter. She said it lingeringly and lovingly. And for the first time I really understood how it was possible to love food as an artist rather than as a glutton.

Her love of the countryside and of peoples' funny ways is as strong. It comes over in her books and to the people who knew her well it came over too in her life. She didn't give of herself as easily as her lovable little heroine did ... but in giving us these people she has given as much as we have any right to demand.

Maeve Binchy,
London, 1984

CHAPTER 1

IT WAS strange to come home after my father's funeral and see the shuttered window of our shop and the bunch of black crepe hanging on the door, while Duffy's and Regan's and the other shops were bright and busy with the Saturday afternoon trade.

'James Scully, Draper' was what the sign over the door said. The sign caught my grandmother's eye. "He was never cut out for a draper, God rest him," she said, writing my father's epitaph.

We did not go in by the front door because the lock was broken and could only be opened from the inside. We all went down the lane at the side of the house and in through the back door. There was a big crowd of us: Gran and my mother and Aunt Rose — my father's sister from Kilkenny — and five of us children. There was Paddy, the eldest, who was apprenticed to a cabinet-maker in Dublin. He was eighteen and nearly out of his time. There was Joe, the second-eldest and my favourite brother, who was serving his time to a grocer down in Borris-in-Ossory. There were myself (I was nearly fourteen) and the two little lads of seven and nine, Jim and Tommy. Peg, the girl who was next to me, had stayed at home to help Moll Slevin, our servant-girl, to look after Ned, the youngest, and Josie and Celia, the five-year-old twins.

The smell of death was still in the house. It met us as soon as we opened the back door. The others went into the parlour behind the shop and I went upstairs to put away my new black coat and hat.

The smell was so heavy in the front bedroom where my

1

poor father had been laid out two nights before that there was no staying in the room at all. I went in for a minute but it drove me out — that and the fear of what I might see if I stayed looking at the bed. He had lain there dying for a year and a half, and it was hard to imagine the bed without him.

When I went down to the parlour the smell was not so bad. It was nearly drowned by the left-over smell of the whiskey and stout that had been drunk at the wake.

The grown-ups were sitting around the fire. They were talking about the big crowds who had attended the funeral and the lovely wreaths. My mother sat on one side of the fire with Ned on her knee. She was pale and composed. Her eyes had a drained empty look as if they would never find another tear to shed. God help her, she had cried enough for a life-time during the past five years. Not that she was a snivelling woman or that she cried during the day. To tell the truth, she did not get much time for crying, between the dress-making and looking after the shop and running in and out to the kitchen to make sure Ned was all right and that Moll Slevin was not spoiling the dinner. And since my father's illness she had had less time than ever, for she was up and down the stairs all day to him.

But she often cried at night. Since she first found out he had made away with the money, I woke up many a night and heard her praying in the dark and crying to herself.

Peg, who was my mother's favourite and who had a great love for her, stood beside the chair, with an arm around my mother's neck. Josie and Celia sat in under the square mahogany table sucking oranges. They kept dribbling the juice down the front of their good velveteen dresses and nobody said a word to them for it. All around their mouths was red and raw-looking from the stinging of the juice. Jim and Tommy were playing draughts at the little rush table under the window.

Aunt Rose sat in the centre of the circle with Paddy on one side of her and Joe on the other. She was a big comfortable-looking woman, with a high bust pushed up almost to her chin by heavy stays that made a ridge of flesh stand out under her shoulder-blades. She kept a fine furniture shop in Kilkenny where she had the reputation of being a great manager. It was hard to believe that my father and herself had come from the same mother. She would have made two of him in size, for he was a short man and very thin. Where she was go ahead and practical and energetic, he was careless and listless and a dreamer.

My mother was very like Aunt Rose in character and they got on well together.

You would wonder how two such different people as my father and mother had ever come to get married. She was a dressmaker in the Leinster House in Kilkenny when she met him. She was twenty-two and engaged to a boy about her own age. He was one of the best hurlers on the Kilkenny team. My father had just come in for a farm and four thousand pounds from his uncle in Inistiogue. He was twenty years older than my mother, but it seems he fell so deeply in love with her that he gave her no peace until she gave up her hurler and agreed to have him.

My mother never pretended to have married for love. Often and often, when worry made her tongue sharper than usual, I heard her turning up to my father the number of times she had refused him before she gave in.

After they were married, she thought it would be a good idea to come home to Ballyderrig, her native place, and start a high-class drapery and dressmaking business. There really was not an opening in a town like ours for such a business, but my mother believed in her idea and she hoped that with herself and an assistant or two making up the goods on her shelves she would make a double profit.

She had a poor opinion of my father's commercial ability, and she allowed him no part at all in the running of the business. That was a pity, for it left him with nothing to do all day but go fishing in the Mill Pond. It was when he got tired of this that he took to attending every race meeting in the Curragh, and that was the beginning of the end. The craze for gambling got into him and he was soon making the money fly.

Here is something I have never been able to understand. When my mother elbowed my father out of the business, she left the managing of the money entirely in his hands. The account was in his name and she herself never signed a cheque in her life. I am sure he would have transferred the money to her name if she had asked him, for he was entirely dominated by her and could refuse her nothing on earth. But the mistake was made, and my father was able to gamble away his money in secret. It was not until about five years before his death that she found out. A wholesale firm in Dublin to which she had made my father send a cheque wrote her a very stiff letter enclosing the cheque marked 'R.D.'

From that day, there was no living in the house with

her. It was nag, nag, nag, at my father, all day long. And he, shamed and cowed, would never raise his voice while she raged. He would only say, "Hush, girl, hush! Not before the children," and out with him to the Mill with his rod. With the exception of Peg and Ned, we would all get the edge of her tongue then. But I came in for it more than the others, for I was most like my father, being quiet and shiftless and lazy. But unlike my father, I could not be silent under a tongue-lashing. I answered back, which only made things much worse.

But all this is not to say that my mother did not do her duty well by us. Leaving aside the nagging, she was the best wife and mother in the world. During my father's illness she would not let him be sent away. She nursed him herself and stitched to support us at the same time. And the nursing of a man with my unfortunate father's complaint was no light task. Everything he ate during those last eighteen months had to come out through a tube in his poor side. I saw my mother get up morning after morning before anyone else in Ballyderrig was stirring, and take my father's sheets down to the river at the back of our house to wash them.

She was a great woman with a great spirit.

Gran sat in my father's chair on the opposite side of the fire from my mother. As I stood at the door and looked in at them, my eyes went from one to the other until they rested on Gran. Her glance caught mine and she made room for me in the big chair. As I squeezed myself in beside her I was conscious of the quick surge of love that always rose in me when she made a gesture of affection towards me.

Oh, Gran! was there ever anyone like you?

There she sat, a little withered apple of a woman. For all her sixty-eight years, her back beneath its black cloth bodice was as straight as a sergeant-major's. She was unloved by the slovenly and malicious and foolish. They resented her neat briskness, her wide charity, her impatience with fools. Such souls apart, everyone else in Ballyderrig loved her.

I had always been Gran's favourite grandchild and she was everything in the world to me. I spent far more time at Derrymore House, her snug farmhouse two miles outside Ballyderrig, than I did in my own home. I was happy when I was with her, for she made me feel useful and necessary, whereas my mother never tired of telling me that all I was good for was novelette-reading.

They finished talking about the weather and the funeral and there was silence for a little while.

Gran raised her head.

"Well, it's neither this nor that, Sis," she said, "but the question is, what are you going to do with the insurance money?" There was five hundred pounds coming to my mother on a policy of my father's to which she had stuck through thick and thin.

My mother looked across at Aunt Rose who fiddled with the gold brooch that was pinned on the shelf of her bosom.

"Sis and myself were talking about that last night, Mrs. Lacy," she said. "We were saying that it might be a good idea for her to sell out here and to open up in Kilkenny. Next door to me in King Street, Mag Hickey's grand shop has been lying idle since she died two months ago. The rent is reasonable, and I know Sis could make a go of it. She'd have half Kilkenny coming to her to make for them, for they all remember her since she was in the Leinster House. Mr. Lawler, the manager, was saying to me only the other day that he never knew anyone to put a cut on a costume like Sis."

A pleased expression played across my mother's face. She *was* a good dressmaker and it gave her great pleasure when anyone praised her work.

"I see," Grandmother said. "You're suggesting that a widow of over forty with a houseful of children should break up her home and leave the town where she's known and respected to go and settle among strangers."

"Oh, not *strangers*, mother," my mother protested. "Sure I'm as well known in Kilkenny as I am here. After all, the children's father belonged there. And we'd be next door to Rose, so we wouldn't be lonesome."

"I can see that it's all settled and arranged," Gran said dryly. She was hurt that my mother and Aunt Rose should have gone so deeply into the matter without consulting her.

"Now, don't take it like that, Mrs. Lacey," Aunt Rose said in her comfortable way. "To my way of thinking — and Sis here agrees with me — there's nothing like a fresh start. Ballyderrig brought nothing but bad luck to herself and James since the first day they set up here. And what opening is there for a good dressmaker in a place like this? A handful of farmers' wives who wouldn't know whether a coat was well cut or not."

"Will you listen to the city woman talking?" Gran said impatiently. "Maybe the women of Ballyderrig aren't well up in the latest fashions, but we know how to dress to suit our ages, anyway — and that's one thing we could teach the Kilkenny people." Pointedly, she eyed Aunt Rose's low-necked black blouse and hobble skirt.

"Anyway it's as good as settled, Mother," my mother said then, "so there's no use arguing about it."

This was the first I had heard of their going to Kilkenny, and fright and dismay had been growing in me as they spoke. So we were leaving Ballyderrig with its bog and its blackberry hedges and its fields of mushrooms for the grey dankness of that back street in Kilkenny? I had stayed there once with Aunt Rose and I hated it. Hated its smell of urine and wet ashes and the way you had to climb out of it into brighter High Street by a long queer flight of stone steps. I hated, too, the thought of living over that grimy shop next door to Aunt Rose. And — worst thought of all — there would be no Gran there . . . no Derrymore House wherein to find love and understanding and sympathy. I knew it would kill me to leave Gran.

In my anguish, I pressed closer to her side.

She knew well what was wrong with me, for she put her hand reassuringly on mine when she spoke.

"What about the children?" she demanded. "What's going to become of them in Kilkenny?"

"They'll be better off in a town where there'll be some kind of opening for them when they're of age to earn their own living," my mother said practically. "They won't have to go miles from their home like Paddy and Joe here."

"And what did you think of putting Delia to?" Gran persisted.

My mother gave a short laugh. Paddy and Joe and

Aunt Rose, their attention drawn to me, looked at me as if they had never seen me before.

"Poor Delia is it?" said my mother. "God knows what she'll be good for. I used to think I'd put her at the stitching, but it would break your heart to see the way I have to rip everything she sews."

"That's queer, now," Gran said. "I thought that little tablecloth she made me for Christmas was lovely."

"Oh, she'll do embroidery all right," my mother conceded. "Give her a bit of fancy work and let her sit all day with it like a lady, and she'll ask nothing better than working flowers and curicaries. But that'll never earn her her bread. Peg here is worth twenty of her for stitching and making."

Peg tried hard not to look smug at this praise, and I could feel myself getting redder and redder. But I felt no inclination to cry. It was queer that my mother's tongue could never sadden me — it only made me bitter and anxious to answer back. She was off now on her favourite horse and there was no stopping her.

"Delia is the most useless girl that God ever made," she went on. "But sure I often heard tell that a light-heeled mother makes a heavy-heeled daughter."

"It's a queer thing *you* are not heavy-heeled, then," Gran retorted with spirit. "God knows I was always light-heeled enough."

"That's right — take her part," my mother said. "You've always spoiled her — though it's little enough spoiling you ever gave me."

It must have cost Gran much not to answer this. But it did not suit her to quarrel just then, so she kept silent.

After a minute, she said quietly, "I was talking to Sister

Mary Patrick down at the school the other day and she told me that Delia has the makings of a good teacher in her. She says that Delia's way with children would surprise you."

"Maybe so," my mother said. "I'll grant you she'd sit telling them stories all day long. But ask her to wash them or mend their clothes and it would be a different kind of story." My mother shifted impatiently in her chair. "But this is foolish talk anyway. Where would I get the money to make a teacher of her?"

"Where, indeed?" echoed Aunt Rose.

It was then that Gran spoke up and changed the whole world for me, bringing me from despair to wild happiness.

"I have a few pounds between myself and the Union," she said. "Leave Delia here with me. In a year or so I'll send her away to school, and we'll make something of her yet. That is, if you can spare her, and if she's willing to stay."

If my mother could spare me — ! I could almost feel her making the effort to refrain from saying how well she could spare me.

And was I willing to stay? Oh, Gran, you sleeveen, nobody better than yourself knew how willing! No one better than you knew the joy I felt at the thought of living with you in Derrymore House, sleeping with you at night, waking up with you in the morning, cooking with you in the buttery, picking mushrooms with you in the Hollow Field.

And when my mother finally agreed that it was all settled, my happiness was so great that I nearly forgot my father had been buried that day.

* * *

Was I an unnatural and callous child not to have been saddened at the prospect of separation from my mother and sisters and brothers? Maybe I was. But let me explain how it was with me.

My father was gone. My gentle father who came second only to Gran in my heart, and for whom I felt a deep and pitying love. I loved my mother, of course, but it was different. There was between us the same curious antagonistic relationship that existed between herself and her own mother. Deep love, but no liking. There was something of the same feeling between Paddy and myself — something that prevented us from being conscious of our natural love for each other until we were apart. I adored Joe, but the pain of separation from him had already been faced and got over two years before when he went to Borris. Then there was Peg, my mother's loving little shadow. Peg was a darling, but my mother's marked preference for her had created a jealousy in me that kept us two apart.

I felt no deep pang at the thought of being parted from Jim and Tommy and the twins. These two pairs found their perfect complement in each other and were independent of the love of outsiders. Now, I have always been reciprocal in my affections. I mean I have never been able to love where my love was unasked or unwanted. I could never understand women breaking their hearts over men who were indifferent to them. I have been told this denotes a great lack in my nature and that it makes any love of mine a poor thing without spontaneity or vitality — a mere echo of another's emotion. But there it is and I cannot help it. I mention it now to explain why the thought of being separated from the four little ones did not grieve me.

But the baby, now . . . Ned . . . that was different.

I loved Ned. At the thought that he was going from me, I leaned quickly over and took him out of my mother's arms. The feel of his thin little body in its red knitted suit sent a pain of love and sadness through every bit of me. He was such a miserable little scrap of a thing . . . pale, watery-white face, a wide sensitive mouth, and two enormous grey eyes that were the image of my father's — quiet, you know, and full of queer sad thoughts of his own. "Little Scaldie-bird," I whispered to him, kissing his thatch of weak silky hair.

He was on my knee and my arm was around him. His little bony hand started playing with the row of buttons on my sleeve, and when I looked down and saw how small the hand was and how thin the wrist, a great wave of something came up in me and a hard lump of pain tore at the back of my throat. And suddenly, it was not poor Ned's little wrist I saw but my father's tortured eyes following my mother around the room and he dying. I saw Joe sitting lonely and frightened on the outside of the mail-car and he starting off for Borris-in-Ossory. I saw every sad tearing thing that I had known in my life and it was all there in that little bony white wrist. I shut my eyes hard and I tried to keep it all back. I tried my best to pray to Our Lady to keep me from crying, but all my heart would say was, "Father! Father! Father!" while a terrible stinging hurt my eyes and the lump in my throat pressed harder and harder.

Poor little Ned felt the queer jerky way my chest was

going up and down with the sobs I was trying to keep inside it. He turned around and looked up at me in wonder. I must have nearly frightened the life out of the child with the burst of crying I let out of me then, for he started to cry too. The twins took it up and soon it was Hell opened to sinners with the four of us.

My mother took Ned out of my arms and tried to quieten him.

"It's a damn shame for you!" she said to me angrily. "Imagine carrying on like a madwoman before the children! And the size of you, too. It would be fitter for you to be out helping Moll Slevin to make the tea. Go do it now."

Snivelling and shamed, I went out to the kitchen.

"I'll be with you," Gran called, coming after me. "I'll be glad of a chance to stretch my legs. I declare I'm stiff sitting this day."

Luckily, Moll had gone down the back yard to shut up the hens for the night. Grandmother closed the kitchen door on the pandemonium in the parlour.

"Oh, Gran," was all I said.

Her kind old arms went around me and she let me have my cry out. "Here, blow your nose," she said at last, fishing a clean handkerchief out of her pocket. "Is it fretting for Ned you are? Sure, we'll have his lordship down to stay with us for the whole summer — and longer, if your mother will let us have him. Stop crying, now, or I'll be thinking you don't want to come live with me, and I'll ask Peg instead."

That threat and a drink of water brought me back to normal, and by the time the kettle was boiling and the table set, Gran and I were making plans for Hallow-e'en.

She brought me home with her to Derrymore House that evening.

Six months later the family moved to Kilkenny. People from Newbridge, by the name of Flood, took our house and started a grocery shop. And 'James Scully, Draper' was painted over with a new sign: 'The Bridge Stores.'

CHAPTER 2

I WENT to live with Gran on October 4th, 1920. I cannot forget the date since it was also the date of my father's funeral.

It was settled that I should continue to attend the convent National School until the following summer twelve-months when Gran would send me to a boarding school. When I came from school every day, Bran, our toothless sheepdog, met me at the foot of the long boreen that we insisted on miscalling 'avenue.' His rheumaticky caperings accompanied me between the rime-touched hedges where fat scarlet haws and orange Johnny-M'Goreys glowed defiance to the frost.

Derrymore House was a comfortable two-storeyed building with a slated roof. The ground floor was cut in two by a hall that ran from back door to front door. To the right were the parlour and the little bedroom where Mike Brophy slept. On the left was the big kitchen and, opening off it, the storeroom and the buttery. None of us ever entered the house by the hall-door. We always went around to the back where a big clamp of turf standing about twenty feet from the house shut off from the kitchen windows the haggard with its cow-house, pig-stye and hen-run.

On cold days it was good to reach the bright comfort of Grandmother's kitchen where the big fireplace that could hold a kish of turf sent out a scorching heat. Judy Ryan, Grandmother's servant-girl, always had my dinner ready for me on the white-scrubbed table that stood against the wall in the space between the two big windows with their ribbon-looped lace curtains and pots of geraniums. Sometimes Mike Brophy, the labouring man, would be sitting at the fire having a shin-heat before going out to milk the cows. More often than not, Heck Murray would be there, too, hugging himself with his short arms and giggling now and again at some private joke of his own. Poor Heck was a simpleton who practically lived at Gran's house, where he got his meals, an odd few shillings and a corner of his own beside the fire.

Judy and myself enjoyed Heck. A red-headed little block of a creature with a toothless grin and poor unsteady eyes, he might have been any age from forty to sixty. When he wanted to wheedle anything out of Gran, he always referred to himself as "a poor orphint." "Sure you wouldn't turn the back of your hand to me, Mrs. Lacey?" he would whimper. "I'm only a poor orphint wid me father and mother lyin' undher the sod." He was always talking about a great match that was arranged for him with a girl in Robertstown, and from time to time he had invited everyone in Ballyderrig to the wedding. Judy and myself used to tease him about the Big Night that never came off, but he always made out that we were jealous. He had a grand way of half-remembering riddles and of throwing them out at us, running question and answer together inextricably.

"Ha! this'll tie yez into a knot!" he would gloat. "Undher - the - wather - and - over - the - wather - an - egg - in - a - duck's - backside — what's that?" Naturally, we were without an answer, whereupon Heck would rock with triumph. "Ha! Heck's too smart for yez! Heck has yez puzzled!"

While I ate my dinner, Gran sat beside me with her

knitting, questioning me on the day's events. She had an insatiable curiosity, and I'm afraid I often made up gossip concerning the doings at school just to please her.

When I had finished and the dishes were washed and placed on the dresser, Grandmother beckoned me into the buttery to help her with her baking. It was then I entered Heaven, for my life held no keener pleasure than helping Grandmother to cook. It was lovely to hustle around at her command, to watch that busy spare little figure in its black dress and check apron and see the brown loaves and currant cake and soda bread take form under her quick hands.

The buttery was a place of delight. It was lit by a small window placed high in the wall and covered with wire netting to prevent the entry of cats. Reaching halfway up its sides were bins for flour and oatmeal and flakemeal, and the yellow Indian meal for stirabout for fowl and humans. Above the bins was a stone ledge that held blue-rimmed crocks of cream and butter and eggs. And above these were wooden shelves for currants and raisins and sugar and spices. Directly under the window the ledge was left bare, for it was here that Gran did her cake-mixing.

Gran was different to most other women in Ballyderrig in that she took a great interest in food. She was a splendid cook. Nothing new-fangled, mind you. None of your dressed up dishes with fancy French names. But good honest Irish food cooked to perfection — ah! there Gran excelled. And if the savour and goodness of her cooking trapped you into eating more of it than was good for you, you could rely on her to make things right. Her head was a card-index file of amazing old herbal remedies.

Many of them, I now suspect, were more amazing than remedial.

In my mind, Grandmother's cooking was inextricably mixed up with red-headed Johnny Doyle, the head of the tinker clan that descended on Ballyderrig at regular intervals, their carts piled high with children and tinware, and accompanied by herds of little shaggy black asses.

We found the tinkers decent people and honest to deal with, and Gran bought nearly all her cooking utensils from them. There was hardly one of her dishes that was not connected with Johnny Doyle's tinware, and as she cooked, her directions to those assisting her were punctuated with repetitions of the tinker's name.

"Grease me Johnny Doyle's big cake-tin," she would say. "I'm going to make a treacle cake." Or, "Get out Johnny Doyle's piedish, Judy, till I set the beestings to curdle." "Take Johnny Doyle's little three-quart can with you," she would tell me when I set out to gather mushrooms for the breakfast. And, on my return, "Take one of Johnny Doyle's tin mugs and get yourself a drink of fresh buttermilk."

Occasionally, the McCanns, a rival tribe of tinkers, would drift into the town on the same day as the Doyles. At first, they would be friendly enough. But after two or three hours of steady drinking, they would begin to remember old feuds, and then the fun would commence, providing the people of Ballyderrig with the only excitement that ever came our way.

To describe the battle-scene, I shall have to describe Ballyderrig. The approach to the town is over a high canal bridge. The bridge slopes steeply down into a triangle out of which run Ballyderrig's two streets, with the village pump in the centre. The men of the village always ran to the top of the bridge to watch the fight in safety, for it wasn't wise to get in the way of the McCanns and the Doyles when they were settling old scores and running up new ones.

Those were the days of the old R.I.C. The members of the British Constabulary were discreet men, and the sergeant and his three peelers always shut themselves into the barracks to play twenty-five until the tinkers had settled their differences.

No one took a greater interest in these fights than poor Rafferty, Paddy Lee's crazy son. A pale attenuated wraith of twenty-five, Rafferty would become wildly excited as he watched the fight from his vantage point on the bridge. Jumping with excitement, he would look down on the battle that raged around the pump. For some unexplained reason, his boots never possessed laces. In Ballyderrig, the laces which the men wore in their heavy hob-nailed boots were called 'fongs.' I was twenty before I knew the word should be 'thongs'.

Rafferty would shuffle up and down the bridge, his thin feet threatening at every step to leave behind them the heavy boots. Bursting with a desire to join in the fray, he would mutter over and over again:

"If I'd only a pair of fongs in me boots I'd bate the heads off the lot of them!"

I don't pretend to explain Rafferty. He was a phenomenon whose ways hinted at reincarnation, dual personality and other things beyond the ken of ordinary people. On moonlit nights in the midst of his ceaseless meanderings up and down the bridge, he would often stop suddenly and lift his pale, hollow-cheeked face to Heaven. At such moments, the idiocy would leave his eyes which would blaze with a holy fire, and from the lips of this poor soft-brained creature would issue a flow of beautiful words in the accent of some place that was certainly not Ballyderrig. Where did he get these words? Not from the people among whom he lived. And the world of books was, of course, closed to him.

I remember watching him in fascination during one of those trances, frightened and thrilled by his words.

"A withered stick in a gap . . . a witch in a shivering rath," Rafferty was murmuring. And then he saw his father coming to take him home. All the fire left his face with its weak fuzz of fair beard. The old muddled look returned to his eyes and he broke into some jumbled non-sense about "Freddie on the ice-cream."

Rafferty was christened Patrick. I have often wondered if his nickname had anything to do with those poetic trances . . . if there lingered in the minds of those who dubbed him Rafferty some vague remembrances of Raftery, the blind poet.

I always felt a great pity for Paddy Lee, the lad's father. He was a silent, heavy-footed man who went about the place with a stricken look on his white, grim face. His tender gentleness towards his idiot son was heart-breaking to see.

When Rafferty died, I went to his wake. I hope I may never again hear such terrible sobs, dry and racking, as came from the man who would not be led from the little room where his son's corpse lay. And I am sure I shall never again see such beauty on a dead face as I saw on Rafferty's. To keep the flies from settling on his mouth and nostrils, his mother had covered his face with a veil

such as children wear for their First Communion. Under
the veil, the face might have been the death mask of some
great thinker. . . Noble lofty brow, sensitive mouth, fine
arched nose. And as I looked at him, ludicrously there
leaped into my mind a picture of poor Rafferty hopping
about on the bridge and begging for a pair of 'fongs' for
his boots so that he might beat the tinkers.

It was the women of the Doyles and McCanns who
fought out the battle to the bitter end. When the men of
both sides had sustained a few cuts and bruises they always retired to one of our many public-houses — eight of
Ballyderrig's twelve shops sold liquor — to wash away their
bitterness with porter. They lacked both the stamina and
vindictiveness of the women. Great strapping women,
they were, with hair bleached like straw by the sun.
Winter and Summer, they wore their heavy mustard-col-
oured shawls. Enduring women, strong in fight and
child-birth.

I often heard my father tell of how he passed a cart-
load of tinkers when on his way to Kildare one day. The
cart was drawn up by the side of the road. A woman,
obviously in labour, was being helped out of it and into a
field.

Later in the day, when my father was returning from
Kildare, he met the cart proceeding on its way. Sitting
bolt upright in it, looking wan but at ease, was the mother.
From the folds of her shawl came the wails of a new-born
infant.

I'll never forget the day my Grandmother delivered the
tinker's baby.

Judy Ryan had just put the dinner on the table — pot-roasted rabbit, it was. Occasionally Mike Brophy would bring in three or four young rabbits . . . tender little co-neens. Grandmother had a way of her own of coddling them in the baker with onions and slices of fat bacon and a little milk.

We were about to sit down to our meal when the cart clattered into the yard and came to a rest outside the kitchen window. A big bronzed giant of a fellow jumped from the cart and came to the door. He had the fear of death on his face.

Huddled on the floor of the cart was a woman who, at minute intervals, moaned hoarsely.

Grandmother sized up the situation at once.

"Bring her in," she told the tinker briskly. With the help of Mike Brophy, the man got his wife out of the cart. She was a magnificently-built woman. Her shirt-blouse of red plaid had slipped from her shoulders, disclosing the full rounded breasts that were white as haw blossom by contrast with her browned neck and face.

"Tch! tch!" said Gran, who was prudish about such things. "Such a sight before the men!" She grabbed the woman's shawl from the cart and threw it hastily about her. Between them, the sobbing dark-eyed creature was half-carried up the stairs to the room over the kitchen.

"Get me plenty of hot water, Judy," my grandmother called down. "And tear up a couple of the old sheets for me."

The tinkerman would not be coaxed from the foot of the stairs.

His frightened eyes, startlingly light blue in that dark face, looked at us from beneath the tousled fringe of black hair that came to his eyebrows.

"If I'd 'a known she was so near her time," he said apologetically, "we could 'a stayed in Edenderry. They'd 'a took her in at the Union."

Suddenly, the gypsy seemed to reach the end of her endurance. Or maybe it was the relief of knowing herself in safe hands that brought about a reaction. In any case, she lost all self-control. Terrifying animal shrieks rent the house.

Mike Brophy, feeling that this was no place for a man, and obsessed by the average male's impulse to run away from suffering he cannot alleviate, sheepishly left the kitchen and wandered back to his work.

Between the shrieks I could hear my grandmother scolding the woman. She had little sympathy with complainers.

"You ought to be ashamed of yourself," she was saying. "A big strong woman like you to be carrying on like that. Stop it at once I tell you, or out you'll go."

This threat checked the tinker's hysteria and her shrieks ceased. Her husband continued to hang around the foot of the stairs, mumbling prayers and watching for my grandmother's appearance. Every now and then he'd shout up: "How is she, ma'am? Is the babby all right?"

My grandmother afterwards told us that when she tried to comfort the suffering woman by commenting on this proof of her husband's solicitude, the tinker checked her moaning and smiled bitterly as she said:

"Aye, I know what's wrong wid him! Three months ago he gev me a batin' at the Fair of Athy. Ever since he's been out of his mind for fear it'd harm the babby."

He had no need to worry. The baby arrived within an hour — a lovely black-eyed boy with plump sturdy limbs.

When the exhausted woman saw him, she stretched out a roughened but very gentle hand to fondle the little head that was covered with a surprisingly thick mat of silky black hair.

"Will you look at the head of hair on him?" she whispered proudly. " 'Tis meself was nearly dead from that head of hair. Wasn't I kilt wid heartburn while I was carryin' him?"

From the sacred black trunk in her room that no one else was ever allowed to touch, Gran rooted out some of the little yellowed garments that had clothed her own babies, for the tinkers had come unprovided with as much as a shift for their firstborn. When the little one was dressed, I was allowed to sit and hold him.

Although Gran pretended to grumble at the extra work which the tinker's accouchement had brought on us, I could see she was in her element that evening. She hustled happily around, beating up eggs and milk with sugar and ginger for the beverage which we called "smacks." "This'll put strength in the creature," she said, pouring the smacks from one jug to another until it was a mass of sweet eggy froth.

To her horror, the tinkers wanted to move on that very evening. She looked at the man aghast.

"Is it mad you are?" she demanded. "It would be the death of that woman to move her before the week is out."

The tinker's eyes shifted before Gran's irate glance. "I'm beholdin' to you for your kindness, ma'am," he said. "But, meanin' no offence, me mother never lay undher any of us for more'n a day."

Reluctantly, he finally agreed to remain that night and the next. He refused to sleep in the house, saying that he'd feel smothered. "If you'll take no exception," he said, "I'll sleep in the hayrick." And so it was settled.

Not until the very last minute could he be brought to tear himself away from the baby that night. He sat there gloating over his son.

"Go on with you, man," Gran said. "You'd think there was never a baby born in the world before. With that fine woman you have upstairs, sure, you'll have a dozen more like him."

On the third day, Gran saw that by no threats or coaxing could she keep the tinkers any longer. They were restless and ill at ease in this restricted world of walls and roofs and regular meals. They were eager for their own domain that was bounded only by the green hedges and the length of the long white road. Besides, they were anxious to join the rest of their clan at the Curragh Races.

Grandmother made them up a great basket of food.

"That woman of yours will be needing nourishment," she said, putting in a dozen of brown eggs, a cartwheel of a currant cake, a fine piece of smoked bacon and a roll of freshly-made butter wrapped in muslin.

The broad-shouldered pair almost cried with gratitude as they said good-bye.

There were tears in my own eyes as they went, for I hated to see that sweet-smelling, sloe-eyed baby going out of my life. I watched them as they jolted down the boreen in their little cart drawn by the black ass, that kicked its heels as if it, too, was glad to be facing once more the long days on the roads and the quiet nights under the stars.

When they reached the end of the boreen, the man turned and waved his whip in farewell to the leggy little girl in her home-made check frock. And the tinker-woman lifted up the little bundle in her arms so that I might have a last look at her son.

The tinkers still meet in Ballyderrig, but they tell me that the fire has gone out of their fights and that the feud between the Doyles and McCanns is dying down. Well, the fights could not be the same, anyway — with poor Rafferty no longer there to shout encouragement at them from the bridge.

CHAPTER 3

THAT WAS a happy winter for me. Very quiet and never a cross word said to me. To be truthful, there was no need for it, for in Derrymore House I was as tractable and obedient and willing as I had been impudent and difficult at home. It was just that Gran and I reacted on each other in such a way that we always gave, one to another, our very best. With my mother it was the opposite, although with others of her children she enjoyed the relationship that Gran enjoyed with me. I have since found that it is the same with people everywhere. Kinship has nothing to do with it, nor virtue, nor lack of virture. Human nature is like bread, I think. Soda bread calls for buttermilk and baking powder bread for new milk. Use the wrong kind of milk and the bread is sodden. Gran was the right kind of milk for me.

I went to school every day and in the evenings I helped Gran to bake. After tea I did my home exercise and in the evenings I knitted or had a game of cards with Judy and Gran and Mike before going to bed. Often some of the neighbours would come in to pass the evening and then we had singing and stories and sometimes a half-set.

On Fridays after dinner, I always went back into the town to do Gran's shopping at Duffy's. Duffy's was the biggest shop in Ballyderrig. In one long, low-ceilinged room it had three departments. On the right as you went down the two steps leading to the dim interior was the grocery counter where in addition to foodstuffs of all kinds, you could buy farm implements and hardware from Ned Connelly. On your left was the drapery with

27

its bales of strong calico and flannelette for honest under-
wear, and the hats and dresses which Miss Derrigan, who
presided there, declared were the latest from Paris. At
the end of the shop was the bar, where Mickey O'Neill
dispensed thick glasses of foaming stout and half-uns of
pale Irish whiskey.

Mickey was a small thin elderly man with a foxy moustache and a bald head across which he plastered a few
fronds of sandy hair. He was a dapper little fellow who
favoured shiny navy suits and a butterfly bow to his collar.
He was the staunchest support of the Church in Ballyderrig. He stood with the collecting plate at the chapel
door for both first and second Mass every Sunday. Half-
seven every week-day morning found him kneeling in the
chapel and when there were evening devotions during
Lent and May and October, Mickey never missed them.
He was a pillar of righteousness and had not broken his
pledge for ten years.

When I knew him, he must have been close on sixty
years of age. He had not always been so religious. The
people of Ballyderrig sometimes recalled those days before
his conversion when he had been a hard-drinking rake
and had not set his foot inside church, chapel or meeting-
house for years.

Whenever any of his friends had tried to point out to
him the error of his ways, Mickey would always retort:
"Och, I've plenty of time to repent. To hear you talking
anyone would think I was an old fellow with one foot in
the grave. Sure I'm a young man yet. Let me have my
fling, can't you?"

And he had gone on being a scandal to the neighbourhood and acting the part of a gay young blade.

When Mickey was fifty, a couple of Passionist Fathers had come to give a mission in Ballyderrig. There were few in Ballyderrig who would have braved Father Dempsey's wrath by staying away from the mission, even though attending it meant taking the pledge. Mickey openly avowed his intention of not going, but his wife nagged him so much that, for the sake of peace, he gave in.

"Well, I'll go," he said, "but I won't take the pledge."

By a superhuman effort, he did not touch a drop of drink during the nine days' retreat. On the last evening of the mission he stood with the rest of the men, lighted candle in hand, while they renewed their baptismal vows.

When it was all over, he came out in the street and put on his hat. It must be confessed that Mickey could not have benefited greatly from the sermons, for he walked straight from the chapel to the hotel bar, where he proceeded to slake the accumulated thirst of a long week.

Young Joe Mooney and Tommy Neale were playing on the flagstones outside Regan's shop as he walked unsteadily home. He stopped when he came to the children and, in the grand accent he always assumed when in drink, he said to them solemnly:

"Boys," — Mickey wagged his finger — "Boys, always be thankful for youth. You see me, a young man, making the most of his youth. I leave the snivelling and the praying for the old people."

The two boys looked at him and suddenly young Neale burst into hilarious laughter.

"Eh, Mooney," he said, "will you look at the candle grease on the auld lad's hat?"

Mickey looked around for the 'auld lad' to whom they were referring, but there was nobody there but himself.

An incredible thought struck him and he took off his hat. The crown was thickly covered with the grease which had dripped from a carelessly-held candle in the chapel.

He walked home, a very thoughtful man. From that day, Mickey O'Neill, the Peter Pán of rakes, was no more. That aspect of him had died when Tommy Neale and his friend made him realize that he was an 'auld lad.' When Mickey's wife told the story of his conversion to my grandmother, she murmured something about "the strange and wonderful ways of God."

My family had a particular interest in Ned Connelly, who managed the grocery end of Duffy's business. A few months after my father's death he proposed to my mother. What induced him to do this is difficult to imagine, since beyond bidding her the time of day, I don't believe he ever exchanged two words with her in his life.

Other considerations aside, common sense would have made my mother refuse Connelly. He was a widower with thirteen children and she felt a natural reluctance to add this horde to her own brood of nine.

Connelly was a flabbily handsome man of forty-five or so, with a pallid good-natured face and protuberant blue eyes. He was distinguished for his exceedingly voluminous trousers which always looked as if they had been handed down to him from a taller and fatter brother.

My young brother Tommy who even at nine gave evidence of a sharp and witty tongue, liked to tease my mother about her rejected suitor by putting to her a riddle he had composed.

"What two towns in France are Connelly's trousers like?"

The answer was, "Toolong" and "Tooloose."

There was nothing very passionate or private about Connelly's proposal. He called Tommy one day when he was whipping his top with a crowd of his buddies on the flagstones outside the shop.

"Give this to your mother," he said, handing Tommy a note written on one of Duffy's billheads. "Here's a ha'penny for yourself."

The innocent man had not even put the note in an envelope. Naturally, Tommy and his friends read it, with the result that the proposal was all over Ballyderrig before it reached my mother.

It was brief and to the point:

"Dear Mrs. Scully,
Your children need a man's hand over them. Mine have no one to put in a stitch for them. I am earning thirty shillings a week and my keep and my chances. If you are agreeable, leave the shop door open tonight and I will call in after Duffy's is shut.
                    Your obedient and loving servant,
                    Edward Connelly."

My mother was not agreeable, and the shop door was closed and locked that night at nine o'clock as usual.

* * *

My grandmother, who was so very thrifty in other ways, was extravagant about clothes. She liked to go up to Dublin for her coats and dresses and hats and shoes. She bought them, as her mother had done before her, at an old-fashioned shop in Henry Street, where she paid for them what seemed fabulous sums to the people of Bally-derrig.

From Miss Derrigan she bought only odd lengths of calico and such sundries as tape and buttons and thread. Consequently, Miss Derrigan was inclined to be a little short with me when I approached her counter with Gran's shopping list.

Not, indeed, that Miss Derrigan was over-amiable with any of her customers. She was the only woman I have ever known whose appearance and manner really justified the term "acidulous." She was a spinster lady of forty or more, thin-lipped, sharp-nosed and frosty-eyed. Even in Summer, her hands were purple, and swollen with chil-blains. Her hair, which was iron-grey, was worn in an elaborate erection of coils and twists that needed a perfect armoury of big black hairpins for its support.

The unkind corner-boys of Ballyderrig christened Miss Derrigan "Cotton-Craw." In some mysterious way they had got wind of her habit of disguising her withering maidenhood by padding the bosom of her grey alpaca blouse with cotton wool.

When I was thirteen, Miss Derrigan had been serving in Duffy's shop for twenty years. For fifteen of those years she had been keeping company with Jim Burke, an insurance agent who lived in Kildare. Every Sunday afternoon of her life, she dressed herself in her lady-like grey tailor-made, her black buttoned boots and her navy boater and walked out the Kildare road to meet her fiancé, who cycled from Kildare to meet her.

There was nothing very unusual in their courtship. Most Ballyderrig people hesitated before marrying. In our town, age did not seem to be measured as in other places. Few men married before they were fifty, and as long as men and women remained unmarried they were referred to as 'boys' and 'girls' no matter how old they might be.

Miss Derrigan lived in a room over Duffy's shop. In one corner stood a high-wheeled ancient baby's pram. A family called Murphy had auctioned off the contents of their house a week after Miss Derrigan had first become engaged. She was a thrifty, far-seeing woman with an eye for a bargain, and as the pram had been offered very cheaply, Miss Derrigan had bought it, hoping to find a use for it one day. To be sure, her purchase of the pram had given rise to ribald jests among the Ballyderrig people, but she was a strong-minded, independent woman. She wheeled home the pram herself, hauled it up the stairs and stood it in a corner of her room. At regular intervals, she polished and oiled it.

Miss Derrigan's long courtship ended at last. Jim Burke married her, and she left Ballyderrig on an outside car, with her trunk and the pram tied on beside her.

The Burkes settled down in Kildare, and news of them reached us from time to time. Two years after the wedding we heard that she had died giving birth to a stillborn baby. We were again reminded of her six months later, when Bid Behan, a beggar-woman from Kildare, walked down the bridge one day wheeling the pram. It was piled high with bottles and rags and jam-jars.

Money never entered into Grandmother's dealings with Miss Derrigan and Ned Connelly. Barter was largely practised in Ballyderrig. Like the other farming women, she paid for her goods in eggs and butter.

Frequently, I got a lift home from the town for myself and my basket. My shopping expeditions took place on Friday, when the pensioners came to the post-office to draw their money, and as Granny Lynn and Tom Martin and Dinny Mulpeter all lived our way, I got a seat in the cart of one or other of them. There was even competition among them as to which of them should drive me home, for it was an understood thing that whoever gave me a lift should have supper at Derrymore House.

To these old people, whose diet consisted mainly of bread, tea and potatoes, Grandmother's suppers were well worth competing for.

There was usually a ling stew waiting for us when we reached home. Nobody seems to eat ling nowadays, but at that time this dried fish, which cost only fivepence a pound, was a very popular fast-day food. Grandmother always kept a side of it hanging in the buttery, all white and floury with dried salt.

On Thursday nights she cut off a large piece and cut it into two-inch squares. These were left steeping in cold water over-night. The ling was given a parboil in fresh water next day. This water was thrown away, and when the ling was picked free of bones it was returned to the saucepan with sliced onions, potatoes and milk, to simmer for an hour or so.

Living so far inland, our fish dishes were mostly ling or red herrings. Occasionally, however, Mike Brophy took his fishing-rod and went down to the mill pond, returning with a few eels or perch. Although Judy Ryan would never touch an eel, saying that they were cousins to the serpent and that life remained in them even when cut in

pieces and sizzling on the pan, I had no scruples about
eating their tender milky flesh.

After skinning them and rolling them in flour, Grandmother always gave them a parboil before frying. " 'Twill
take the grease out of them," she used to say. They were
good fried, but I liked them even better stewed. She set
them to parboil while she made a creamy white sauce
with plenty of chopped parsley and scallions in it. The
eels were drained and set to stew in this sauce until tender.

There was always a hot seedy cake on Friday evenings.
It was a good rich mixture of flour, half its weight in butter and sugar, a teaspoonful each of bread soda and cream
of tartar, a pinch of salt, and eggs, buttermilk and caraway
seeds. Grandmother did not hold with newfangled foreign methods of beating butter and sugar to a cream. Except in the case of Christmas cakes, she always rubbed
the butter into the flour. The seedy cake batter was
poured into Johnny Doyle's flat round tin and put to cook
in the baker.

The indescribably appetizing cloud of spicy vapour that
rose from the baker when the lid was at last lifted and the
cake pronounced cooked would have cajoled a dying man
to eat. The cake was split and eaten hot, thickly spread
with butter that melted into luscious little pools on its
speckled surface.

CHAPTER 4

I SLEPT with Grandmother in her big iron bed, white-enamelled, with its enormous feather tick. The room was sparsely furnished. Between the windows and opposite the bed stood a mahogany chest of drawers surmounted by a swinging mirror that sometimes made your face look round and fat, and others long and thin, depending on the angle from which you viewed yourself. To the right as you entered the room was a wardrobe ornamented with sprays of heavy carved leaves. We always called it "the press." Under one window stood Grandmother's black trunk where she kept, among other things, the habit in which she would be laid out, and a carefully laundered cloth, a crucifix and two blessed candles in readiness for the 'sick call' that would one day be sent to Father Dempsey.

Under the other window stood her commode. Against the far wall was her little altar-table with a coloured statue of the Sacred Heart, a white plaster statue of Our Lady holding a gilt Rosary and a little metal Child of Prague. A red lamp with a wick floating in colza oil always burned on the altar. Close to the altar were a photograph of my grandfather and a picture of the Good Shepherd. The floor was covered with brown linoleum patterned with prim yellow flowers that had worn raggy in parts. Starched lace curtains hung stiffly in the windows that looked out over the green and brown fields to where a purple ridge marked the beginning of the bog. It was a bare room, but airy and sweet-smelling. The red and pink geraniums in the window sent gusts of spicy acrid fragrance into the room, and from the press and drawers and trunk stole the breath of Gran's pot-pourri — little jars of which stood in every receptacle for clothes.

No one could make pot-pourri like my grandmother. She knew the fragrance value of such combinations as sweet briar, bay, myrtle, lavender and thyme. And she knew to the last fraction of an ounce how much cinnamon, cloves, lemon rind, nutmeg and orris root should be added to the bay salt and saltpetre in which the leaves were 'pickled.'

We went to bed early in Derrymore House. After we had said the Rosary at ten o'clock, Gran raked the fire, putting the glowing turf into the hole at the side of the hearth and adding a fresh sod before covering it with ashes so that there might be plenty of kindling next morning. When the fire was raked she always drew a cross in the ashes with the tongs saying, "I rake this fire in the name of the Father, Son and Holy Ghost."

I was always first in bed, for Gran had her own private prayers to say when she reached her room. These were very lengthy because she held that it was a pity to break a good habit, and once she had learned a prayer and had made a habit of saying it, that prayer remained to swell the long list of her orisons. At seventy, she continued to say the prayers she had learned at her mother's knee. This custom was such a part of her that I found nothing ridiculous in hearing the grey-headed old woman conclude her prayers each night with:

> "Infant Jesus, meek and mild,
> Pity me, a little child."

The neatness of her movements made it pleasant for

me to lie between the coarse fragrant sheets and watch her drowsily as she undressed in the candle-light.

First her black woollen waist-coat was taken off and left on the cane-bottomed chair beside the bed. Then her check apron, her serge blouse and her heavy black skirt. A black sateen petticoat came next and a red flannel bodice and under-skirt. Now she peeled off her long black stockings and the heavy knitted knee-caps of white wool which she wore beneath them to ward off rheumatism.

When Gran reached this stage in her disrobing, I would hand her the grey flannel nightdress I had been warming for her against my tummy. She would pull this over her head and, screened by its ample folds, would remove her stays, chemise and long flannelette drawers. Sitting up in bed, she let down her thin little wisp of hair and twisted it into two weak plaits. Then having dipped her fingers in the holy water font over the bed, she was ready for sleep.

She turned her back to me and I drew up my knees to make a seat for her. Then, with my arm around her thin little body, I cuddled close to her and we were soon dreaming.

On days before the heavy washing was done, we went to bed an hour earlier than usual. When leaving the house for school on the eve of washing day, Gran always said to me:

"Go around to Glin's on your way to school and ask Sylvia Gorry to tell her mother I want her tomorrow." And I would go into the town and go around to the back door of Glin's where Sylvia worked in the kitchen.

It was an unwritten law that under no circumstances

should I go direct to The Bawn where Sarah Gorry lived in one of the four miserable hovels inhabited by the dregs of Ballyderrig society. Other than this ban on approaching her home, I can remember no way in which my grandmother ever showed her disapproval of Sarah's calling.

As a side-line, Sarah followed one of the oldest professions in the world. When the public-houses had closed at night, furtive kerchiefed men from the canal boats that were anchored at the lough slouched down the bridge and turned into The Bawn.

Sarah's two sons and two daughters had not a father in common. For a small village that was saturated with the natural prudery common to all small villages, Ballyderrig's attitude to Sarah was surprising. She made no secret of her profession, we accepted her for what she was, and that was all there was to it.

There wasn't a woman in Ballyderrig, however respectably married, who wouldn't stop and chat to Sarah when she met her on the road or in the street. Even those who turned with horrified loathing from any young girl who anticipated her marriage by a few months, never shunned Sarah. My mother was kind to her and often gave her bundles of our cast-off clothes for her children.

She was a handsome, heavily-built woman with an untidy mass of cloudy black hair, a sallow skin and sleepy brown eyes. Slow-moving and languorous, she had a wonderful capacity for hard work, and could foot turf or snag turnips better than any man. She was constantly called upon to do the heavy washing in the farmers' houses.

When not washing or working on the bog or in the fields, Sarah would carry her little three-legged stool to where The Bawn joined the street, and sit nursing her latest child while she read a novel. She had an insatiable appetite for books, particularly romantic novels. Her romantic leanings were shown in the names she gave her children — Annabel, Sylvia, Hubert and Alec.

Sarah and I often exchanged books, and after school on the days she came to wash for us I liked to sit in the washhouse discussing books with her while she rubbed and wrung and rinsed. Grandmother never objected to my being closeted with Sarah, for she knew her to be as correct in manner and conversation as any woman living.

Sarah's neighbours in The Bawn were a queer lot. Hers was the first cabin. Next door to her lived Polly Dunne who was called 'Side-o'-Ling' because she was so flat and long and colourless. 'Side-o'-Ling' was a pedlar who went off each morning with her basket of oddments to canvass customers in the lonely cottages in the bog.

The next cabin was occupied by 'Head' Butler, an old British Army pensioner who had fought in India. 'Head' was a harmless old fellow except on the days he drew his pension, when he would drink himself into a fighting mood and offer to take on all comers. In drink, he was a dangerous man with the strength of ten. Frequently, it required the combined efforts of Sergeant Ginnell and his three constables to drag him to the barracks.

In the last cabin in The Bawn lived Roach Doyle, a truly horrible old man and his equally horrible brother. The Roach was the only person I hated and loathed in Ballyderrig. He had a foul tongue and a dreadful cackling laugh.

He never worked, but hung around the door of Duffy's

pub all day, trying to cadge drinks from the men who went in and out. He wore a greasy cap with a broken peak and indescribably filthy clothes. His light shifty eyes and ragged grey moustache that fringed a mouth ornamented with a few blackened stumps of teeth horrified me.

He suspected my loathing of him and for years he made my life miserable by muttering beastly things at me as I ran past. He took a fiendish joy in tormenting small children. I wished sincerely that sudden and violent death might strike Roach Doyle when I saw the trick he played on Annabel Gorry one day.

Annabel was Sarah's eldest child. She was an unfortunate little creature, lame and nearly blind. It was hard to believe she could be the half-sister of the other Gorry children who were handsome and well built like their mother.

I was coming down the street. In front of me hobbled Annabel Gorry. The child was eleven or twelve at the time and I was considerably younger. Annabel was singing as she dragged her lame leg laboriously along. Annabel always sang, for, mercifully and wonderfully, she did not suspect that her life held any reason for tears. And so she sang as she approached the corner, her thin little grime-covered hand shielding those terrible sore eyes from the sun.

At the corner Roach Doyle lurked in wait for his prey.

As Annabel drew near, he took his blackened stub of a pipe from his mouth and spat carefully.

"Eh, young Gorry," he called. "There's a shillin' for you. Look! it's on the ground — there at your feet."

Annabel's song stopped short and before I could shout, before I could warn her of the Roach's vileness, she groped in the direction of the white circle of spittle.

The Roach's dreadful cackle destroyed the evening as the child's fingers met in the spittle.

May I never feel for anyone else the searing passion of hate that descended on me for The Roach in that moment, and that even now can stir me whenever I remember that day!

"Oh, God, please strike him dead," I prayed passionately.

But my hate received no outlet beyond the storm of crying that sent me running home.

And the most shocking part of the dreadful incident was that Annabel Gorry was neither hurt nor enraged nor disgusted. As I ran, I was horrified to hear her thin little treble of laughter joining that loathsome cackle. . .

Soon after I went to live with Gran, Annabel went into a decline and Sarah came frequently to Derrymore House to ask Grandmother's advice. It was pitiable to see the woman's distress as the crippled child slipped slowly from the clutches of her miserable life. Sarah had a very real love for her daughter and she was passionately grateful to Gran for the cures she concocted for her.

"She's troubled with a looseness, Mrs. Lacey," Sarah said, her face drawn with anxiety. "That bottle the doctor gave me is no good. Would you know of anything to help her?"

Grandmother had a remedy for 'the looseness' as she had for everything else. She pricked a nutmeg full of holes, toasted it on the point of a knife and boiled it in a quart of milk until most of the milk had evaporated and the nutmeg was soft enough to break up.

The potion, nutmeg and all, was sent to Annabel to be taken last thing at night.

In a few days Sarah came back, her face heavy with fear.

"She's coughing blood, Mrs. Lacy. They tell me you know of a cure. . ." Her voice trailed off miserably,

"To be sure I do, Sarah," Grandmother said kindly. "But you know yourself that if God means to take the child to Heaven, no cure in the world will do her any good." Just the same, Grandmother made up her approved remedy against spitting of blood.

She gathered a great basketful of nettles and bruised them with a beetle until the juice ran. This was strained and sweetened and was sent to Annabel to be taken — two teaspoonfuls of it — morning and evening.

Grandmother's cure did not prove so efficacious in this case as usual, for Annabel continued to fail, and finally Dr. Mangan gave her up.

When Sarah came to wash for us the following week, she was sullen and uncommunicable, like a wounded animal. She worked furiously all morning in the washhouse and refused to come in to share the cup of tea which Gran always wet at eleven o'clock.

At dinner-time she came into the kitchen when the coddle was ready. On washing days we always had coddle for dinner. It was a simple dinner to prepare, for once the finger-thick pieces of bacon, quartered cabbage hearts, sliced carrots and halved potatoes had been put in the baker, they could be left to simmer without further care until dinner-time.

Sarah took her plate of coddle from Gran and brought it over to the fire, as she always did, to eat it in solitude. She would have been welcome to sit at the table with us, but this she always refused to do with a dignity that left no room for persuasion. It was her only gesture of acknowledgment that she recognised herself as being . . . different.

She sat staring into the fire with heavy brooding eyes, but she didn't touch the coddle nor the apple-dumpling that followed.

When Mike Brophy had left the kitchen, Grandmother took Sarah's untouched plate from her and she drew up a chair beside her.

"There's no use at all in flying in the face of God, Sarah," she said kindly. "The Lord loves those He marks and, loving Annabel, isn't it natural He'd want her for Himself?"

The kind sympathy in Grandmother's wise old voice was more than Sarah could stand. Great, heavy tears rolled slowly down her sallow cheeks and grief suddenly broke up the mask of reserve behind which she shielded her shame and her sorrow.

"It isn't only the child," she said chokingly. "Don't I know she's a poor object and that she'll be better in Heaven? But her father was the first, and though he made me what I am, I'll always love him."

Grandmother looked at me and with her eyes commanded me to leave the kitchen. Obediently, I went into the buttery, but I was careful to leave the door open so that I mightn't miss any of this interesting talk. There was nothing disloyal to Grandmother in this, for she had sent me out of the kitchen more to spare Sarah's feelings than to protect my innocence. Grandmother knew that uncensored reading had made me precocious, though I remained very hazy about certain aspects of the facts of life.

In any case I had grown up with the realization that something set Sarah apart from the other women of Ballyderrig.

In the kitchen Sarah was sobbing quietly and, little by little, the whole story was tumbling out. It went back twenty years to the time when she had been in service with the wife of a British officer in the Curragh. A blond blue-eyed jockey had come courting her, and poor Sarah had been in heaven until the day she had begged him to marry her quickly, only to be told he was married already.

That may seem to be a very ordinary little story, cheap and sordid, but as I leaned that day on the flour-bin in the buttery and listened to Sarah sob it out, it was stark bitter tragedy.

When Sarah's sobs ceased, she rose to finish her washing, but Grandmother pressed her gently back into her chair.

"If the doctor gave Annabel up last night, you'll be wanting the loan of a few things," she said. She went upstairs, where I could hear her throwing back the lid of the black trunk. Presently she came down carrying the starched white cloth with its beautiful drawn-thread work and hand-crocheted border, the black-and-silver Crucifix and the wax candles, together with a pair of brass candlesticks from the mantelpiece in her room.

"You'll be needing these for the wake, Sarah," she said, "and here's something towards the little habit." She pressed a note into Sarah's reluctant hand. "Take it, woman, and don't be foolish. Can't you work it off?"

Everyone in Ballyderrig followed Annabel Gorry's funeral, but I doubt if Sarah, in her battered black velvet hat and long green coat, saw any of us.

CHAPTER 5

IN MARCH, the family moved to Kilkenny. None of us cried much when we said good-bye at Kildare Station for, as Gran said, it wasn't as if they were going to America. Kilkenny was only four shillings' worth of a journey away, and we would be up and down to see each other.

I never saw my mother looking so well as she did in her new black sealskin coat with the puce lining. There was a fresh young look on her face, and anyone would think she was afraid the train would never start by the way she kept looking at her watch.

Peg got into the carriage and sat between the twins, and Jimmy and Tommy sat opposite her. They were so excited about the journey that they were quiet for once.

I held Ned in my arms as long as he let me, but he had a bad cold on him and was fretful and uneasy and he wanted to go to my mother.

"Well, God bless you, Sis," Gran said when the whistle blew. "Don't forget that I'm here if you want me."

"God bless you," my mother said in a husky voice. They clung together for a moment, their antagonism temporarily wiped away, as it always was when it came to the really big things.

"Be a good girl and do as your Gran tells you," my mother said to me, leaning from the carriage window to kiss me and holding Ned down so that I might have a last hug at him.

Then they were gone. Gran and I got into the trap and she handed me the reins.

"You drive, Delia," she said, pretending that she wanted to keep her hands warm under the rug. But I know now that it was just to give me something to keep my mind on, for she guessed how I was feeling.

I did not speak until we were beyond the railway arch and out under the shoulder of Dunmurry Hill.

"He looked very dawny, didn't he, Gran?" I said.

"He did, indeed," Gran agreed. "Sure he's barely in it. But wait till you see the change in him after a few months in Kilkenny. It's wonderful how a change of air will make a child thrive. You won't know him when he comes down to us in the summer."

That was Gran's way. She never tried to fool you by pretending that the cause for your worry did not exist, but she always managed to find a comforting thought for you.

They settled down quickly in Kilkenny. At Easter my mother wrote to say the shop was opened and doing well. She had taken on an apprentice to the dressmaking and Aunt Rose had found her a grand girl to serve in the shop.

"Peg has started at the Loreto Day School," she wrote. "Please God in a year or two she'll be a great help to me in the business. Tell Delia Ned often asks for her — above all at bedtime. I think he misses the stories she used to tell him. He's picking up very slow and he still has that cold on him. I'm threatening to take him to Dr. Griffin if he isn't rid of it soon."

I was fourteen on the second of May and two days later a letter came from Peg to me:

"Dear Delia,

Poor Mother isn't able to write to you and she asked me to. We buried Ned to-day. He died of pneumonia on

Wednesday evening at seven. Mother said to tell you you're not to fret for him and that he's better off in Heaven. The shop is shut this three days but we're opening again to-morrow. Aunt Rose was very good to us. She got the coffin and everything. It was a little small one and he had a blue habit. Mother said you're not to fret and that he was not long for this world anyway. This is all for the present, and Mother will write to you herself when she is better.

Love to Gran and yourself,

Peg."

I had a bad time for a while after that, for I was in a black world where even the light of Gran's comfort could not reach me. I was shut away from her by the misery which prevented me from telling her what was in my heart.

How could I hurt her by confessing that I bitterly regretted having stayed in Derrymore since my staying had lost me those last months with the little Scaldie-bird? And how could I tell so religious a woman of the dreadful thoughts that possessed me before I went to sleep at night? She would have been shocked and worried to know that my faith was not sufficiently lively to help me to see Ned safe and happy beside Our Lady in Heaven. Instead I had awful moments when I saw him shut up in that small coffin, his heart-breakingly thin little hands folded on the breast of his blue habit, and all around the coffin a weight of damp black earth pressing . . . pressing . . . pressing . . .

Let no one believe that children cannot grieve deeply and intensely. Fortunately, this very intensity makes their grief short-lived. Within a fortnight of Ned's death the sharp edge was gone from my sorrow. I lost my morbidity and began to be once more a part of the life of Derrymore House. But it was a long time until I could hold in my hands a young chicken or any small-boned sparse-covered thing without feeling once more Ned's thin little body in its red-knitted suit as I had felt it that evening of my father's funeral.

It was fortunate for me that we were caught up in an unusual whirl of activity just then. No one could remain wrapped in grief, however poignant, while the bustle of the turf-cutting season was going on.

Realising that a change of occupation would help me to get over Ned's death, Gran suggested that I should stay away from school for a week or so to give a hand with the extra cooking.

At such times as this, additional men were hired to help Mike Brophy, Gran's one labouring man. Her ideas of catering for them were lavish and entailed much extra work.

The bog was never so beautiful as in May, when we cut the turf. A white road stretching straight and true as a taut ribbon ran gladly through that gentle spread of lovely colour. For a little distance, the full beauty of the bog was screened by the hedges that bordered the road — hedges of foaming May-blossom and twisted mountain ash and swaying bog-willow. Later, the wild convolvulus would join each bush and tree with wildly-flung vines dripping with purple and white bells, and the honeysuckle and sweet briar would do their most fragrant best to kill your memories of the scent of departed hawthorn. At each side, a grassy bank climbed from the dust of the road to meet the green of the hedge. Innocent dog-daisies, slim-fingered ferns and tenacious Robin-run-the-hedge mingled with the waving little pink flags unfurled by the wild vetch.

There were gaps in the hedge that gave you occasional tantalizing glimpses of the bogland's wonder, but you did not linger at the gaps. Like an impetuous confident lover who scorns such sops to his passion as the kissing of the loved one's hand, you disdained these half-promises of joy and hurried on, impatient to reach the end of that screening hedge so as to possess completely and at once the bog's beauty.

As far as the eye could see stretched that prodigality of colour. The heather had ravished every shade of blue for its cloak, from palest mauve to deep purple. Here and there, the ridges of fluffy white bog-cotton danced into the tender green of fresh young bramble shoots. And the gorse-blossom, new-minted and clean, sent out a sweet winey smell where the sun shone hotly on it.

At intervals over the bog were scattered the little white cottages with their roofs of amber thatch and, close to them, in the rushy fields reclaimed from the bog, the red cattle grazed lazily. Wind-burnt men and women bent over the long banks of new-cut turf that was chocolate brown and richly sodden.

Grandmother's turf-bank, which she leased for ten shillings a year, was almost opposite the Reddins' cottage. This was convenient, for the Reddins always cut and reared our turf.

They were artists at their craft. Mick Reddin and his three sons, Joe and Willie and Ned, could wield a slane better than any man in Ballyderrig. Working together, they could cut and foot and heap the turf more quickly than a dozen other men. The pity was that they were never available together. Every day during the turf-rearing season the four of them were in constant employment at different banks up and down the bog.

If they had not been such splendid men at their trade they would have been boycotted, for the Reddins were not popular in Ballyderrig. We feared and distrusted them. We could tolerate Sarah Gorry but we could not accept the Reddins. Theirs was that gravest taint of all . . . they were anti-clerical.

Old Mick Reddin read much, and when he went into Duffy's for a drink in the evening he liked to horrify religious Mickey O'Neill, the barman, by hinting darkly that Ireland would one day follow the lead of France.

He would take a long drink from his pint and lean across the bar to Mickey, his eyes narrowed and his grey moustache bristling.

"What's wrong with you isn't just that you're iggorant — it's that you know nuthin'. Take a look at Spain, man." Mickey obligingly took a look.

"Well," Reddin would demand, "what did the priests ever do for Spain? Battened on it, they did. Sucked the blood out of it like vampires."

Now Mickey knew nothing of Spanish ecclesiastical history. His ideas of the land of Perez de Ayala and Goya were confined to a hazy suspicion that all Spaniards went about looking for bulls to fight when not engaged in growing onions and oranges. To Reddin's sacrilegious allegations he could only retort weakly but logically:

"Well, Ireland's not Spain."

Reddin would bury his moustache in his pint, and when he had drained the thick glass would utter darkly:

"Ha! Just wait awhile, me lad. There'll be changes in this country yet. Red revolution — that's what we'll have."

And he would stump out of Duffy's leaving Mickey wondering if he shouldn't run up and warn Father Dempsey of the impending revolution.

Even the fact that the Reddins came to Mass every Sunday and went to their duties regularly did not reconcile us to them. They were dark restless men, wild in looks and dour in speech, always talking about the wrongs of Ireland. From living so near the Curragh with its English population we had grown apathetic about such improbable things as Irish freedom, and the three Reddin boys were the only Ballyderrig men who went up to Dublin in Easter week.

Father Dempsey had no great liking for the Reddins. His dislike of them dated from the time when he first came to Ballyderrig. He was a city man, and it took us a long time to get used to his fine accent and his queer pronunciation of our names. When at Mass on Sundays he read out the names of those who had paid their dues, a wave of something that was half amusement, half irritation would sweep over the congregation as he read, "Kate Braw-han, half-a-crown," instead of Kate Moroccan. Yes, we knew Kate's name was spelt 'Broughan.' But wouldn't you think an educated man like a priest would know that 'Broughan' was always pronounced 'Moroccan' — in our part of the country anyway? Similarly, he insisted on calling Martin Kehoe, Martin Kay-hoe. But, though these strange habits of Father Dempsey irritated us, we were prepared to overlook them and to put them down to the general queerness of Dublin people. None of us would ever have dreamed of showing the disrespect to his cloth that Mick Reddin did.

It seems that about a month after his coming to Bally-derrig, Father Dempsey was upset to find that his horse had toothache. He was a great believer in raw potatoes for curing toothache in his horse, and he inquired of his housekeeper as to who among his parishioners grew the best potatoes.

She told him, as truthfully she might, that Mick Red-din of the bog was known throughout the country for his splendid Arran Chiefs. She glanced out of the window at that moment and saw Mick driving into the town in his horse and cart.

"There's the man himself now, Father," she said. "If you go to the door you'll catch him."

Father Dempsey went to the door and hailed Mick. It must be confessed that the good priest had rather a lordly manner which was aggravated by his refined accent.

"Come here a moment, my good man," he called. "I want to speak to you."

Mick pulled up the horse. Even then he suffered from rheumatism brought on by working in the dampness of the bog. He climbed stiffly from the cart and walked to where Father Dempsey stood in the doorway of his house.

"Yes, Father?" he said, respectfully enough.

"Er — my horse has the toothache and I was wondering if you had any of those large, ordinary potatoes. You could bring them in to me, say a stone or two, some time to-morrow. You know the kind I want — those large ordi-nary ones. You have plenty of them, I'm sure."

Mick was silent a second.

"I have, your reverence," he said, "but I've plenty of

those large ordinary childher to ate them. Good-day to you."

The Reddin family always seemed to be in trouble with the clergy. When the boys were young and going to school, Mr. Byrne said he would rather teach Latin and Greek to a deaf-mute than prepare the Reddins for the diocesan examination. No matter how well they answered their catechism in class they were bound to make some awful bloomer when Father Mahon came to examine them. They made these bloomers in all innocence. They just seemed incapable of absorbing the finer points of religious instruction like the other children.

There was that awful year when Mr. Byrne, wishing to outdo himself in grinding the children, coached them in the lives of the saints in addition to teaching them the prescribed course. There was one story in particular that seemed to go down very well with the boys. It concerned some holy hermit who wore a leather girdle.

When Father Mahon arrived, Mr. Byrne mentioned the lengths to which his enthusiasm had carried him and begged that the priest might be good enough to question the boys on this additional course. As ill luck would have it, Father Mahon picked out Ned Reddin.

"Well, son," he said, "what saint would you like to tell me about?"

Poor Mr. Byrne was mortified to hear Ned answer promptly,

"The one who wore the leather girl around his waist, Father."

The following year, his brother Joe surpassed this effort. For months, Mr. Byrne had been drilling into him the meaning of the infallibility of the Pope.

When Father Mahon arrived, Mr. Byrne was overjoyed when he questioned Joe Reddin on the very subject in which he had been so carefully coached.

"What does the infallibility of the Pope mean?"

"It means he can't tell a lie when he's teaching."

So far so good. Mr. Byrne was smiling openly with satisfaction.

"And why can't he tell a lie?" Father Mahon persisted. The smile left Mr. Byrne's face. He had not pursued the question so far as this with Joe. He waited fearfully while Joe searched his brain for the answer.

"Come on, son," Father Mahon said. "Why can't the Pope tell a lie when he's teaching?"

A beam of intelligence that almost shouted "Eureka!" suddenly shone on Joe's heated face.

"Because he reads it out of a book!" he said brightly.

I liked to sit and watch the men cutting the turf. One of the Reddins wielded the triangular slane. He had three helpers. As the dripping sods were cut, one man lifted them, two at a time, into the barrow. Mike Brophy wheeled the heavy barrow along the bank, and a fourth man went before him laying out the turf to dry. Later, the women would come to pile the turf loosely into little footings of five sods each, and when the footings had partially dried, they were erected in waist-high stacks to finish drying. Afterwards, the turf was wheeled out to the side of the road where it was built into a clamp and left there until the time came to draw it home.

Grandmother always sent me out to the bog with Judy Ryan to take the men their dinner.

We brought them stacks of round spongy griddle cakes, and crusty loaves of currant bread. A whole shoulder of bacon which for the sake of extra flavour and tenderness had been cooled in the water in which it was boiled, was cut up for the hungry men.

We lit a fire on the bog to make their tea. Four big sods were selected and made into a square to form a hob. In the centre we piled little branches of withered heather and scraps of flaky dry turf. When the kindling had taken, we piled on bigger pieces of turf and soon we had a glowing fire. The blackened can of brownish water from the stream was set on the hob to boil. When it was bubbling, Judy dropped in a handful of tea and sugar, lifted off the can, and set the tea to draw while the men came running in answer to her call.

They ate enormously and then lay on their backs for a little while in the heather before returning to their labour to work up an appetite for the still more enormous supper that awaited them in Gran's kitchen when day was done.

My grandmother always said that a day without potatoes was a day without nourishment. She took a great pride in feeding her employees well, and for the turf-cutters' supper she always had, not ordinary boiled potatoes, but steamed potatoes, and sometimes thump.

The potatoes to be steamed were scrubbed and put into the baker with a cupful of water. The baker was then covered, coals were piled on its lid and the potatoes were left to convert themselves into balls of flour. Knowing that butcher's meat would be a treat for these men who rarely tasted it except at Christmas or Easter, she generally had a big joint of John Dooley's good juicy beef for them, although the men would have been well content to make their supper off the steamed potatoes, topped and buttered and eaten with a spoon like eggs.

But she gave them boiled beef as well, cooked with peas and carrots and onions and chopped cabbage, barley and dumplings. Sometimes she prepared a mock goose, spreading a great slice of steak with mashed potatoes, chopped scallions, lard, pepper and salt and a sprinkling of dried sage. The meat was rolled up, tied with tape and roasted. She basted it with milk and served it with a good brown gravy to which was added a tablespoonful of her mushroom ketchup.

The only drawback to those evenings when she made thump for the turf-cutters was that no matter how much she prepared, the men never seemed to have sufficient of the creamy fluffy potato mixture. For thump, she boiled the potatoes whole in their jackets. When they were cooked, I peeled and beetled them with the big wooden beetle, while Gran boiled a handful of scallions to tenderness in a half-pint of milk. The milk and scallions were added to the potatoes together with pepper and salt and a generous lump of butter and then the mixture was beaten until it was as white and light as freshly-fallen snow.

With thump she gave them succulent chops browned to perfection before the fire in her big Dutch oven.

Often the main dish was followed by a big rice pudding, yellow with eggs and richly spotted with raisins and sultanas, spicy cinnamon, and coated with a fragrant brown skin of nutmeg. Sometimes she unearthed a few of last year's apples from their bed of hay in the loft and made them into a dumpling.

Gran's apple dumplings, served with drawn butter, were a meal in themselves, rich, satisfying and full of flavour from the cloves and brown sugar. The tender pastry that wrapped the apples was a delight.

She took five or six freshly cooked potatoes and bruised them on the baking-board with the bottom of a big delft mug. A cup of melted butter was sprinkled over them and a good pinch of salt. Then she worked in enough flour to bind the mixture and rolled it out. When the chopped apples, cloves, brown sugar and scraps of butter had been encased in rounds of pastry, the dumplings were tied up in scalded and floured squares cut from a well-boiled flour-bag and put down to cook in boiling water.

When supper was over, the men liked to sit around the kitchen fire. Drowsy with food and their day's hard labour on the bog, they were content to sit without speaking. Whichever of the Reddin boys happened to be present would usually take a French fiddle from his pocket and play softly the plaintive old tunes of Carolan and Rose Mooney and the other Irish harpers.

His playing was good, for all the Reddins were natural musicians, but we were always relieved when he put the mouth-organ back in his pocket, and after a curt "Good-night to yez, now," set out for his home in the bog.

"He's terrible nacky with the French fiddle," Mike Brophy would say when he had gone, "but them sad tunes he plays belong to the banshee."

The unrest of the Reddin clan that made them despise our apathy and our contented acceptance of whatever government was in power, that drove Willie and Joe to fall fighting on the edge of the Curragh a few years later, had disturbed our quiet kitchen while the boy played, and comfortable peace came to us once more when his footsteps died away down the boreen.

CHAPTER 6

UNTIL the June of my first year with Gran, no one had ever told me frankly and exactly where babies came from. By that time I had, of course, a pretty good idea, but it was the result of private observation and not of reliable information.

A straight question to my mother on the subject had always brought a snub or an evasive answer. We were encouraged to believe that all babies were bought from Nurse Cassidy, the midwife, who had a monopoly of them, and that she catered for the Ballyderrig baby-demand from some mysterious source of supply in her garden.

This explanation was just another proof of the way most grown-ups seemed to underrate our intelligence. No normally-intelligent child could have failed to pick on the weak spots in this improbable story. Why, for instance, did Nurse Cassidy never have babies of her own if she could come by them so readily? Why, if you had to pay dear money for them, did rich Mrs. Roche have only one while the poorest among us had eight or ten? Further, why was Nurse Cassidy so thoughtless and inconsiderate as to bring a baby to a woman just at a time when it was least convenient for her to look after it? I know she never failed to bring a baby to our house immediately my mother had to go to bed with a sore leg. That leg was surprising. Never a sign of a scar or a sore or a vein on it. But there it was — a periodic visitation. And it always coincided with Nurse Cassidy's arrival with a new baby.

When I realized I was being lied to, I asked no more

questions. Looking back, I cannot say when exactly I finally rejected the story, or when and how a suspicion of the truth dawned on me. I suspect my knowledge came to me as such knowledge comes to all children. A word overheard here and there, a look noted, a gesture observed — odds and ends that were slowly fed to the subconscious until gradually and unnoticeably a semblance of a fact was assimilated.

Although my own observation was sufficient to explode for me the Nurse Cassidy fallacy, there were no looks or signs to give me an inkling of the mysteries of adolescent girlhood.

When Gran came up to our room one night in July, she found me sitting up in bed white-faced with fright because of something I had observed while undressing.

"In the name of God, child," she demanded, "what's come over you?"

Grey-lipped, I told her the reason for my terror.

"What's wrong with me, Gran?" I asked tearfully. "Am I going to die?"

"The devil a die," was Gran's comforting answer. "But, tell me child, did your mother never say a word to you about this?"

"She didn't, Gran," I said.

"Well, that beats out," Grandmother said. "God knows I gave *her* plenty of warning. I can't make out your not having found it out for yourself and you so well up in other ways. You know where babies come from, don't you?"

I did, of course. An incredible thought struck me.

"Oh, Gran," I breathed, half in fear and half in delight, "am I — am I going to have a baby?"

At this Gran threw back her head and laughed so heartily that I found myself laughing too.

"You little oinseach!" she said to me at last. "It isn't as easy as all that to have a baby. Here, move over a bit and let me sit on the bed and I'll try and explain it all to you."

I moved into the middle of the big bed and Gran sat on the side of it.

"From to-night you're not a child any longer, Delia," she said. "You're a little woman now. From now on your body is fit to do the work that God created it for, and that is to bring children into the world. Listen to me . . . do you know that little stream at the bottom of Loughlin's Grove? It flows on, doesn't it, without rhyme or reason, down into the river? And what happened to it last month?"

"It stopped flowing," I said. "It stopped flowing for two days because the Loughlins dammed it with scraws and rocks above at the bend to make a big pool for washing the sheep."

"Exactly," Gran agreed. "To look at that little bit of a stream, you'd think it was no use for anything on God's earth. You'd say it was there for a nuisance — indeed, many is the time I called it that myself when I had to pick my way over it on stepping-stones. But the same stream turned out very useful last month when the Loughlins dammed it and turned it into a fine deep pool for the sheep-shearing. It's the same way with what's after happening you to-night. It happens to every girl when she comes to your age. Month in and month out, that will go on happening to you, and it will last a few days with you every month. If ever you're tempted to say to yourself that it's a useless thing and a nuisance, remember Loughlin's stream. For when you're married, please God, and when your time comes to have a child, you'll find out the reason for it and the use it has. It will stop the way the stream did. It will stop for nine months and all the time the baby inside you will be growing bigger and stronger — like the pool above at the bend got bigger and deeper when the water was dammed."

Grandmother's knowledge of biology may not have been very accurate, but there was nothing lacking in her honesty and delicacy.

"It's a grand and a wonderful thought," she went on, "that God should have gone to so much trouble when He was creating a woman. Women have a lot more than men to thank Him for and be proud of."

Since, when I have heard women complaining of "the curse of Eve" and "the plague of women," I have remembered Gran's words.

Emboldened by her sympathy and by the easy natural way she had disposed of my fears, I voiced a problem that had perplexed me for some time.

"What did Sarah Gorry mean, Gran, when she said the Corporal was the first?" I asked. "You know — what she said that day when Annabel was dying."

Gran withdrew from me for a moment and her mouth tightened a little.

Then, "We'll leave poor Sarah out of this," she said gently. "When you're older you'll know that some of us are weaker than others and that none of us have more virtue than what we pray for. What you want to know, I take it, is what men have to do with women having babies."

Yes, that was what I wanted to know. I had already guessed there must be some connection, but what it was I could not hazard.

"It's like this," Gran said, searching for the right words. "God never intended for women to bring children into the world and then have the whole bother and responsibility of looking after them. Neither did He intend for men to be just the bread winners for their children and not have a real share in them like a woman has. So He fixed things so that part of both the father and the mother goes into a child and they own it between them. You're a lucky girl to have been born and bred in the country, for you'll find what I'm going to say to you real easy to understand where a city child wouldn't take it in in a million years."

She smoothed down her checked apron and then put a wrinkled hand on mine.

"Making a child is very like farming," she said. "When harvest time comes, you can't rightly say that the farmer owns the crops entirely, for there wouldn't be any crops at all only for the earth that feeds and nourishes them. The crops don't belong entirely to the earth, either, for it could lie there fallow for all eternity if the farmer didn't sow seed in the spring. It's just the same with a man and a woman. The man carries in his body the seed that God gave him. It's only a fool of a farmer who'll sow seed in any old bit of ground, and the man who's a good Christian and a pure man will be just as careful in the sowing of human seed. He'll wait until he finds the woman he wants for the mother of his children. When he marries her decent, he'll give her his seed then and not before."

"How does he give her his seed, Gran?"

"That's something that needn't trouble you till you're married yourself, child. It's a sacred thing and a holy thing and not to be talked about."

"And what does the woman do with the seed when she gets it?"

"What the earth does with seed—she keeps it deep inside of her and feeds it and nourishes it with her substance. When the harvest-time comes and the baby is born, the two of them have an equal share in it. Now do you see?"

Of course I saw, Gran, God bless you! No shame, no shock, no disgust . . . only a grand happy understanding and a great thankfulness that God had ordained everything so wisely and so well.

But there was another question. Gran saw it trembling on my lips.

"I declare you'll keep me sitting here all night!" she said in mock irritation. "You ask more questions than Father Mahon. Well . . . come on. Out with it. What's troubling you now?"

"Why is it a sin for a girl to have a baby before she's married?" I asked.

Any other woman would have said, "Because it's forbidden by the Sixth Commandment and that should be reason enough for any Christian." But it wasn't Gran's way to take the easy road out.

"Well, there's many a good reason for it," she said. "In the first place, if a girl lets a man give her the seed of his body without being married to him, it means they're both committing adultery — and adultery, as you know, is forbidden under pain of mortal sin. And then, as I was saying a minute ago, every child needs a mother and a father and a proper home, and the child of a girl who isn't married can't have these, God help it. You see poor Sarah's children for yourself and how they're reared. That's why every girl should keep herself to herself and wait for the right man to come along — the man who'll love and respect and marry her. Once they're married, they can have all the babies they want, and good luck to them."

"Why don't people always wait till they're married then?"

"Because, God help us, the wanting of a man for a woman and a woman for a man is like a craving in our poor bodies. It is something like the appetite for drink, Delia. But decent people don't let it master them, just like decent people don't go and make beasts of themselves in drink."

"Why is it a craving, though? I mean, does a person get a lot — a lot of joy out of it?"

Gran looked across at the picture of my grandfather which hung under the Good Shepherd picture on the opposite wall. Her face was soft in the candlelight.

"Done in love and with the blessing of God on it, there's no joy on earth to come near it. It is being lifted right out of this world and into the next in the arms of the person you love more than yourself. But done in lust, it is nothing but brute drunkenness, with a disgust and a shame and a vomit after it. For you see, child, though the devil can make us forget for a while that we're made in God's image and likeness, he can't make us forget it all the time. And it's when we stop forgetting and let God into our hearts once more that we could die with shame for fouling the temple of the Holy Ghost."

She rose from the bed and untied the strings of her apron.

"And now turn around there while I take off my clothes," she said. "Here's a last word to you. Mind you guard and look after the body that God gave you, and keep it safe and pure. His Holy Mother'll help you if you say this little prayer every night of your life: 'Through thy sacred Virginity and Immaculate Conception, O Most chaste Virgin, obtain for me purity and sanctity of soul and body.' Say that after me, now."

Obediently, I said it again and again until I had it off by heart.

When Gran was in bed, she said, "Maybe we'd go for mushrooms to-morrow morning. Mike Brophy tells me the Hollow Field is white with them."

I went to sleep with my mind filled — not with the weighty facts of life we had been discussing — but with glad anticipation of the following morning's excursion to the Hollow Field.

From late June until the middle of August was mushroom time. I loved those dewy mornings when Grandmother and I rose at five o'clock to gather the platters and the white cuppeens that, fresh and tender and pink-fleshed, pushed through the grasses with the first rays of the sun. In Ballyderrig it was held that mushrooms went back into the ground as the day advanced, and that early rising was essential if you wanted a good basketful.

Gran was ready dressed next morning when she wakened me by making the Sign of the Cross on my forehead with

holy water. She wore an old tweed cap of my grandfather's on her head, and the tail of her skirt was turned up
and pinned around the waist so that it might not catch the
dew in the long grass.

She left me to dress while she went downstairs to boil
Johnny Doyle's little tin kettle for an early cup of tea.
When we had drunk our tea, we took our baskets from
the buttery and set off.

There was a magic in the boreen at that hour. From
the leafy hedges came the sleepy twitterings of early birds,
and far away in the bog a lone curlew sent out his sad call.
Faint stirrings among the grass-hidden roots of bramble
and hawthorn and sloe bush told that we had disturbed
some little furry creature, wary-eyed and timid, by our
passing. And dew gemmed the delicate lace which grey
field-spiders had woven on the shiny red branches of sweet
briar.

The best place for mushrooms was the Hollow Field at
the bottom of Carroll's meadow. To enter the meadow,
we had to climb a stile directly opposite our boreen.
Grandmother needed no help in getting over the stile.
She crossed it with more agility than myself, and, once
over, she swung along the little path that edged the meadow
with the keen enjoyment of a young girl.

As we walked along the narrow path, one behind the
other, we kept close to the hedge so as to avoid the mois-
ture of the dew-drenched meadow grass that grew waist
high. It rippled smoothly in the light morning breeze,
and the tall fringed dog-daisies and glowing poppies that
dotted its surface nodded their heads to the sun. As we
walked, an occasional grinning frog leaped out of our way
into the sea of meadow-grass.

On this side of the road all the land for miles around belonged to the 'Shift' Carrolls. In Ballyderrig, where almost every family was given a nickname, the 'Shift' Carrolls possessed the queerest name of all. They were wealthy people with a big family of boys and girls. Mrs. Carroll had married above her. Her mother, in spite of her son-in-law's wealth, still lived in the little two-roomed cottage where Maggie Carroll had been born and reared.

"Why do they call them the 'Shift' Carrolls, Gran?" I asked, as I followed her along the little meadow path.

"Because it was an American shift that got Maggie Carroll's man for her," Grandmother said back to me over her shoulder. "There's not a word of a lie in that, for Maggie Carroll — Maggie Doyle she was then — told the whole story herself to Mary Regan of the shop shortly before she got married. She was a fool to tell it to Mary Regan for Mary could never keep her own secrets, let alone anyone else's."

Bit by bit, Grandmother told me the story as we went along through the stirring scented morning, but it is only now that her dry little sentences take on life and meaning. It is only looking back from a long distance that I can focus the fragments into a complete picture.

From the time Lizzie Doyle first went to America, she sent home a plentiful supply of clothes to her sister Maggie. Her mistress, it seems, was a carelessly generous woman and when she had tired of her clothes, which was often, she passed them on to Lizzie. Lizzie kept the best of them and sent the remainder home to Maggie.

All kinds of lovely things came Maggie's way — furred coats, leather handbags, silk stockings and clinging, vivid, wonderful frocks. These American frocks did something to Maggie Doyle. Always a good-looking girl, with her wide grey eyes, milky skin and auburn hair, she became a raving beauty when she dressed herself in the gorgeous frocks that Lizzie sent home.

It was an American frock that first made Denis Carroll take notice of Maggie. He overtook her one evening on his way home from the town. The elegance of the soft green velvet frock she was wearing made him think she was some visitor, but when she said, "Good evening to you, Mr. Denis," he recognized the soft little voice of Maggie Doyle. Still, he had to look twice before he could convince himself that this glowing creature was the quiet-spoken girl who had lived all her life in the little cottage at the very gate of his home.

With every step of the road they walked that evening, Denis Carroll discovered in Maggie beauties that he had never noticed before. How white her teeth were, and how perfect. How small her hands and how neat her feet in their ridiculous little American shoes of fawn kid. How very long and black the lashes that fringed her grey eyes, and how snowy the skin around her mouth by contrast with her red lips. By the time they reached Doyle's cottage, these discoveries had so impressed Denis that he had made an appointment with Maggie for the following night.

They met frequently after that, but secretly, for Denis knew his parents would not smile on a romance between their only son and Maggie Doyle. But in Ballyderrig it has always been impossible to keep anything secret. The whole story came out, and Denis was threatened and coaxed and bullied by his angry father and his weeping mother until he promised to give up Maggie and agreed to let himself be sent away to England.

Maggie was heartbroken, and even the arrival of a fresh parcel of clothes from America did nothing to cheer her. Mrs. Doyle opened the parcel and unfolded the lovely garments. Among them was something the like of which neither Maggie nor her mother had ever seen in their lives. It was a chemise — but what a chemise! A wisp of sapphire chiffon, it was edged with the finest and most delicate of creamy lace through which was drawn a narrow velvet ribbon.

In spite of the heaviness of her heart, Maggie was thrilled by the loveliness of the wispy silken garment. She held its blue against the auburn of her hair and looked in the small cracked mirror opposite the door to see the effect.

Mrs. Doyle clicked her tongue when she took the little chemise in her hand and saw its transparency.

"Imagine wearing the likes of that to keep out the cold," she said sarcastically. "The American women must be queer and hot in their leather. Still an' all, Maggie, it'll make a nice little front for you to wear with your blue costume. I'll bring it into the town to-morrow and get Mrs. Lawler to make it up."

That night when her mother had gone to bed, Maggie again took out the chemise and looked at it. All her life, she had never worn other than a flour-bag shift. An irresistible temptation came over her to slip on the chemise just for a moment and feel the magic of its delicate caressing silkiness against her skin. Knowing that her mother would condemn the experiment as foolishness, she first tiptoed into the room off the kitchen to make sure her mother was asleep. Mrs. Doyle was sleeping soundly.

Maggie had taken off her blouse and skirt when she reflected that it would be almost sacrilege to put the shimmering, gorgeous garment, lying like a sapphire pool on the table, on a body that was not newly-washed. She filled the tin basin from the kettle, washed her young body with yellow soap and dried herself in the inadequate little towel from behind the door.

At last she reached for the sapphire chemise and drew it over her head. It was only then that Maggie Doyle realized her body's beauty. In spite of the ache in her heart for Denis Carroll, she was young enough and woman enough to feel exultant that her limbs were white and slim against the sapphire of the silken chemise and that her small breasts pushed trim and pointed under the creamy froth of lace edging.

The cool silky feel of the beautiful garment against her skin gave her an airy headiness. She kicked off her shoes and, suddenly, the confines of the smoky, peat-grimed little kitchen seemed to stifle her. Through the window, the moon poured down on a quiet silvered world. As in a trance, Maggie raised the latch and stepped on bare white feet into the cool beauty of the night.

She walked to the big rowan tree that stood just inside the cottage gate and leaned against it, suddenly weary and saddened by the moon's loveliness and by the return of her own temporarily forgotten heartache.

Across the road, the boy who planned to leave for England next day and who had come to look for the last time at the nest of his beloved, stared white-faced at the lovely vision. "Maggie," he called softly and unbelievingly. "Maggie."

At her name, Maggie Doyle looked up into the face of

Denis Carroll. All at once his eyes made her aware of her nudity, and a hot flush of shame mantled her as she tried to cover herself with her hands.

"If you look at me for another minnit, I'll screech for me mother, Denis Carroll," she said.

"I love you, Maggie," Denis said before tearing his eyes obediently away. "I'm never going to leave you."

Denis flatly refused to leave for England next day. His determination wore down his parents' opposition and he married Maggie Doyle before six months had passed.

The story, as I have told it, is how I now believe it to have happened. On that morning long ago, when Gran outlined it to me, I merely felt that Maggie Doyle had been very immodest in walking out into her garden dressed only in a shift, and I was relieved when we left the story behind us on reaching the gate leading into the Hollow Field.

I kept to the centre of the field, for it was here one was most likely to find the cuppeens, compact little mushrooms that grew in semicircles and in groups of three and four. Grandmother kept to the hedges, for she concentrated on finding platters to make ketchup. The platters were the big flat mushrooms, dark-fleshed and heavy with juice.

Long practice had made us both adept in finding the mushrooms. Instinctively, we knew in which clump of grass they were most likely to be hidden. We seemed to recognize a sheepfart from a distance of yards, and were never lured out of our path by the deceptive promise of these little white fluffy balls that broke into yellow powder when you stepped on them.

By eight o'clock we had filled our baskets and were ready for home and breakfast.

When we turned in at the kitchen door Judy had the table set and the kettle boiling and was standing in the buttery cutting thick rashers from the side of bacon. Mike had already milked and was preparing to feed the calves. I liked to help him to feed the calves. As they butted each other gently in their awkward babyish efforts to reach the pail of linseed meal and milk, I felt the same half sweet, half sad stirrings within me that I had felt when Grandmother placed the tinker's baby in my arms. To fool the little calves into an illusion of motherhood, we held our hands below the surface of the liquid food and let them suck our fingers. They drank in the food as they sucked.

When we went into the kitchen, our breakfast was on the table — soda bread and brown bread and ash cakes, butter and parsley jelly, and a big blue dish of sizzling hot bacon and inviting mushrooms. Some of the mushrooms were fried. Judy had broiled a special portion for me on the gridiron, because that was how I liked them best. She pulled a light raking of red coals under the griddle-stand and set the greased gridiron on this. The mushrooms were stalked, sprinkled with salt and set to cook on the gridiron until they slowly filled with juice and grew brown and tender. You had to be very careful in dishing them up, for to spill that delicious juice was to lose all the goodness of the mushrooms.

Some of the cuppeens were reserved for supper, to be stewed in milk with butter and pepper and salt, and eaten with tiny new potatoes. More often than not, at the last moment Gran stirred a cupful of clotted cream into the mushroom stew. She had her own way of preparing clotted cream. Overnight, a wide pan of milk was left on one side for the heavy cream to form on top. Next morning, the pan was heated over a slow fire to set the cream. When it was cold, the thick coating of cream was lifted off and beaten smooth with a spoon.

During the mushroom season, Gran made ketchup every five or six days. Each fresh gathering of platters was bruised, emptied into a big crock and covered with a layer of salt. When the crock was full, she added cloves, mace and spice and red pepper. The contents of the crock were then simmered gently for four hours, strained and bottled. She made countless bottles of the piquant winey sauce, for there were few in Ballyderrig to whom she did not present a few bottles.

CHAPTER 7

THE Convent school re-opened on the second Monday in August. I was put into seventh class with Mary Joe Heffernan and Bridie Murray of the bog. I had no great taste for lessons and it's little work I would have done if Sister Mary Patrick who taught Fifth, Sixth and Seventh, and knew that Grandmother wanted to make a teacher out of me, had not kept a close eye on me.

Sometimes I was sent in to mind the babies while their teacher, Sister Mary Anthony, who was in charge of the Convent garden, went to make sure that Paddy Moloney, the gardener, was not idling or eating the pears.

I was green with envy when I reached school that first morning after the holidays. Mary Joe Heffernan, whose father was one of the biggest farmers around Ballyderrig, and Bridie Murray, whose mother kept a public-house at Brackna Cross-Roads, had each of them a new bike.

The two-mile walk home from the town was hard on me that evening. The road to Derrymore had never seemed so long, and I kept thinking of how short it would be if only I had a bike. To make it even longer, a partridge flew down on the road right in front of me just as I came abreast of Doran's wheat field. It seemed to have a broken wing or an injured leg, for as I neared it, it fluttered lop-sidedly across the road and through the hedge into the field. I followed the partridge through a gap in the hedge and was just in time to see it alight in the centre of the wheat. Well, there was no following it there, for like every country child I had a respect for growing things, and if Maeterlinck's blue bird had alighted three yards

76

from where I stood and I had recognized it for what it was, it would not have tempted me to tread on the ripening wheat.

I plucked an ear of the wheat and, as Grandmother had taught me to do, I blessed myself with it three times — once for the food it stood for, once for the prosperity it represented, and lastly because the Consecrated Host was made of wheat.

When I reached Derrymore House I was later than usual.

"You're late," Gran said to me. "What kept you?"

"Ah, it's a long old road, Gran," I answered.

"That's the first time I heard you complain of it," was her dry comment. "Are your legs going on you?"

"If I'd a bike, I wouldn't be long covering it," said I.

Judy Ryan let a laugh out of her as she put my dinner before me — stewed ribs, it was, with a plate of baked apples and cream to follow.

"Maybe it's a bike you want," she teased. "You'll be looking for a canal boat next."

I attacked the stew. It was lovely. Plenty of sweet juicy pork on the ribs and with the potatoes just the way I liked them — some of them cooked to briseach to thicken the oniony gravy and more of them whole and firm.

"What's after putting the notion of a bike in your head, may I ask?" Gran brought her knitting over to the table and sat near me as I ate. She used to say that nothing gave her more pleasure than to watch me enjoying my food. I refused nothing, and I had an appetite like a bogman's.

I lowered the bone I was picking from my mouth.

"Oh, nothing," I said casually. Then, a moment or

two later, "Mary Joe Heffernan and Bridie Murray have a new bike apiece."

"H'mmm —" was Gran's comment. "Isn't it well for them that have money to burn?"

She said no more about the bike, and I never guessed a word of what she was up to — though it should have made me suspicious when she dressed herself and went into the town alone the following Saturday, for that was a thing she rarely did.

On the next Sunday week, Gran gave me a basket to take to an old crony of hers, Mrs. Doolin.

On Sunday evenings, I was often sent to call on bed-ridden Mrs. Doolin with small gifts of jelly and cake and smacks. If we had chicken for dinner, the cold breast was wrapped in butter-muslin and added to the contents of the brown basket with its lining of cool fresh cabbage leaves.

The invalid lived with her unmarried daughter in a small thatched cottage on the other side of Loughlin's Grove. I did not like going into the cottage which was dirty and ill-kept. If I went in, politeness forced me to accept the glass of buttermilk which Maria Doolin always offered. She was a sweaty untidy woman with dark greasy skin, heavy loose breasts and varicose legs. The thought that she had churned the buttermilk made it repugnant to me, and I hated to drink from the smeared glass which always smelled of dirty dishcloths.

I found it even more repugnant to enter the little room off the kitchen where Mrs. Doolin lay. The window had not been opened for twenty years and the fug of stale air, unwashed clothes and sickness was nauseating. To make matters worse, Mrs. Doolin always drew me down to her with a skinny claw and insisted on kissing me. My lips shrank from contact with her toothless mouth and bristling upper lip.

Whenever possible, I handed in the basket with a gabbled inquiry for Mrs. Doolin's health and, telling some lie about having to be home by a certain hour, I made a hasty escape.

There were compensations for these unpleasant visits.

In summer, there was joy in walking through the slowly gilding fields where corncrakes scolded in anger and tiny field-mice clung precariously to swaying stalks of grain. In Loughlin's Grove, a narrow belt of wood which fringed the road opposite Doolin's, the mystery of the cool green shade was very pleasant. I sometimes lingered here when I had delivered my basket and spent an hour picking the sweet wild strawberries that grew so plentifully on the little ferny hillocks in the Grove. To carry home the strawberries, I plucked long wiry stalks of wild wheat and threaded onto them the juicy red berries. Often, I brought home as many as ten hanks of strawberries.

I was forbidden to paddle in the stream that ran through the wood. Gran, who imposed so few restrictions on children's play, was unreasonable in her hatred of water. It dated from the time when my Aunt Alice, a child of six, had been found in the canal after having been missing for a day and a half. In Gran's trunk, carefully wrapped in tissue paper, were the little clothes Alice had been wearing that day. The clothes had never been washed — only dried and folded. I expect Gran felt that to wash them would be to lose the essence of contact with her child's body which the clothes retained. I had seen them once. Scraps of dried weeds from the canal's reedy bed still clung among the pleats of the stained little dress. In her prayer book Grandmother kept a strand of Alice's hair, a little golden circlet, unbelievably fine.

I am afraid I often ignored the ban which was placed on the stream. I could never resist the temptation to peel off shoes and stockings and dip my feet into the icy water, wriggling my toes luxuriously in the slimy black mud that lined the bed.

When bending over the stream I was always careful to keep my mouth tightly closed. Like all Ballyderrig children, I lived in mortal dread of the fat black tick-like creatures which we called darkie-lukers, and which were reputed to have a horrible tendency to leap from the water right into an open mouth. If you were so unlucky as to be invaded by a darkie-luker in this way, the only cure was to return to the stream on a moonlit night, and sit on the bank with your mouth open. It was believed that the sight of his fellows basking happily in the moonlit water might induce the fishy intruder to leave his human habitat through the door by which he had entered.

Personally, I never had much faith in this method of getting rid of a darkie-luker. I felt that, moon or no moon, to sit open-mouthed beside the stream was to ask for trouble. It was barely possible that the black tick would jump out your mouth, but it seemed to me just as likely that a whole shoal of darkie-lukers might be tempted to join their exiled brother. There was more sense in Judy Ryan's story of the Athy man who had got rid of one of these pests by standing, open-mouthed, over a pan of rasher gravy. The enticing smell of the gravy had lured the darkie-luker from his hiding-place.

There was another forbidden pleasure in which I oc-

casionally indulged on my way home from those visits to
Mrs. Doolin. If, instead of entering the Grove and coming home through the fields, I walked along the road, the
walk led me eventually to Mitchell's Forge.

The forge, deserted and silent, stood at the cross-road
where you turned to the right for Derrymore House. Instead of turning to the right, I frequently turned through
a gate on the left to watch the maypole dancers. I often
wondered why they called it a maypole, for there was no
pole. Just a number of planks laid side by side on the
grass, on which the boys and girls danced half-sets and
reels to the music of a fiddle and melodeon. The musicians were sometimes relieved by amateurs like the Reddin
boys, who could play for hours on a French fiddle — without once repeating an air.

There was no mixing of the sexes between dances at
the Maypole. The girls stood at one side, chatting and
laughing. On the other side stood the boys, to all appear-
ances completely unaware of the girls' presence. But
when Willie Beckett, who acted as M.C., shouted out,
"Take your partners for a half-set," there was a stampede
as the boys rushed for the best dancers.

One of the most light-footed of the girls and most often
in demand was Peg Molloy. Peg was a stout red-haired
girl with a freckled white face and a rather stupid expression. The girls who were jealous of her popularity as a
dancer cruelly called her 'the divil.' "Swing up 'the
divil,'" they would call to some boy who danced by with
Peg floating in his arms. Peg did not mind this taunt.
Long ago she had become accustomed to the notoriety
that had come her way as a result of having been possessed
by an evil spirit.

The possession of Peg Molloy was an old story in Bally-derrig. As a child of fifteen she had gone to service in England. Her employers were ardent spiritualists. Apparently, they found Peg with her dull brain and complete lack of self-will an ideal medium. During one of her trances, something dark and frightening happened to Peg. When she returned to Ballyderrig a year later, she was skeleton-thin and her eyes held a vacant terrified look.

She had not been home a week when her mother came in to Father Dempsey one day with a terrible story of cups that moved on the dresser of their own accord, of beds that lifted themselves towards the ceiling when Peg lay down to sleep, and of peculiar inexplicable noises that filled the house at night.

Father Dempsey was at first inclined to be sceptical, but investigations proved Mrs. Molloy's story to be tragically true. It was said that when he entered the house Peg had a terrible seizure, rolling herself on the ground and frothing at the mouth. The table in the room rocked like a ship, sending the cups and saucers to the floor. Mrs. Molloy herself said she felt unseen hands beating her face and pulling her hair.

There were repeated manifestations of this kind. It was proved conclusively that the spirit was not in possession of the Molloy house but of poor Peg herself, for when she was brought into other houses the same phenomena took place. Reluctantly, Father Dempsey was forced to the ugly belief that the unfortunate child was really possessed by an evil spirit.

He consulted the parish priest who in turn invoked the help of our Bishop. I have vivid recollections of those days, tense and anxious for all of us, when everyone in the parish joined their prayers with the solemn exorcising ceremonies performed by the clergy. There were dozens of priests at those ceremonies, and we heard afterwards that their intensity was so trying and so arduous that one poor priest died as a result of them.

But he did not die in vain. Our prayers were heard and the evil thing that had taken possession of innocent Peg Molloy was driven out. She grew plump and healthy again, and soon could be seen driving happily into the town in her mother's ass and cart and dancing gaily at the Maypole.

That was not the only case of possession we had in Ballyderrig. There was another case and the girl concerned went to school with me. Mary Reilly was her name. She was a queer dull silent child with black hair and thick pale lips. She was always getting slapped for not keeping her mind on her books. Anyone could see that half the time her thoughts were not in the class at all. She never played with the rest of us in the school yard. She didn't even sit with us to eat her lunch on the bench that ran down the length of the shed. She always went off to a corner of the yard by herself to eat her bread and butter and drink her naggin bottle of milk. And on rainy days when the rest of us sat on the concrete floor of the shed and played jacks, Molly Reilly withdrew from us. She would go and stay in the closet until Sister Mary Joseph came out ringing the big bell and it was time to go in to school again.

Mary Reilly's father was a decent, hard-working handy man who, although he had never served his time could do any kind of carpentry job as well as the best tradesman who ever lived. Her mother was an ordinary Ballyderrig woman, who looked after her husband and her children and her home and who went to her duties regularly. They lived in a narrow little two-storey house just beyond the rath. It may be thought that I am inventing the rath to make what I am going to tell more credible. But there is no lie in it. We have a rath in Ballyderrig and what is more it is right beside the graveyard. At the top of the town there is a small railed-off triangle set with laurel and holly-bushes which we call the Green. On the left, the street suddenly stops on a dead level with the Green. On the right, it continues for a further three houses. First the barracks and then Doctor Mangan's house and lastly, right beside the Protestant Church and the common graveyard, is the house where Mrs. Lane, the Protestant teacher, lived when I was a child and where in the front parlour she taught the seven or eight children of our small Protestant community.

Mrs. Lane took a great pride in her garden which ran flush with the graveyard. She had a couple of magnificent plum trees which in autumn spread golden globed fans against the graveyard wall. Moll Slevin, who used to work for my mother, and who went to service with Mrs. Lane after my family left Ballyderrig, sometimes came to see me at Derrymore House, bringing a pocketful of those lovely plums. Grandmother always advised me against eating them, saying that their size and plumpness were due to their proximity to the graveyard. She swore that Mrs. Lane had once given her a present of some of her plums. To test out a private theory of her own, she said she had placed them in a bowl of warm water when going to bed and that when she came down next morning there was a cake of grease a half-an-inch thick on top of the bowl.

When you passed the Protestant Church, you came to a breast-high wall that ran at the foot of the rath. The rath was covered with a clump of gnarled, hungry-looking trees, and was such a forbidding place that even the bravest of the Ballyderrig children never intruded there. On the other side of the rath was the Reillys' little house.

I feel myself that its nearness to the rath and the graveyard may have had something to do with the haunting of Mary Reilly. The rest of Ballyderrig must have thought so, too, for the house remained empty from the day the Reillys moved out of it.

There were four children in the Reilly family — Mary and three younger brothers. The first that was known of the haunting came out when Mr. Byrne, who had been puzzled and annoyed by the boys' sleepiness in class, asked them at what time they went to bed at night.

Joe, the eldest boy, burst into tears. He confessed that no matter how early they went to bed they got little sleep because of the queer noises that woke them up at all hours of the night. Noises which for over three months now had been heard in the little room over the kitchen that Mary shared with her father and mother.

"What kind of noises, Joe?"

"Like — like a horse kicking the wall, sir," the boy said. "But don't say anything to me mother, Mr. Byrne, sir! She said she'd kill us if we let on a word!"

Notwithstanding the frightened child's plea, Mr. Byrne

felt it his duty to investigate. After school that day he went to see Mrs. Reilly. Confronted with a direct question, the poor woman told the whole story. The noise had first been heard about three months before. The children were in bed and Mrs. Reilly and her husband were having a cup of tea before going to bed. Suddenly, this kicking started right over their heads just in the spot where Mary's bed stood. With their hearts in their mouths, they raced up the stairs. Mary was sitting up in bed, her face full of life and she talking what seemed to be gibberish to some unseen person or thing at the foot of the bed. And every time the child ceased speaking, the kicking sound was heard as if in answer. They managed to bring Mary to herself after a while but she was sullen and reticent and all she would say was that she had been talking to a friend. Since then, this strange and frightening noise had been heard night after night, with Mary answering to it in a strange jargon, but with everyone else in the house petrified with terror. Neither threats nor coaxings were successful in making the child divulge a word of information concerning the strange "friend."

Mr. Byrne told the story to Father Dempsey, who came and blessed the house. But his prayers were not successful, for the knocking went on until the Reillys were driven nearly out of their minds. At last Mr. Byrne suggested that a change of locality might help. A collection was made around the town and the afflicted family moved to Edenderry. Sure enough, they left Mary's "friend" behind them, and in Edenderry the Reillys were able to sleep in peace once more.

I always thought of the Reillys with gratitude, for their

departure for Edenderry provided me with inspiration that won ten-and-six for me in the Poet's Corner of a Dublin weekly paper. On the day they were moving, Sister Mary Joseph sent me to their house with a Reader and a Sum Book which Mary had left in school. I could get no answer at the door of the house, so I went around to the little shed at the back that Joe Reilly called his workshop. It was here he did his odds and ends of carpentry. The tools had been packed and the workshop was bare and empty.

Reilly stood in the middle of the floor, his face full of sorrow and loneliness. You could see that it was breaking his heart to have to say good-bye to the workshop.

He looked up when he saw me.

"Well," he said philosophically, "I'm no worse off than Saint Joseph. Sure he had to say good-bye to his workshop, too, that night of the Flight into Egypt." Joe Reilly was probably the first man ever to express a fellow-craftsman's sympathy with that particular aspect of Joseph the Carpenter's hurried evacuation.

It was a good thought. It was a thought that seized hold of my imagination. I went home with my head full of it, and by slow degrees the rhyming soft-falling words of a poem were forged out of it. Unknown to anyone, I sent my poem to the Dublin paper. When it won the weekly prize of half a guinea a few weeks later, I nearly went out of my mind with joy and excitement. Gran was afraid I might get too stuck up on the head of it, so she made little of my success. But anyone with half an eye could see she was bursting with pride and delight. This was the poem that Joe Reilly's loneliness inspired:

FLIGHT INTO EGYPT

It was hard on you, man, to rise up in the night
    And break in on their rest,
To waken the woman who smiled as she slept
    With the Child on her breast;
Hard in the telling the news that you bore
    As you bade her make haste,
And heavy your heart as you saddled the ass,
    Not a minute to waste.

Lonesome your thoughts when you stood at the door
    With your tools in your hand;
Your glance lingered long on the pile of new wood
    For the work you had planned.
Bitter it was to start out in the night
    For a man of your years,
To look back from the top of the hill at your home
    With your eyes filled with tears.

Hard though it was, all your lonesomeness went
    And your sorrow was done
When Mary leaned down from the hurrying ass
    And said "Carry my Son."
You carried Him, Joseph, with grandeur and peace
    Like a man who is blest,
Like a man who walks down from the altar of God
    With the Host in his breast.

I wanted to spend my ten-and-six on presents for everybody, but Gran made me put it towards the price of a pair of new shoes.

But I started off to tell about that Sunday evening when Grandmother sent me to Mrs. Doolin with the flummery and cake. As I came home around the side of the house swinging the empty basket, I heard a strange voice from the kitchen. Before opening the door, I looked in through the division in the curtains. Gran was there, sitting beside the fire in the big wooden chair with the red woollen cushions. Heck Murray was in the corner of the settle-bed drinking a big mug of tea. In the other corner of the settle, Judy Ryan and Mike Brophy sat side by side. Sitting before the fire was a visitor. His back was turned to me, but by his bald head I recognized him for Paddy Fitz, who kept the bicycle and harness shop in the town.

I opened the door and went in, but once inside the door the power left my limbs and I could not have got out a word of greeting to save my life.

What was leaning against the dresser but a brand-new girl's bike!

Suddenly, I was struck with a wild fear that my joy might be premature or unfounded and that the bike might not really be for me. Dry-mouthed, I looked quickly at Gran.

She gave a little nod of her head and from her smile and the flush on her face it was plain that she was as pleased and excited as I was myself.

"Well?" she demanded. "How do you like it?"

What could I say to her? Thank God for her understanding that let her see right into my heart and realise the love and joy and gratitude that were welling up there and were keeping me from thanking her in words.

"I wanted it to be a surprise for you," she said. "Paddy Fitz sent to Dublin specially for it. Sit up on it there till Paddy sees will he have to let down the saddle."

"Did it cost a lot, Gran?" I asked later when the saddle had been adjusted and every part of the bike down to the last tube of solution in the repair outfit had been examined and admired.

"Never you mind how much it cost," Gran retorted. "If it cost twice as much, I wasn't going to give Tommy Heffernan's daughter and Bridie Murray of the bog the laugh over you."

CHAPTER 8

DURING the weeks that followed I lived in a state of ecstasy induced by the heady delight of speeding over the roads of Ballyderrig on my lovely shining new bike. Mr. Mangan's sow brought me to earth. I was turning the corner at Mitchell's Forge when the sow crossed the road in front of me. September rains had made the road greasy and a quick braking sent me and my bike into the ditch.

The bicycle had to be returned to Paddy Fitz for repairs, and I was once more reduced to dull pedestrianism.

I was particularly upset that the accident should have occurred when it did, for the following day my monthly visit to Leadbeater's Mill fell due, and I had been looking forward to showing Miss Hope my new bike. I had a very deep affection for the little Quakeress and for her father, the Ballyderrig miller.

At one time, our town had been the centre of a large and prosperous colony of Quakers. The Odlums, the Goodwins, the Shepherds, the Langs and the Hanks families all attended the meeting-house on Sundays and in times of stress. They sent their children to be taught forbearance and a love of order at the little white schoolhouse. And their dead were buried in the garden-like burying ground where peace lay down with the sleeping Friends.

The meeting-house was a low white building, one-roomed, with brown-painted doors and windows. It was neat and modest, like the Quaker women themselves. It stood well back from the road, about a half-mile outside

Ballyderrig. Several times I indulged my curiosity by climbing over the white-painted gates and running up the gravel path with its neat border of white-washed stones, to peep in through the uncurtained casements of the empty meeting-house. Although the austere bareness of the cold white walls and prim wooden seats was a little forbidding to my Catholic eyes, I was conscious of the piety that lingered in the deserted little room. Somehow, this feeling made me ashamed of my prying and sent me scurrying away.

When I was a child, the schoolhouse was empty of scholars, for the Society had dwindled to a mere handful of widely-scattered people who came, twice a year, to pray in the meeting-house, and the only Quaker family left in Ballyderrig were the Leadbeaters of the Mill. But the Quaker buildings were not neglected, for Sam Leadbeater painted the woodwork and whitewashed the walls each year, and every spring he clipped the tall quick-set hedge that bounded the burying ground.

I liked old Sam Leadbeater. He was a quiet-spoken bearded man with eyes that were wise and kindly. He had a fine library of books of which he allowed me free use when I had proved myself careful in handling them and punctual in returning them. He always dressed in suits of dark grey cloth on which the mill dust lay in a thick film. Unlike other Ballyderrig men, he wore his starched white front and black tie even on weekdays.

He and his daughter Hope lived alone in their big gloomy old house, where the murmur of the millrace provided an accompaniment to all their words and activities. The mill had been declining for years, and I often heard

Grandmother say it was a pity that Frank, Sam's son, would not come home to help his father.

Hope Leadbeater was a small-boned slender woman of middle age, with faded fair hair that was smoothly-parted and coiled into a heavy bun behind. She had a gentle glance, and a pink and white skin marked by innumerable tiny lines. When she spoke, most of her sentences trailed away into a deprecating little ghost of a laugh that sounded as if, on second thoughts, she felt she had been over-daring in speaking. With the exception of the fact that she wore her fair hair uncovered and not hidden by the white cap of the Quakers, she observed the traditions of the Society in her dress. A tight-bodiced, full-skirted gown of light fawn clothed her meagre figure. I never saw her without her snowy muslin apron and the fine lawn kerchief which was crossed meekly over her little bosom.

The people of Ballyderrig liked to think that Hope had not always been so meek. They said that as a young girl she had been wildly in love with a Catholic boy from Dublin who came to stay with the Fulhams, and that she had even run away with him. Sam Leadbeater, the story went on, had overtaken the runaways before they got as far as Naas, and had brought Hope home again. I never believed the story, for I found it impossible to connect gentle mild Hope with the thought of any strong emotion. I found it equally difficult to picture kind tolerant Sam Leadbeater as the type of man who would prevent his daughter marrying the man she loved.

Friendship and understanding existed between Hope and my grandmother, although two more opposed characters would be difficult to imagine. Yet their love of thrift and their great interest in good food bound the shy little Quaker woman and my forthright strong-minded Gran.

They liked to exchange recipes and samples of preserves, and frequently Sam Leadbeater sent Gran small gifts of game. Once he sent her a hare, and on that occasion Grandmother invited the Leadbeaters to share it. It made a very piquant dish, steamed in the baker and stuffed with a dressing of beef suet, breadcrumbs, parsley, sweet herbs, onion, lemon peel, grated nutmeg, pepper and salt and the hare's liver chopped fine. The dressing, which was bound with a couple of beaten eggs, sent an indescribably good flavour through the flesh of the hare. Grandmother cured the skin of the hare and got Patsy Ennis, the cobbler, to fashion the rich dark fur into a pair of slippers for me.

I liked to be sent down to Leadbeaters to order our monthly supply of Indian meal and wheaten meal.

We used a big supply of both.

The fowl, of course, got the lion's share of Indian meal. In addition, Grandmother had many delectable ways of making it into bread and cakes. One of the best of these was ash cakes, which we ate with rashers and eggs. The meal was first scalded with boiling salted water. It was then made into a dough, rolled out thinly and cut into little scones. A bed was made on the hearth by raking away the spark-sprinkled ashes on all sides. Each scone was rolled in cabbage leaves and placed in the bed. Hot ashes were then piled on top of them and they were ignored until half an hour had passed, when they were lifted out and the scorched leaves turned back to disclose steaming fragrant little cakes, perfectly cooked and firm.

Sopped in rasher gravy and egg-yolk, they had a very sweet nutty flavour.

Grandmother also made the Indian meal into tea-scones. She mixed the golden meal with its weight in flour, added salt and bread soda and rubbed in a big lump of fluffy fresh lard. A cup of buttermilk with an egg or two were used to bind the mixture. She cut it in rounds with the handleless cup she kept for the purpose and baked the scones on the griddle. They were delicious eaten hot with butter and jam.

Two or three times a week we had Indian meal stir-about. When there was any left over, Judy Ryan scraped it into a bowl and left it on one side to set firm. When it was cold, Gran cut it into slices, fried it in butter and served it hot with golden syrup.

Occasionally, the order also called for a small quantity of sids, the finer husks of the oats. When Grandmother's digestion gave her trouble, she made herself a dish of sowans from the sids. She had great faith in the medicinal value of sowans for all kinds of stomach trouble.

The sids were mixed with oatenmeal and covered with buttermilk and warm water. After the mixture had been left to ferment for a couple of days the liquor was strained off, seasoned, and boiled until thick as jelly. She ate the jelly with milk before going to bed at night and swore next day that she felt a new woman.

You entered the Mill grounds over an old stone bridge with very low walls. I have since learned that the walls were built low to allow the passage of the pack donkeys that in olden times passed over the bridge with creels of flour and meal strapped to their sides.

The avenue leading to Leadbeaters was dark and silent from the chestnuts that sent embracing branches from each side. In early spring, snowdrops and crocuses splotched the avenue's grassy border with white and purple and gold. Later the wild hyacinth sent spreading stains of blue through the long grass, and blood-cowslips nodded their fringed red heads in lonely little clumps of twos and threes. When May came, it was good to walk beneath those trees with their great thick spikes of peppermint-pink blossoms.

I always brought Grandmother's order around to the back door where Miss Hope worked in her neat kitchen. She brought me in and sat me down at the white-scrubbed table under the muslin-curtained window. On warm days I was given lemonade and fairy cakes. In cold weather, Miss Hope gave me hot buttery pancakes speckled with sultanas, and a glass of warm milk sweetened with honey and with a dusting of cinnamon on its surface.

This hospitality never varied.

While I ate, Miss Hope went down with Gran's order to her father in the mill and I was left alone in the high dim kitchen, where golden flitches of bacon hung from the mellowed rafters, and the flicker of the fire was reflected in the gleaming delft on Miss Hope's dresser and in the burnished preserving pans that hung on the wall.

When Miss Hope came back to the kitchen it was time for me to return the book I had borrowed on my last visit and to select another. She brought me along the dark passage running from the kitchen and up the wide staircase with its thick mahogany banisters and bare shallow steps, to the room on the first floor where her father kept his books.

From the moment you entered the Leadbeaters' house you noticed a distinctive smell. The smell one notices in convents. A smell of cleanliness and orderliness and austerity. It triumphed over the cooking smells that pervaded the kitchen. It lingered in every recess of the dark passage and waited for you on every step of the broad staircase. But the convent smell was lost when you opened the door of the library, for here it was vanquished by an odour of mildewed leaves and bindings. The damp which penetrated every room in the time-scarred old house was most noticeable in the library.

Having conducted me thus far, Miss Hope left me to make my selection from the thousands of books that lined the shelves and lay in heaps on the floor.

Mr. Leadbeater had amassed his library by attending auctions all over the country and by buying bundles of books wherever they were offered for sale. The collection was a curiously mixed lot. Shakespeare and Voltaire, Dickens and Victor Hugo, Milton, Thackeray, Sir Walter Scott . . . these and hundreds of others were there, incongruously rubbing shoulders with school primers, medical books, weighty legal volumes and paper-backed novels by Ouida and Mrs. Henry Wood and Charles Garvice.

I have often suspected that it wasn't a love of reading that made Sam Leadbeater spend his scant shillings on that queer mixture of volumes. I feel it was more probably a love of books, a love of all that printed paper stood for: romance, tolerance, wisdom, culture — all the things that those of us who were born and bred there mistakenly believed were scarce in Ballyderrig. I even doubt if he had read more than half-a-dozen of the books he sacrificed so much to buy. Several times, he betrayed himself by fibs — notably on that occasion when I unearthed Volume One of *The Geography of Ireland* from under a pile of yellow books. I had selected Mrs. Hall that day, not because I had ever heard of her, nor because her strange versions of our folklore were at all likely to appeal to my strongly Catholic nationalism. I had selected the book, as I usually selected others, because the cover was clean and of a colour that appealed to me.

As I walked down the avenue with it, I met Sam Leadbeater himself, walking along happily, his hands clasped behind him under his full coat tails.

"Well, what did you get today?" he asked me kindly. "No blood and murder, I hope." I held out the book for his inspection.

"H'mmm . . . *Ireland*, by Mrs. Hall. I read that from cover to cover in one evening last week and I enjoyed it. You'll like that."

When I got home and opened my Mrs. Hall, I found that not more than half-a-dozen pages of it had ever been cut. This incident only made me like Mr. Leadbeater all the more. Lying was a habit that frequently got me into trouble with Gran, and I found it warming to know that someone I liked so much as Mr. Leadbeater was tainted by the same fault as myself. The knowledge formed a bond between us and I never gave him away.

On that day in autumn when I turned into the avenue on foot instead of whirling up it, as I had hoped, on my new bike, the chestnuts were dropping thick layers of golden leaves and the shining red nuts, still sticky from their recently burst casing of white-lined green, lay waiting to be gathered. In Ballyderrig, we had three uses for chestnuts. They could be bored by a red-hot steel knitting needle and threaded singly onto strong lengths of string. Used in this way, they became conkers and provided great fun in battles in which you tried to smash a rival's conker with your own. The second alternative was to make long strings of them and use them as bandoliers when playing Indians. A third was to cut a lid from the top of the chestnut, scoop out the firm juicy flesh and pierce a hole in one side to receive a fat oaten straw. Thus you turned the chestnut into a very realistic pipe in which shaggy turf-mould could be smoked.

I filled my pockets with chestnuts and kicked my way along the avenue. As I went, I wondered whether Miss Hope would consider the day hot or cold, and whether fairy cakes or sultana pancakes would be my lot. I had a preference for the pancakes, and as I approached the back door I pulled the collar of my coat up around my neck and tried to look as cold and as miserable as possible.

From the moment I knocked on the door, I knew that something had happened. It wasn't merely that I could hear a baby crying inside and the unaccustomed sound of animated conversation. It was that the atmosphere of retirement which pervaded the Mill House was gone — the atmosphere which had seemed to insist that the Leadbeaters, though in the world, were not of it.

When Miss Hope opened the door, her little mild face was flushed and excited. To my great surprise, she put her arm around me and kissed me warmly. Over her shoulder I glimpsed a strange man sitting at the fire. He had a little boy on his knee. Opposite him sat old Sam

Leadbeater, his face suffused with happiness. He was holding in his awkward arms a small baby and leaning over the child was a woman I had never seen before.

"Forgive me if I don't ask you to-day, Duckie," Miss Hope said. "We're all excited, for Frank, my brother, came home this morning with his wife and babies. Run home and tell your Gran. Ask her to call over to-night. And tell her Frank has come to stay!" In her gladness, Miss Hope for once forgot to be apologetic for speaking and she concluded her happy speech without the usual deprecating little laugh.

I hope — though I doubt it — that I rejoiced sufficiently in my friends' unexpected happiness not to regret the sultana pancakes as I ran home with the good news.

CHAPTER 9

WE GOT our holidays from school on the Friday before Christmas week. Two cans of boilings were shared out between us, and there were prizes and a concert.

The concert was short, but lovely. First the whole school sang *Ban Cnuic Eireann O* in unison. I had a cold that day, so I didn't join in. I was just as glad, for you got more out of the singing by just keeping quiet and listening to it. It was grand to hear the song begin softly and simply and sweetly with "Take a blessing from my heart to the land of Ireland," and then find it commencing to pulse with a tearing sadness as the exile remembers his lost fields and hearth and the brown bog. Just for a moment the sadness faded and a great gladness leaped up with the memory of the Irish hills and "the shining of the sun on them," but then loneliness came again and the last verse was hardly to be borne, holding as it did all the heart-hunger of all exiles who had ever longed for the things of home.

After that, Fourth and Fifth classes sang *Eibhlin a Ruin* in harmony. It would have done you good to hear the way the firsts and seconds blended into a throbbing joyful sweetness that filled the school with spring and thrushes and love-promises and fidelity, and you forgot every sadness and that it was December and that outside a cold grey sleet was falling.

It was the Babies' turn to show off next. Anna Maria Casey recited *Eire is Ainm an Tire Seo*, and Josie Flaherty gave us "A Little Bird Always Tells," which had been recited every year by one of the Babies for as long as I could remember. Father Bracken, the parish priest, who came to give out the prizes at our concerts every Christmas, laughed in all the right places with as much enjoyment as if he had never heard the recitation before.

We finished with *Brighidin Ban mo Stor* from Annie Broy of the Canal Bank, who had won First Prize in all Kildare for the under-sixteen singing at Newbridge Feis. Annie was a short, fat girl with red hair, light brown eyes and a wide nose. When she opened her mouth to sing and let that clear rich voice of hers wing its way into your mind and heart, she put such a spell on you that you forgot her lumpy figure and plain face, and you loved her so much for her singing that you imagined her as beautiful as Queen Maedhbh herself.

The prizes were mostly prayer books and rosary beads and little scapular sets that the nuns had made — small pocketbooks of leatherette with button-holed edges. They were lined with white satin and contained scapulars, an *Agnus Dei,* a Sacred Heart badge and a miraculous medal. There was one outstanding prize that year — a big box of milk chocolates which Father Bracken had brought from Kildare as a prize for the girl who had attended school throughout the year with the greatest regularity and punctuality.

The prize was won by 'News-of-the-World' Burke, as well it might, for her home was right next door to the school.

Let me hasten to add that it was not any tendency to gossip that won for Rosie Burke her peculiar nickname. It arose out of a circumstance connected with our school lunches. When Sister Mary Anthony, who was the portress of the school, had closed the wooden door in the high grey wall at ten o'clock in the morning, no power on earth would induce her to reopen it until it was time for us to go home. Many of the children had to come to school without their lunches. By lunch-hour, however, when we were turned into the yard for a half-hour's play, the mothers had generally managed to knock out a loaf or a soda-cake. Those who had not, boiled potatoes for their lunchless daughters. Because of Sister Mary Anthony's obduracy in the matter of the door, the belated lunches could not be handed in. The mothers kicked in turn on the door. Each child was adept in recognizing her mother's code kick. She left her play and stood by to catch the paper-wrapped lunch which presently came sailing over the wall. Katie Burke's mother always brought her a dollop of thump for her lunch. The thump was wrapped in newspaper and the steam of the hot potatoes made a transfer of the print. As she ate her ball of thump you could read the news of the world on it. And so Rosie became 'News-of-the-World' Burke.

That was our way in Ballyderrig. We did not mean to jeer or to be unkind, but we could never resist bestowing a nickname. The victim did not resent this, and soon became so accustomed to the new name that he or she answered to it more readily than to the name acquired in Baptism.

We all clapped loudly when 'News-of-the-World' went up to receive her box of chocolates from Father Bracken, for she was a popular girl. I got a prize for needlework — a black *Key of Heaven* with red edges. I was very proud of that prize, for I had worked hard for it. I won the prize with a nainsook chemise that was gathered at the neck into a band covered with feather stitching. The front was decorated with little tucks and with three ornate stripes of drawn-thread work. The elbow-length sleeves were finished with fine hemstitching. The chemise was intended as a Christmas box for my mother and my satisfaction in winning the prize arose chiefly from the fact that now she would have to reverse her opinion concerning my usefulness. Although I say it myself, the garment was beautifully made. I had always found a joy in careful sewing. I do still. The steady brilliant flash of the needle, the satisfying precision of neat careful stitches, the gradual growth of a small fine seam . . . these things have always given me something of the thrill a composer might feel, or an artist. Possibly, it is the artistic thrill that lies in doing well and carefully any work that gives pleasure to the doer.

Even today I prefer stitching by hand to using a machine, and I often waste hours sewing a long seam when a machine would do it for me in quarter the time.

After school that evening, I posted the chemise to my mother, and I sent Peg the *Key of Heaven*. Grandmother sent a hamper of Christmas gifts to Kilkenny: one of her own turkeys, plump and white and tender, a sugar-cured ham that had mellowed to perfection in oaten-straw smoke, a half-sack of apples and an enormous Christmas cake.

On the following morning Judy Ryan got the letter about her legacy.

It was Judy herself who had confided to me that she was a love-child. She had told me about it one morning that summer when we were walking home together from first Mass.

I don't think I was surprised, for I had always known

that there was some mystery about Judy's birth. Once, when I was very small, I had heard Gran say that Judy had "dropped from Heaven." Not knowing then that this was Gran's fanciful way of saying that a child's parents were unwedded, I cherished for years a dim image of Judy, chubby and naked, drifting down from the sky like a rosy snowflake.

Judy's father had run away to America shortly before she was born. Her mother, who came from beyond Naas, went to England to service when Judy was four years old, leaving the child with her grandmother. She had never returned to Ireland, and Judy had long given up expecting to hear from her.

She came to work for Gran when she was fifteen, a stout raw-boned girl with fine dark eyes, big strong teeth and a high colour. She had a ready laugh and was unfailingly good-natured.

When Gran first got her, Judy was incredibly ignorant of the ways of good housekeeping. As Gran said, "she didn't know 'B' from a bull's foot." Under Gran's painstaking tuition she quickly improved, and by the time she was twenty-two she had become the best bread-maker in the County Kildare.

A few months before I came to live with Gran, Mike Brophy came to Derrymore House from Athy, a shy awkward fellow of twenty-five or twenty-six who wore his years sheepishly and peered apprehensively at the world from under a dull thatch of yellow hair. He was tall and gangly and walked in that plodding fashion which is the normal gait of men who have bent their backs in heavy labour from boyhood and who have always worn the hobnailed inflexible boots that take the spring from one's foot.

If Mike were only crossing the kitchen floor, his gait gave you the impression that he was climbing laboriously a steep hill or plodding his heavy way through a ploughed field.

From the first, he fell a hopeless victim to the cheery good-nature of Judy's loud laugh. Though he showed his infatuation only by an increasing shyness and a complete inability to form a sentence of more than four or five words when in Judy's presence, she was quick to sense how he felt about her. Judy was cruel to him. She laughed openly at him and teased him at every opportunity. In her heart of hearts she was pleased and flattered, for she liked the tongue-tied Mike and admired his quiet dependability about the farm.

Mike had been with Gran about a year when he asked Judy to accompany him to Robertstown Sports. How he plucked up sufficient courage to do this and where he found words to make himself intelligible, I do not know. Judy refused to give him her decision until she had consulted Grandmother.

My grandmother, who was an inveterate match-maker, was all in favour of Judy's going.

"Go with him by all means," she said. "He's a quiet decent lad, Judy, and you could do worse than encourage him."

Judy was of the same opinion, but a sudden shyness had descended on her with this first oblique avowal of Mike's interest.

She stood before Grandmother, one strong red hand patting at the bun of black hair on the back of her neck. This was a habit of Judy's when she was embarrassed.

"Well, I don't know, ma'am," she said. "Supposin' he

gets to hear of me father and mother?" To poor Judy, her birth was a shameful topic and the high colour in her cheeks flamed redder than ever as she spoke.

Grandmother clicked her tongue impatiently and raised her eyes from the apron she was making.

"Well, aren't you the foolish child?" she said. "Don't you know well that in a gossiping place like Ballyderrig, Mike is bound to have heard everything there is to know about you by this? And what could they tell him beyond that you're a nice respectable hard-working girl? That your father and mother weren't married? Pshaw! That wasn't your fault, and it's a poor kind of man Mike would be to hold it against you. Get along with you now, and don't be wronging Mike by making him out to be a weak-minded thing that would let gossip stand between him and the girl he likes."

Judy's face brightened.

"He does like me, doesn't he, ma'am?" she said with a satisfied toss of her head.

"Anyone with half an eye in his head could see the poor oinseach is daft about you, you big lazy lump," Grandmother said indulgently. "Go on now and tell him you'll go to the Sports on Sunday."

Judy still hung back. "I'm not in love with the notion of going with him by myself," she said. "Couldn't Delia come with us?"

This condition was agreed to, and on Sunday the three of us set out for Robertstown in the pony and trap. Mike sat on one side driving, looking very stiff and uncomfortable in his Sunday suit of navy serge and a new cap of black and white check worn well back on his head. His feet were encased in his best boots — 'box' boots was how

we always described the finer boots that were sold in cardboard boxes to distinguish them from the heavy everyday
boots that, unwrapped and greasy-looking, hung suspended
from hooks in the ceiling of Duffy's shop.

Judy looked lovely, I thought, though her laugh rang
out less readily than usual, for she was still suffering from
shyness. She wore a black skirt and a blouse of pink silk
with the lace of her best chemise carefully pulled up to
show at the high V of her neck. A pair of beige cotton
gloves with black stitching on the backs encased her
hands, and her shiny black laced shoes with the bulbous
raised toe-caps that were popular at that time, looked very
smart. A white straw hat trimmed with bright red roses
and glossy green leaves completed the ensemble.

It was not a very enjoyable drive, for I thought it mean
of Judy to ignore Mike so completely and to address her
remarks so exclusively to me, but all this was forgotten
when we reached Dan Kelly's field where the Sports were
being held. Once inside the gate, Mike went off to join
the men and Judy and I prepared to enjoy ourselves.

We spent twopence each on an orange and a stick of
Peggy's leg. These delicacies were on sale at a table near
the gate, together with bottles of fizzy lemonade, great
slabs of plum-duff and piles of dry little yellow cakes
topped with pink icing.

Sucking our oranges we went to join the admiring
crowd that stood looking at a table covered with the prizes
donated by the local shopkeepers. There was a lovely
pair of china dogs from Dunne's that I thought would
look grand on the mantelpiece in Grandmother's parlour.
Duffy's had contributed six handsome cups and saucers

festooned with improbable pink flowers clinging to gilt leaves. Mrs. Donoghue of the sweet shop gave a big can of 'boilings,' and Jim Glin's contribution was a razor and strop. But among all these splendid prizes what most won Judy's envy and mine was the big bottle of scent which Miss Regan had given. For years that bottle had stood in the very centre of Regan's window, the admiration of all Ballyderrig. It was labelled *Joie d'Amour*, and its exotic presence overshadowed the hair-slides, mouth-organs, delft, lucky packages, scour specific, babies' soothers, paraffin lamps and other articles with which Miss Regan filled her window. It nestled in a case of dark blue plush with a satin lining that had once been sapphire but now was faded white.

Judy looked longingly at that emblem of luxury and romance.

" 'Joey Daymor,' " she whispered ecstatically. "I'm sure it smells lovely."

We tore ourselves from the table and went to watch the sports. Mr. Byrne, the schoolmaster, was doing valiant work as starter and judge. The tug-of-war between Ballyderrig and Monasterevan ended in a victory for the Ballyderrig men. The high jump, the long jump and the various sprinting events were contested and decided. At last we came to the big event of the day — the hammer-throwing. The contestants discarded their coats and waistcoats and took up their position.

Judy suddenly gripped my arm.

"Will you look at who's in for it?" she said excitedly. "It's Mike Brophy himself!" Sure enough, Mike was lined up with the other contestants. Oh, the wild elation as Mike stood in the circle, lifted the heavy weight, swung it around his shoulders and flung it with one grand strong throw to beat the others by a full foot!

Judy's face was beetroot with pride and satisfaction.

"I never thought he had it in him," she said over and over again. "I never thought he had it in him."

When it was time to go home, Mike joined us. Shame-facedly, he handed Judy a package. "That's what they gave me for winning the hammer," he said, his eyes averted. "It's for you."

Judy took the package. Her hands trembled as she un-wrapped it to disclose Miss Regan's bottle of *Joie d'Amour*.

Judy used that perfume liberally. She and I thought it lovely, and we could not understand why Grandmother sniffed disgustedly whenever Judy was especially generous with it.

"Bad luck from you anyway, Mike Brophy!" Grand-mother would say. "If you'd stayed away from Roberts-town Sports we wouldn't be stunk out of the house!"

After that Sunday, it was generally recognised that Judy and Mike were keeping company. They were undemon-strative lovers and they had none of that urgency for soli-tude which usually devours those in love.

On fine evenings and on Sunday afternoons they set out together for a walk. More often than not, they took me with them.

Their walks usually led them down the banks of the lazily-moving canal where yellow water irises and velvety fawn bulrushes clustered close to the banks.

Mike walked as far from Judy as the narrow path would allow him, swinging an osier and emanating peace and content.

It would have been hard to feel otherwise as one walked along the canal bank in the cool of the evening beneath a sky where pink-flushed clouds were rolled back to show the steady blue. Dragon-flies skimmed the surface of the water and occasionally an industrious perch would rise to snap at them, spreading ripples that slowly widened from bank to bank. The far bank of the canal sloped gently down to a hedge where melody-drunk birds tried out a few last sweet motifs before retiring.

They never walked farther than the little slated house where Tim Doyle, the smith, lived. Tim was a quick-limbed little man with light blue eyes and skin as dark and as leathery as his smith's apron.

We respected and liked Tim though we laughed some-times at the stories that were told of his queer ways. He had a family of twelve children who suffered when their father gave way to the religious mania that possessed him at times. It was said that at such times he was likely to order the whole family down on their knees at any hour of the day. To quell any tendency to levity among them while in this position, Tim would stand over them threaten-ingly, a sod of black turf in either hand.

"Think of the Man above!" he would urge solemnly. "Think of the Man above."

For years Tim Doyle and his wife had borne a heavy cross which may have accounted for the old man's queer-ness. They had twin sons who, though paralysed from birth, had lingered to be eighteen years of age. They died within a month of each other. In my thoughtless youth, I looked on Tim only as a rather eccentric old man. Since, however, I have sometimes tried to picture the awful martyrdom of mind he must have endured as for eighteen years he helped his wife to nurse those crippled boys in the restrictions of that poor little house.

Tim's invalid sons were confirmed with me. I can remember their father and mother carrying the long wasted bodies up the chapel to the Bishop, helpless limbs trailing. That was the only occasion when the boys were ever seen by anyone in Ballyderrig.

After the boys died, Tim was very distraught for a time and custom fell off in the forge. One evening, his eldest son had to fish him out of the canal. In a fit of religious frenzy he had tried to walk on the water. As the poor man sank, his voice could be heard a long distance away, crying piteously, "Lord, I must have sinned!"

When the bouts of religious mania left him, Tim was one of the most sensible men in Ireland. He was a fine fisherman, and in memory of those days when Grandmother had been in the habit of sending Carrigeen shapes and flummery to his invalid sons, he would often give Judy and Mike perch and roach to take home.

Grandmother fried the fish for our supper. She would gut and wash them, seasoning the opening with salt and pepper. Then she would roll them in oatmeal and fry them in butter. They tasted very good eaten with brown bread and cress from the stream below the garden.

The courtship of Judy and Mike progressed smoothly and uneventfully until the American letter came on the day after I got my Christmas holidays.

I'll always remember that day because it was the day that Nora, the black heifer, had her twin calves. Jimmy McDermott, the vet, had just gone, and Grandmother was talking about the beestings curds she would make us the next day. Whenever a cow calved, we had beestings curd. Beestings were the first milk the cow gave after calving. Grandmother would strain the rich yellow beestings and set them in a pie dish in the baker. They were heated very slowly until they set in a curd. We ate the curd with cream and sugar.

The beestings were always shared with the neighbours. When they heard the cow had calved they would come over to Derrymore House with jugs in their hands and a blessing on their lips.

"God bless her," were their first words as they came into the kitchen. The jugs were for their share of the beestings. The blessing was for the cow.

Judy stood at the table mixing a soda loaf.

"Here's Willie Beckett," she said suddenly. The excitement that entered the kitchen with Willie Beckett almost made us forget the twin calves, for the postman came so seldom to Derrymore that his coming was almost a sensation.

Willie Beckett took off his blue cap as he came into the kitchen.

"God save all here," he said cheerily. We stood in suspense while he fished in his canvas bag for the letter.

" 'Tis for you, Judy," he said at length, producing the letter — a big square envelope with a strange-looking stamp. "It's an American letter."

Half fearfully, Judy took the letter with floury hands.

Willie Beckett sat down on the settle to hear the news. We accepted it as a sign of friendship that Willie should be interested in the contents of the letters he brought us. The fact that he rode two miles to deliver them made him a kind of third party to our correspondence.

Judy scanned the letter.

"I can't make it out at all," she said helplessly. "Here, Mrs. Lacy, you read it. You've a betther head than I have for reading writing."

Grandmother took the letter, keeping us agog with impatience while she hunted for her steel-rimmed spectacles.

"Well, can you beat that?" she said at length. " 'Tis from a firm of American solicitors and it seems there's money coming to you, Judy, if you can prove you're the daughter of Mary Ryan, 'formerly of Kilnantick, Naas, and late of 1245 Wabash Avenue, Bronx, New York!' "

Grandmother had to reduce the letter to its very simplest terms before Judy got the meaning of it. At first, the big good-natured girl could only understand that her mother was dead, and, young though I was, I must admit that I thought the grief Judy displayed for the mother who had abandoned her and to whom she had not given a thought for years was rather superfluous.

"But, what on earth are you crying for, Judy?" Grandmother demanded, not unreasonably.

"Me grandmother always said she had the dawshiest little hands and feet," was poor Judy's muffled answer.

Here Willie Beckett joined in. "The Lord have mercy on the poor woman," he said. "Say a prayer for her, Judy, and don't be breaking your heart crying. The best thing you can do now is to make sure of the legacy that's coming to you."

The reminder that she was an heiress checked Judy's tears at once.

Derrymore was a changed house during the next few weeks. The smooth-running stream of our ways was transformed to a whirlpool of excitement. We talked and thought of nothing but Judy's legacy. Judy sent off her birth certificate and the affidavits secured for her by the village schoolmaster, and while we waited for a reply from America our speculations as to the amount of the legacy grew increasingly ambitious. Mike Brophy took no part in these speculations. From the moment he heard the news he had grown more silent than ever. Rarely did he address a word to Judy these days, and the quiet pleasant walks down the canal bank were no more.

Judy watched Mike's withdrawal with amazement that finally gave way to hurt indignation. She was not the type to nurse a grievance in silence, and on the Sunday afternoon following the arrival of the letter she confronted Mike when, dinner over, he rose to leave the kitchen not saying a word to Judy about his plans for the afternoon.

"Would it be any harm to ask if I done anything on you, Mike Brophy?" Judy demanded. "To see the way you've been carryin' on since the letter came, anyone'd think you begrudged me the bit of money that's comin' to me."

Mike flushed to the roots of his tow-coloured hair as he searched for words. "You know well I wouldn't begrudge you anything in the world, Judy," he said quietly.

"Well, what's wrong with you then that you haven't a word to throw to a dog?"

Mike took his check cap from the back of the door before replying.

"Now that you've come in for money it isn't words from the likes of me you'll be wanting," he said. Without waiting for a reply, he plodded his lonely way out of the kitchen.

Judy's mouth dropped open and she stared after him in angry amazement.

"Well, did you hear that?" she demanded of me. "The — the bad-minded omadhaun! If that's the sort you think I am, Mike Brophy, good-bye and good riddance!" And she commenced to clear the table with such vigour that Grandmother, who was taking her Sunday afternoon rest upstairs, called down to know if Judy wanted to break every bit of delft in the house.

That was an exciting Christmas for us. Every night the kitchen was filled with neighbours who came to discuss the good news and to offer Judy friendly suggestions as to ways of spending the legacy. Feeling that the occasion demanded festive fare, Grandmother regaled them with tea and plum cake.

"A little business in the town, now, would bring you in a mint of money," Jerry Noone said wisely. "I hear talk of Miss Regan selling out. They say her leg's got so bad lately that she'll soon have to take to her bed altogether."

"Aye, she is poorly, the creature," Grandmother said. "She was hard set to walk up the Chapel aisle on Sunday last."

"You could do worse with your money than invest it in Miss Regan's business, Judy," said Paddy Fitz.

Judy considered for a moment the pleasant prospect of herself as proprietress of Miss Regan's shop. Then she discarded the picture.

"Och, sure I know nothing about shopkeeping," she said. "What I was thinking of, now, was a nice little farm of land and a two-storey house with a slated roof . . ." She glanced at Mike to see if he were impressed by this vision which, with its dreams of a two-storeyed slated house, was, to Ballyderrig minds, the very ultimate standard of prosperity.

Mike continued to stare into the fire.

"But, then," Judy went on, sighing gustily, "how would a lone girl like me look after a place like that?"

"You wouldn't be long finding someone to help you," Tim Dolan said. "There's any amount of snug men in Ballyderrig would be glad to give you a hand to look after your legacy."

"That's what I say, too," Mike said, rising and going out to the clamp for an armful of sods. Judy said nothing. With a toss of her head, she rose to set the table.

One Saturday early in February Willie Beckett rode up the boreen through a thin silver mist that veiled the hedges and fields and bog with cool tenderness and sent the fowl to huddle in the shelter of the turf clamp.

When he came into the kitchen, tiny rivulets were running from his shiny black cape and drops of mist hung suspended from his moustache and nose.

When he handed Grandmother the big square letter with its blue stamp, he said: "Judy'll have to sign for it. It's registered. There'll be money in it."

Grandmother went to the kitchen door. "Judy! Mike! she called. "Here's Willie Beckett with the legacy!"

In answer to the call, Judy left her bed-making and almost broke her neck rushing down the stairs. Mike came more slowly from the haggard where he had been chopping turnips for the cow.

"You open it, Mrs. Lacy," Judy said. "I'm that excited, I couldn't read a word of it."

Grandmother opened the envelope and took out a letter to which was clipped a pale-blue cheque.

We waited in silence while she read.

"Judy, alannah," she said at length. "I'm afraid there's

a big disappointment coming to you. There'll be no farm of land, I'm thinking. Your legacy is only twenty pounds."

"Them solicitors made away with me mother's money," Judy said with finality when the passing of the first shock allowed her speech. All her life, she was to retain the libellous conviction that her fortune had been embezzled by American lawyers. Then she was struck by another thought and one that affected her more deeply than the realization that she was no heiress.

"Oh, Mrs. Lacy," she wailed, "how am I to face the people when they come over to-night? After all me big talk, I'll be the laughing-stock of the place!"

Mike Brophy, who had been sitting on the settle-bed all this time, now spoke. His face was brighter and happier than I had ever seen it.

"Sure, there's no need for you to be here when they come, Judy," he said very kindly. "Can't you and me take a walk down the canal bank after the tea is over?"

Judy looked at him while the colour flamed higher and higher in her cheeks.

"We'll do that, Mike," she said slowly. "Anyway, I'm thinking that twenty pounds is no small sum of money for a girl to be able to put away towards her wedding."

CHAPTER 10

SHROVE TUESDAY was spoiled for me that year because it was the evening I fell into the fire.

I always looked forward to Shrove Tuesday and to Gran's pancakes which were not made in the Kildare way with an ordinary batter of milk and eggs and flour. She made them as they make them in the West of Ireland with grated raw potato. She got her recipe for boxty pancakes from her mother who was a Mary Kelly from Galway. She was a grand-looking woman, Mary Kelly. A tinted photograph of her hung over the cabinet in the parlour of Derrymore House. Though I was never good-looking, I am supposed to have a look of her. My hair is brown as hers was in the photograph and I have the same eyes — grey with a brown tea-leaf in the left one. Whenever anyone commented on this resemblance, Gran was far from pleased, for she had adoration for her dead mother and to have any living creature likened to Mary Kelly outraged her nearly as much as if an ordinary mortal had been compared to Our Lady.

The boxty pancakes were crisp little crumpet-like cakes that were eaten hot with butter and sugar as they came from the pan. Shrove Tuesday was unthinkable without boxty-on-the-pan. They were the fortune-tellers that gave you a glimpse of what the coming year held for you.

Gran made a huge pile of them that year, for seven or eight of our neighbours were coming in to tea.

She let none of us stand with her in the buttery while she mixed the grated raw potato, flour, buttermilk, salt, bread soda and eggs, and beat into these ingredients a handful of little paper-wrapped charms. The cross that stood for a religious vocation, a ring for courtship, a bright threepenny bit for wealth, a button for an old bachelor, a thimble for an old maid. As she dropped the mixture in spoonfuls on the big sizzling pan, we tried hard not to cheat. Tried hard not to watch for the charms and memorize their position in the ever-growing dish of golden boxty pancakes that stood before the fire.

While Grandmother fried the boxty, Judy Ryan and myself covered the white-scrubbed table with a heavy cloth of unbleached linen that was as big as the sheet of a double bed. We cut up the sweet cake with its thick crumbly crust and covered the fruity slices with Gran's fresh butter which, possibly because her cows grazed on bogland, was always tallowy white. In the centre of the table we put the big bowl of flummery, made since the day before to allow it a chance to set firm. The flummery was a dream and Gran's own specialty. A delicious delicacy made from oatenmeal jelly and sugar and whipped cream. There were little wheaten buns and spongy white soda bread and square currant scones. Odd spaces on the table were filled with damson preserve and blackberry jelly and sloe jelly.

As a matter of course, we added a couple of dishes of parsley jelly, sweet and clear and cool-looking. Grandmother insisted on parsley jelly being eaten at every meal. She had implicit faith in its powers to ward off rheumatism, cure indigestion and clear the blood. She made a few pots of it every week of her life. She washed the parsley, filled her speckled enamelled pot with it and covered it with cold water. She simmered it for half-an-hour

and then strained it with infinite care through her flannel
jelly-bag. She measured the juice and returned it to the
fire to boil a few minutes longer. Then the sugar — a
pound to every pint of juice — was added to the parsley
juice and they were boiled together until the jelly set.
During the last ten minutes of boiling, she always dropped
in thin lemon parings tied up in a piece of muslin. I did
not need Gran's urging that the jelly was good for me to
make me spread great spoonfuls of it on my bread-and-
butter.

When our friends came in, the enormous black kettle,
grey-white on top with its coating of light turf-ash, was
swung in on its crane from where it had been steaming at
the fireside all evening for a quick boil-up over the heat
of the fire. The tea was wet and set to draw on a couple
of red embers broken with the tongs to fine griseach on
the hearth.

And then we all sat down to feast, Judy Ryan and Mike
Brophy taking their places at the table with us, naturally
and easily. Gran had no patience with those farmers'
wives who did not treat the servant-boy and servant-girl
as members of the family. "The stranger on my floor gets
the same treatment as anyone else in the house," she was
fond of saying. She had a habit common to most women
in our part of the country of avoiding any servile term
when referring to her employees. She would never say,
"Judy Ryan works for me," but "I have Judy Ryan living
with me."

We were a big crowd that evening at the table. Tim
Dolan was there, with his fiddle in its black sateen bag
waiting for him on the dresser. A quiet fellow, Tim, of
thirty or thereabouts, with a thick thatch of black hair and

the saddest eyes I have ever seen in a human being. He would play the liveliest of gay reels and hornpipes looking all the time as if his heart was breaking. Maybe it was. He was a spoiled priest. No one ever knew the reason for his sudden departure from the ecclesiastical college. He kept the secret to himself, but we all felt that there was something about him which set him apart. The Kenny girls, Nellie and Kathleen, were there, and Corny Flynn who was courting Nellie but who couldn't marry because he was the only son in a family where there were six girls all unmarried. It wasn't to be expected that his mother would let him bring another woman into the house. We had Willie Beckett, the postman, black-moustached and brown-eyed as an Italian, and little dried-up Miss Flood from Killymoore who was engaged to Willie. Socially, Miss Flood was miles above Willie, but from a financial point of view it was well known that Willie was a good enough match for any girl in Bally-derrig. He had plenty of money in the bank — American money. His only brother, who was a fireman in Chicago, had been killed on duty, and the American Government had sent Willie good compensation.

We were nearly finished when old Dinny Mulpeter came in. Dinny made the coffins and drove the hearse for Johnny Dunne, one of our shopkeepers who ran an undertaking business as a side-line. Since the death of his wife a few months before, Dinny Mulpeter had come to live in a little cottage about half-a-mile down the road from us, and Gran made the lonely old man welcome whenever he came up for a chat and a cup of tea.

He was very good to me, and sometimes brought me little figures of saints he had carved. I still have the workbox he made me. God knows he was a forgiving man to talk to me at all, for with the rest of the Ballyderrig children I had given his wife and himself plenty of persecution when I was small.

For years, the Mulpeters lived in a little house down near the school. The downstairs room had a window from which a pane of glass was missing. Never, as long as I can remember, was that pane of glass replaced. Instead, a griddle was set against it to keep out the draught. When passing the window, the impulse to give the griddle a quick tap and send it clattering down onto the floor inside was irresistible. Poor Mrs. Mulpeter, who was bent almost to the ground with rheumatism, would shout threats at us, but the threats never came to anything.

The Mulpeters had one son, Stephen, who was killed in the Dardanelles. I wouldn't like to say that Stephen was out and out simple, but there is no doubt he was not over-bright. I often heard his own father calling him "a poor thick."

The British got Stephen when they held their first recruiting meeting in Ballyderrig. I remember the night well. It was early on in the War, and I was still living at home.

They came one evening late in the year, and it was nearly dark when they arrived. A crowd of them came in a kind of lorry like a covered wagon, which they backed up against the pump. They erected a cinematograph screen almost opposite our shop, and as soon as it got dark enough they commenced to show pictures of soldiers playing football and running races and eating their heads off in a canteen, just to show us the fine times fellows could have in the British Army. They had every man, woman and child in Ballyderrig watching the fun — all except the bedridden, and invalids like poor Mrs. Mulpeter.

Stephen was in the front row of the audience that night, and he drinking everything in. When the last of the pictures had flickered to a standstill, the recruiting sergeant started to address us. He fixed poor Stephen with his eye, and seemed to be addressing his entreaties directly to him. He mesmerized the lad to such an extent that Stephen Mulpeter, who previously had cherished no animosity of any kind towards "the 'Uns" of whom the sergeant spoke, walked like a lamb up the steps to the covered wagon.

Dinny Mulpeter was away with a funeral in Thomastown that day and we young ones thought that Mrs. Mulpeter should be told what her son was up to, so away with us like red shanks down to her house.

Over the half-door we could see her sitting crookedly on a creepy-stool beside the hearth where she was minding a griddle cake.

"Quick, Mrs. Mulpeter," we yelled. "Oh, come quick! Stephen is listin' on you!"

Mrs. Mulpeter was one of those who thought that a respectable woman should never be seen in the street without her cape and her beaded bonnet, and even with the prospect of losing her only son, she waited to dress herself properly before coming back up the town with us.

That was an agonizing procession for those of us who thought that his mother's quick intervention could save Stephen. All our impatience could not hurry poor Mrs. Mulpeter's crippled joints. Slowly, shufflingly, she dragged herself up the street. She might as well have stayed at home.

At the Chapel gate we met Paddy Fitz.

"You may take your time, Mrs. Mulpeter," he said.

"Why? Is he gone?" quavered Stephen's mother.

"No; but he's as good as gone, God help him. He's signed on for the duration. He's above in Johnny Dunne's bar this minnit drinkin' great big pints with the soldiers."

Stephen drove away with his new comrades-in-arms and when his father came home from the funeral that night and heard the news, his only comment was:

"Ah, sure I always knew he was only a poor thick."

Stephen was killed in the Dardanelles.

"God rest the poor thick," said his father when the telegram came. "I'll go bail he walked up to the Germans with his mouth open."

The decoying of Stephen Mulpeter had a sequel in Ballyderrig. The Reddins, with their violent anti-British feelings, were furious that England should have won even this one poor recruit from us. When a second recruiting meeting was announced a few months later, they determined to take no chances. Right in the middle of the meeting, we heard the chapel bell being rung frantically. For the bell to ring at eight o'clock at night could mean only one thing — a fire! Like one man, we left the recruiting sergeant without an audience and rushed to the chapel gate. Joe Reddin was waiting for us.

"Quick!" he shouted, heading us towards Killymoore, "Miss Flood's house is afire!" By the time we got there we found a little miserable bit of a fire in the haggard. When the true story of that night came out later, Willie and Ned Reddin admitted that the hardest job of their lives had been to keep that fire going until our arrival.

But they accomplished their object, for by the time we trekked back to town the British Army had withdrawn to the Curragh with the sad realization that they would have to carry on the war without the help of Ballyderrig.

But all this is a long way removed from our Shrove Tuesday tea-party and my fall in the fire.

When tea was over, we cleared the table and brought down from the dresser the tumblers that were the pride of Gran's life and which my grandfather had brought her from the Cork Exhibition in 1903. They were rimmed with gold and had her name — Mary — written on them in gilt letters. There were minerals for the women folk and stout for the men.

I knelt down to build up the fire. In reaching for the tongs, I over-balanced and fell sideways into the hot griseach. The enamelled tea-pot was still on the hearth and this saved me from falling right into the glowing hearth as I fell. My cheek struck the spout. Someone lifted me up and the next thing I remember is sitting on the settee beside Gran. She had her arm around me and my unburnt cheek was pressed to her shoulder while waves of pain came and receded and came again, leaving me half delirious.

"Mother of God! She's ruined for life!" I could hear Judy Ryan saying, and I could smell the burnt egg-shell smell of my scorched hair.

I was moaning rather than crying, and I heard Gran crooning to me as if I were a baby.

"There now, alanna! There now . . . you'll be all right. . . . You'll be all right in a minute. . ."

Then someone — Gran, I think it was — gave brisk orders.

"Pour out that tea in a bowl, Judy, and stand it to cool in a basin of water. Hand me down that package of wadding from the shelf of the dresser."

And in the middle of all the commotion, Big Bill, the pedlar, was suddenly and unaccountably stooping over me and licking my face.

I thought at first it was some kind of delirium, but it proved to be reality. Certainly, the blessed soothing relief that came to me as the old man's tongue went over my cheek licking away ashes and pain was no illusion.

Afterwards I learned that he had come in his pony-cart with a message for Gran just when the consternation was at its height. Unable to make himself heard at the door, he had walked into the kitchen and had sized up the situation at a glance.

"Give her here to me," he said to Gran, "I have a cure in me tongue."

His entry at that moment and his quick offer seemed to Gran like an answer to prayer. Everyone in Ballyderrig knew that Big Bill had a cure in his tongue, and there were many who had cause to be grateful to him for it. When he had licked my face from forehead to chin, Gran dipped a piece of the cotton wool in the strong tea, which by this time had cooled, and dabbed my face with it. Then she saturated a fresh piece in the tea and spread it gently on my cheek.

"Your poor hair is a sight," she murmured. "But, what matter? God is good that your eyes weren't hurt. You'll be as right as rain."

I was not worrying about my hair. I had been lifted out of a sea of pain, and for that I would have been content to wear a wig for the rest of my life.

"Keep up your heart, Deelyeen," Big Bill said, "there'll be money bid for you, yet. In a month's time there won't be a sign of a burn on your face. I never knew the cure in me tongue to fail. What matter about your hair! Won't it grow again? Anyway the girls that's goin' now are payin' the barbers to cut the hair off their heads."

This made me want to smile, but my smile stopped half-way when I felt how it hurt my cheek.

By this time Judy Ryan had heated a couple of irons and had wrapped them in cloths and put them into the bed. Gran brought me upstairs and took off my clothes and tucked me in.

By Easter there was not a mark on my face except for a little scar near my left eye where the spout of the tea-pot struck me. I have that scar still, but you would hardly notice it. Call it a faith cure, if you will, but I know, and Gran knew, and all Ballyderrig knew that it was Big Bill's tongue that cured me.

I had always liked the big bearded pedlar, but from that day I was devoted to him, and I called into his little cottage at the foot of the bridge whenever he was at home. This was not often, for Big Bill's trade carried him and his little pony and cart far and wide over the County Kildare.

He sold cheap rosary beads which he wired himself, and statues and holy pictures. He also carried a good stock of such things as scented soap, combs, jewellery and delft. He carried a cart-load of these wares when setting out on his travels and came back with his cart piled with the goods on which he made money when he sold them in Dublin — rabbit-skins, rags, jam-pots, bottles and odds and ends of junk. In September he kept the children of Ballyderrig supplied with pocket-money, for he was a ready market for blackberries at three-ha'pence a pound. When he had collected a barrel of them, he sent them on one of the canal boats to some Dublin jam factory. We were all ready to make our three-ha'pences out of this side of Big Bill's activities, but it put all of us from buying blackberry jam or jelly. We knew that the barrel sometimes took as long as three weeks to fill. We also knew that the berries must often have been crawling with worms by the time they reached Dublin.

When I was eight or so, Big Bill had come to Ballyderrig from no one knew where — a brown bearded giant of a man of fifty-five with a pack on his back. He had prospered with us and had settled down, for good it seemed, in the little cottage at the foot of the bridge. He took no one into his confidence regarding his past or his people.

I liked that cottage of his. Although it was crowded with the things he had picked up in his journeyings, and smelled strongly because of his wares and from being shut up for long periods, it was one of the cleanest houses in Ballyderrig. He could cook better than any woman I knew — excepting Gran, of course. It was Big Bill who gave me my first taste of roast kid.

No one in my part of the country had ever heard of anyone eating kid, and they looked on Big Bill as some kind of cannibal because he was willing to pay sixpence for a newly-dropped kid goat. He gave me a plate of it one day when I went in to see him, and I have never tasted anything so sweet and tender.

I liked the way he made tea, too.

"Hot, strong and sweet, Deelyeen. That's the way to drink it," he would say, pouring the mahogany-coloured tea from his little brown pot and adding plenty of sugar and the merest drop of goat's milk.

He was a genius with the tin whistle. It was not the familiar Irish tunes he played, but strange foreign-sounding airs that brought Puerto Rico and the Alhambra and Quatemala and other lovely-sounding far-off places into his crowded little room. His playing made me suspect he had been a sailor in his time — that and the tattoo-marks on his arms.

One day, about a year after he cured my burn, I called to see Big Bill. There was no smoke rising above the thatch and the pony-and-cart were missing. I looked in through the little window. The crowded shelves had been cleared and not a stick of furniture remained. Big Bill had gone from Ballyderrig. Why, or to where, none of us ever found out.

CHAPTER 11

IN MAY I was fifteen, and Gran decided to commence making a teacher of me. I cannot think why she was so set on this particular career — unless it was that she thought it high time one of our family restored the tradition introduced by Michael Kelly, her West of Ireland great-grandfather, who had been a hedge schoolmaster in his time.

Personally, I was never conscious of any strong urge to devote my life to the moulding of youth, but I was quite willing to try to become a tight-rope walker or a female cobbler if that was what Gran wanted of me. Besides, I owed it to my mother. When she had agreed to leave me in Ballyderrig it had been on the tacit understanding that I was to become a teacher. So there it was.

There was a great deal of writing to my mother on the subject and much sending here, there and everywhere for prospectuses, while Gran tried to decide which school should have the honour of educating me. Mary Joe Heffernan helped her to make up her mind. When Mary Joe announced that she was going to a school in County Wicklow the following September, Gran, not to have me outdone by Tommy Heffernan's daughter, decided I should go there, too.

As soon as I got my holidays in July I went to Kilkenny for a month so that my mother might measure and fit me for my school outfit.

Peg was waiting for me when the train drew in. She had grown so tall that I hardly knew her. She had an air of importance and self-confidence that made her seem very grown-up. The twins, who were with her, were changed, too. It was over a year since they had seen me, and they had almost forgotten me. As we walked along John Street, they kept a tight hold of Peg's hands and eyed me shyly and warily.

"We have two girls in the workroom, now," Peg told me with pride. "We're doing a great trade. We have an order for two hundred skirts from the Leinster House and Mother is putting money in the bank every week." She was leaving school after Christmas to come into the business, and was inclined to be a little patronizing with me because my prospects of taking my place among the breadwinners of the world were so much more remote.

The shop *did* look prosperous. It had a double front. One window held a display of children's and babies' clothes. In the other window were ladies' blouses, corsets, stockings and underclothing.

There were a couple of customers in the shop, so Peg did not stop to make me known to the smart red-haired assistant whose name, I afterwards learned, was Bridie Duane. We walked right through a curtained glass door and into the workroom where my mother was sewing away with her two assistants and enveloped in the smell I have always associated with her — a smell of French chalk and new material and hot irons and steam.

Oh, I was glad to see my mother! Neither circumstances nor antipathies can ever completely sever the cord between mother and child and I felt its quick warm tug when she looked up at me and smiled warmly. Always shy of demonstrativeness, her only greeting was a kiss and a "So here's herself!" But in that moment when her lips were on my face I knew that she was moved as I was —

knew that deep down beneath all those little antagonisms that sprung from our widely-opposed characters, there was strong natural love. We were mother and daughter and always would be, and the rest was unimportant.

Until then, I had never realised this. Neither had I realised that she was so good-looking. When Jim and Tommy had come in and we all sat down to dinner in the parlour above the shop, I could hardly keep my eyes off her. There was a glint in her light-brown hair which I had never noticed before, and her grey eyes were as clear and as bright as a girl's. She had lovely skin, my mother. Pale, but very clear and smooth, and her features were good. In spite of her nine children, her figure was young and slender. This good-humoured, contented woman was not my mother as I had remembered her. There was little here to connect her with the distraught creature who had nagged and scolded and made our lives a misery. It was a pity I had not had more understanding in those old days at home in Ballyderrig and that I did not realise her bitterness was the inevitable reaction of an ambitious hard-working business woman who finds herself in a dead end. I would not have been nearly so resentful of her acrimony towards my father if I had only known that her spleen was born of the realization that she had been cheated. When she had given up her hurler and had married my father, she had chosen money instead of love. Small wonder she grew soured and that her tongue acquired a sharp edge when she found she had been done out of the fortune for which she had bartered her heart.

In her new venture in Kilkenny, my mother had come into her own. There, she found an outlet for her business ability that Ballyderrig could never have afforded her.

It was grand to be sitting with all of them in that room which, though strange, was homelike because it contained all the furniture we had in our parlour in Ballyderrig . . . the square mahogany table, the sideboard that sat squat on the floor, with a thick column supporting it at each side and a high, shelved back for tumblers and cruets, the fretwork smoker's cabinet which Uncle Frank had made before he went to Buenos Aires, and the black horse-hair chairs and sofa. It was pleasant to see Peg, as sedate as a girl twice her age, correcting Jim and Tommy for their manners, and beginning to look and act so like my mother that to see them together was frightening. The twins' shyness of me was wearing off, and I was ridiculously pleased when either of them spoke to me. I enjoyed listening to Tommy, with his sharp and witty tongue, as he chatted in the old-fashioned way he had, and it was good to hear Jim, who was fat and good-natured and a stutterer, put in a hesitant word now and again.

Miss Duane, who was still in the shop, had to wait for her dinner until someone went to relieve her, but the two dressmakers, Ettie Sparks and Lil Cummins, had their dinner with us. I liked both of them on sight. Ettie was fair and pretty and young. She had yellow hair which she wore bobbed and pulled down in a heavy soft bang on her forehead. Lil was much older. She was a tall quiet woman and not at all pretty, but she had lovely teeth and a nice slow smile.

Yes. It was a happy reunion. I was so contented that I even found it in me to kiss Aunt Rose with affection when she came in after dinner.

If a pang leaped in me now and then when I thought of little Ned steelily I ignored it. I never once mentioned his name. Neither did my mother. Next to Peg, she had loved him more than any of her children and his death must have gone hard with her.

I got a great thrill that evening when my mother sent me up to her room to bring down a clean handkerchief from the top drawer in her dressing-table. I opened the drawer, and what did I see folded carefully away in tissue-paper but the chemise I had made her! In the centre of its folds was the cutting with my poem. Now, she had never made much comment on either of them, and it gave me a quick rush of pleased satisfaction to see them treasured. But that was my mother all over. When you had made up your mind that she was casual and hard, you suddenly discovered something about her so sweet and soft and feeling that it almost made you cry. But it was fatal to pretend you had noticed this softness, for my mother was so shy of appearing anything but an efficient business woman that if you made any comment she spoiled it all for you immediately. That is what happened when I went downstairs.

Always lacking in restraint and reticence, I was so moved by what I had seen upstairs that I could not leave well enough alone.

"So you liked the chemise, then, Mother? And the poem?" I said, avid for spoken confirmation of what the tissue-papered parcel had made evident.

My mother's face hardened instantly and she withdrew from me.

"So you were rummaging then," she commented dryly. "I never met anyone like you for looking for praise."

The first week went for me in being measured and fitted for my school outfit. Four of everything I had to have, and a Sunday dress and an everyday dress and two pairs of sheets and a coverlet and pillowslips. Cutlery, too, with my initials stamped on the handles, and — what I had never used before in my life — table napkins. Another novelty was my dressing-gown. My mother bought a lovely piece of mauve ripple-cloth in the Leinster House, and Ettie Sparks ran up the gown for me in a day. I fancied myself very much in it and earned a scolding from my mother by wearing it around the house.

That was the way it was with us by the start of the second week. The perfection of the love aroused by our reunion was beginning to be spoiled by my ability to irritate her in a thousand different ways. The way I spoke, the slouching way I sat, my capacity for sitting still for an hour at a time doing absolutely nothing, my deafness to any remarks addressed to me while I was reading — all these things had the power to put her into a temper and make her hurtful and sarcastic. Our old antagonism flared up again, and we were soon resenting and disliking each other as much as ever.

Peg's status with her was another thing that made me ill at ease. I honestly do not believe I was jealous of Peg at this time, but her position as my mother's right-hand man made me feel out of it. I began to long for Gran and for Derrymore House where I was the important pivot around which the house revolved.

The coming of Paddy and Joe for the holidays in the last fortnight of my visit did nothing to improve matters. They were both young men by this, and could think of nothing but girls. They quickly made friends with two sisters called Fitzgerald and we saw little of them at home during their stay.

All in all, it was not a pleasant holiday, and I was not sorry when my outfit was ready and the month was up.

It was the middle of August when I came home to Ballyderrig, with just a little over a fortnight to spend with Gran before starting off for Wicklow. I was hanging out of the carriage window straining my eyes for her long before the train ran into Kildare station.

There she was, the little handful! When I saw her in her black cloth coat with its satin revers and her Sunday hat of black velours, her face with its kind smiling mouth and wise old eyes seemed to jump towards me and I could hardly wait for the train to stop.

Did you ever know just how much you meant to me, Gran? That to me you stood for understanding and sympathy and wisdom and for all the warm uncritical loving I needed? You were the purple bog and a ripe wheat-field and a crab-tree in May. You were good food, and songs in the firelight and the rosary at night. You were a welcome for my coming in and a prayer for my going out. *You were Gran.*

Peace was in my heart as we drove home between hedges that were heady with woodbine. I put away from me the thought that too soon I would have to go away again, and I gave myself up to the grand store of Ballyderrig news which Grandmother had harvested against my return.

"Sheila Clinton is to be married before Christmas," she told me.

"To Red Connolly, Gran?" Sheila had been keeping company with Red Connolly, her third cousin, since she was a child in her confirmation dress.

"No, and more's the pity. If ever two people were made for each other, Sheila and Red were. He has nothing to his name, to be sure, for with four brothers before him, there will be nothing for him out of that little farm of theirs."

"But he has a good job in Dublin, Gran."

"If he has two pounds ten a week he has a thousand," Gran said. "Still and all, they could live on that, for Sheila has a grand pair of hands and she's a good manager. Yes, it's a pity they're not marrying."

"Who is she marrying then, Gran?"

"Frank Price of Thomastown — he's got her at last."

"But didn't Sheila refuse him twenty times in the past year?"

"She did indeed, alanna. But there you are. Constant dripping wears away a stone. And Frank had Sheila's father and mother on his side. They never liked Red Connolly since the first day he started going with Sheila, and when Frank came along they were dead set on marrying her into Thomastown. I don't know what will come of it at all, at all. God knows I'm not against made marriages. Often and often I've seen them turn out better than so-called love matches. But Sheila and Red were different. They were always mad about one another, and where there's real love like that it's a great mistake to interfere. I wouldn't like to be in Mrs. Clinton's shoes this minute. She has a lot to answer for."

"Does Red still come down from Dublin to see Sheila?"

"He hasn't been down since the match was made, and

by all accounts he's never going to set foot in the place again. Well, I'm sorry for the two of them."

So was I. Frank Price was a dull loutish kind of fellow who, judged by our standards, was comfortably well off. If he had been twice as wealthy, I would never have chosen him as a husband for Sheila Clinton.

Sheila was quick-silver — a slight girl with gleaming black hair and splendid grey eyes that were almost black. Red Connolly was ideal for her. He was as red as she was dark, and a fine up-standing good-looking young fellow.

Frank was heavy-moving and slow-brained to stupidity. He had been very carefully and tyrannically reared by his mother, who guarded her only son in virginal solitude, always refusing to allow him to associate with the other boys of Ballyderrig. His stand-offishness became second nature with him for when his mother died shortly after my own poor father, God rest him, he did not take advantage of this release from bondage to make friends. The only use he made of his newly-found liberty was to propose to Sheila Clinton on whom, it seems, he had always had his eye. In spite of the anger of her mother and father, Sheila had refused him again and again. But with the persistence of the dull-brained, Frank had returned to the attack. He even bribed the Clinton parents with sundry gifts of cattle and money. And now he had won.

My sympathy with the lovers was not sufficient to spoil my joy in that home-coming. Judy Ryan was glad to see me. And when Mike came in from the bog with a load of turf half-an-hour later, he pump-handled my arm in inarticulate pleasure. I had presents for both of them. A tie and a white silk muffler for Mike. For Judy a pink silk stockinet petticoat and knickers. She whisked them off the table when Mike came in, and ran away, red-faced, to hide them in her room.

"We won't be having tea for another hour or so, Delia," Gran said with a glance at the clock on the dresser. It was not long after four. "Take off your good clothes and put on a bib and get yourself a glass of milk. That'll keep you going till tea-time."

When I came down, the baker was heeled up against the fire to heat, and Judy was lifting the little black pot off the crane. It held floury cracked potatoes.

"What are we having for tea, Gran?" I called. She was bustling about in the buttery.

"Rashers and eggs and potato-apple cakes. Does that suit your ladyship?"

Potato-apple cakes! Above all our Derrymore House specialties I loved them.

"Come in here and give me a hand," commanded Gran. "Bruise that pot of potatoes for me and peel me a dozen apples."

Obediently, I turned the pot of steaming potatoes onto the baking board and bruised them with the bottom of a mug. While Grandmother scraped the mashed potatoes into her bowl, scattered over them salt and melted butter and kneaded into them barely sufficient flour to bind them, I peeled the early green cookers from the orchard behind the house. Grandmother halved the dough and rolled out each half into a flat round. She cut the rounds into eight triangular pieces. Half of these were covered with sliced raw apple. She placed the other half on top and then nipped the edges of the cakes to seal them.

"Is my baker ready, Judy?" she called. "Coming with

the cakes." There was a clatter of tongs as Judy raked the glowing red embers under the pot oven, and in the cakes went. Later, when they were browned and risen, the sides were slit and the tops burned back. Slices of butter and plenty of brown sugar were added to the apples. The tops were replaced and the cakes were returned to the baker just long enough for the sugar and butter to melt deliciously into a syrupy sauce that oozed from the sides as we ate.

"Delia and myself will wash up," Gran said when tea was over. "You go and get ready for the spree, Judy."

"Where's the spree, Gran?" I wanted to know.

"It's above at Soot Higgins's," Mike said. "Biddy is goin' back to America in the mornin', so they're givin' a joint spree to-night. Half-a-crown for the men, and the women free."

Mrs. Higgins was called 'Soot' because her complexion supported the popular belief that she washed her face only at Christmas and Easter. Gran, who could be so tolerant of what she called 'the human sins' had no charity at all where laziness and dirt and bad housekeeping were concerned.

"You'll nearly want to stand under the pump when you come back," she commented acidly.

Mike laughed.

"We're likely to pick up a few hoppers," he agreed. "I believe the fleas above at Soot's are that hardy they become grandfathers in a night."

"Poor Biddy must have had a time of it for her holi-day, then," said Gran. "It was hard lines on her coming home to a house like that after the style she was used to in America."

"Don't be talkin', ma'am!" said Judy. "They tell me that since she came home she has every bit of Violet Powder in Duffy's bought up trying to cover the marks on her neck."

"There's no doubt it's to be a good spree, though," Mike said. "Mickey O'Neill was telling me Soot ordered a half-barrel of porter for the men an' six dozen of minerals for the women. An' I heard talk of a ham."

"Aye," said Gran unbelievingly. "A ham with lugs on it you mean."

This was a wicked crack at the Higgins's love for pig's head. Now, we all liked our pig's head in Ballyderrig. Nicely cleaned and cooked and lying on a bolster of green cabbage, there were few delicacies to equal it. But there's reason in all things. The Higgins's love for pig's head was like the craving some people have for drugs. They couldn't get enough of it. When Biddy Higgins came home from America, her family had nothing to show for all the money she had sent during her fourteen years of exile but a big heap of bleached jaw-bones out behind the cottage. She complained of this publicly and from that day the Higgins's were known as the family who had squandered a fortune on pigs' heads.

"There's one thing, anyway," Mike said, standing up from the table. "Ould Jem Higgins'll be able to sleep in peace again when Biddy's gone back. I hear she's been making him sleep in pyjamas."

This was too much! The idea of poor old Jem Higgins, who often hadn't a shirt to his back, going to bed all dolled up in pyjamas so overcame Judy Ryan that she laughed until the cups shook on the table.

"You're an awful liar, Mike Brophy," she said with streaming eyes when she got her breath. "Jem Higgins in pyjamas . . . !" and Judy was off again. Small wonder, for pyjamas were so unusual in Ballyderrig that it was doubtful if Dr. Mangan himself wore them.

"There's not a word of a lie in it, Mrs. Lacy," Mike assured Gran. "She got Miss Derrigan to send to Dublin for two sets of them for him. Sure it's all over the town."

Mike was proved to be no liar. On the Sunday after Biddy Higgins went back to America, her mother sailed in to Second Mass wearing a magenta-striped pyjama jacket over her blouse and skirt.

Two days before I went away to Wicklow, Gran sent me into the town for messages. It was late when I started home for there were many good-byes to say. At Doran's field I got a puncture which delayed me further, so that the trees and hedges were swimming in pearly dusk by the time I reached Mitchell's Forge.

Two figures emerged from the shadows of the deserted forge as I approached. Even in that light I knew them both too well to be mistaken as to their identity. They were Red Connolly and Sheila Clinton. Red was wheeling a bike and he had his arm around Sheila.

She was crying, and when I realised this, a sick frightened feeling came over me. For grown-ups to cry always affected me in this way. They were facing the Kildare road, and they never noticed me coming up with them.

As I drew level with them Sheila started talking – little

rushing, sobbing words that increased the misery of sick sadness inside me.

"Oh, God forgive me, Red!" she was saying. "God forgive me! I should never have let you come back. You must never come again till I'm married. Hurry now, alanna, or you'll miss your train."

I turned where the road forked at the forge and they never knew I was within a hundred miles of them.

In bed that night I told Gran what I had seen. She lay silent for a minute. Then, "I knew no good would come out of that match," she said with finality. "It's a forced marriage and they were never good or lucky."

She was silent again while she considered the matter in all its aspects.

"Can you beat it, though?" she said at length. "He must have been coming down on the train from Dublin and cycling over to meet her — and not one in Ballyderrig knew a word about it!"

The rest of the story may as well be told now although there were parts of it I did not hear until years later.

Sheila Clinton and Frank Price got married after Advent, and Mr. and Mrs. Clinton were well pleased with themselves when they saw Sheila finally settled in Thomastown. Their complacency was shattered when, six months after the wedding, Sheila gave birth to a fine son with a flaming red head.

I think I explained that Frank Price was not very bright. In addition, he had been shielded so carefully by his mother, that he was anything but well up. However, even his innocence and dull wits did not keep him from wondering if it was not just a little too soon for his wife to have a son — and a son with such a red head into the bargain.

After a long struggle with himself he carried his doubts to Dr. Mangan. The doctor, who had a great feeling for romance, rose nobly to the occasion.

"What are you complaining of, man?" he demanded indignantly. "That it didn't take your wife as long as it does other women? That's because she's a fine quick woman — a grand quick woman. In all my experience, I've seen only one woman in a thousand who can do it. Let me tell you there's many a man who would give thousands to have a wife like yours. Go home and thank God for her, man." And then, showing Frank to the door, he added, "He's a lovely boy, that son of yours. You know, a man who isn't experienced might think it a funny thing about that red head of his, seeing that yourself and Mrs. Price are so dark. But it runs in the Clinton family, you know, and turns up as regular as clockwork no matter what colour the parents are. I saw it over in Meath with cousins of theirs — all black-headed fathers and mothers and all red-headed children. Aye, indeed — a very common thing in the Clinton family."

Frank Price went home happy and at ease. But he did not enjoy his happiness long. The following spring twelve-months he was ploughing a field when the tractor overturned, pinning him beneath. When they got him out he was dead.

When Sheila married Red six months later, there were some who said her haste was indecent. But gossip could not hurt the Connollys, for they had sold out and sailed for America with their son almost before we knew what they were doing.

CHAPTER 12

"HERE'S Granny Lynn to say good-bye to you, Delia," called Judy Ryan to me the night before I left for Wicklow. I came down from the bedroom where I was finishing my packing and found Mrs. Lynn in the kitchen.

She was a kindly old woman, very simple and very grateful for any little service. My grandmother had been a good friend to her during a time of sore trouble, and Granny Lynn never forgot.

"I was on me way down to poor Lisheen Walsh's wake," she said coming into the kitchen, "so I thought I'd drop in to say good-bye to little Deelyeen." I was 'little Deelyeen' to all the old people in Ballyderrig.

"That was good of you, Mrs. Lynn," Gran said. "We were thinking of going down there ourselves, too. If you'll just sit down here at the fire, Judy won't be a minute making you a cup of tea. While you're drinking it I can be getting ready, and then we'll all be down to the wake together."

Granny Lynn sat down at the fire and Gran went upstairs. Then Granny fumbled at her pocket and brought out a little paper-wrapped parcel which she handed to me. She leaned towards me confidentially. She had a habit of giving everything she said an air of terrific importance by speaking in a conspiratorial whisper.

"I brought you a little keepsake," she whispered. "Open it an' see what's in it."

I unwrapped the parcel. It was a necklace of light blue beads. The colour was lovely — pale as heather when it has begun to fade.

146

"Oh, thanks, Granny!" I said. "Sure you shouldn't have bothered. It's too good of you altogether!"

"Whist, now," Granny whispered. "But take good care of it, for there's a blessin' on it." I looked my impressed surprise, and Granny went on, "Aye, indeed — I codded the Missioner with it. When he told us to hold up our rosaries for a blessin' at the June Mission, I held the necklace up, too, an' he never knew." Her delight at having put one over on the Missioner was lovely.

I put on my necklace, and when Gran had come down and had duly admired it and Granny Lynn had taken her tea, the three of us started for the wake.

The Walsh's house was next door to our old home in the town, separated from it only by a short steep lane. At the front the house was one-storeyed, but when you went down the lane and turned left to the back-door you entered an earthen-floored basement of two rooms furnished with a couple of soap boxes and several ramshackle beds. These Mrs. Walsh let to lodgers, thus adding to the wages her husband earned on the canal boats. The lodgers she kept were tramps, quiet inoffensive men, who came with their red-handkerchiefed luggage at night and departed on their wanderings next morning after cooking themselves a meal on the fire which was provided in addition to the bed for the sum of twopence. She had several regulars, among them a bent old clockmaker called Wolfe. I remember him well for he had taken a liking to me when I was a child. I looked forward to his coming. Ten minutes after his arrival at Mrs. Walsh's I would hear him calling me over our back gate.

"Little Deelyeen. . . Is little Deelyeen there? Send little Deelyeen out to me."

I would come running out and there he would be. Enormous bald head surmounted by a ragged-brimmed bowler hat faded to rusty green by sun and wind and water. Contented light grey eyes forced slightly from their sockets by much peering at minute wheels and springs. A heavy humorous nose, and a smiling toothless good-natured mouth. Winter and summer, he wore a multitude of baggy old overcoats.

When Wolfe saw me, he started rummaging in one of his numerous pockets and presently a gift would be produced and handed down into my eager hands over the back gate. A cotton handkerchief of mushrooms, maybe, or, in the autumn, of small oval hazel-nuts, brown and smooth and shining, that were as good to handle as they were to eat. Sometimes it was a big yellow apple. There was even an occasion when he brought me a little live coneen, but Bruss, our terrier, broke my heart by killing it before it had been mine for an hour.

"Poor little Lisheen went very sudden, after all," Granny Lynn said, as we walked along the moon-white road.

"She did indeed," Gran agreed. "How old would she have been, do you think?"

I was able to tell them that. I had been talking to Lisheen in the town about a month before her death. She told me she hoped to be confirmed in the spring.

"How old are you now, Lisheen?" I asked. In Ballyderrig this was one of the commonest of questions, for we had a deep and insatiable curiosity with regard to ages.

Little Lisheen had snuffled and said, "If I like to live till Christmas I'll be twelve."

Well, she hadn't liked to live till Christmas. Nor

could she be blamed for this, for the poor hectic child not only had consumption. She had the minearach as well. I am not quite sure how that word should be spelled. It is the name we gave in Ballyderrig to the condition which I have since heard city people call calcium deficiency and which manifests itself in children by a morbid craving for lime, forcing them to eat plaster and clay.

Lisheen had the minearach very bad. She ate the whole side wall out of our house. Well, maybe not the whole wall, but she did eat a big patch of plaster out of it. I am afraid, like everyone else in Ballyderrig, I am sometimes inclined to exaggerate a little. We had no intention of lying. It was just our way and came as natural to us as breathing. For instance, we would never think of saying of prolific Mrs. Nolan, who produced a child as often as the laws of Nature allowed, that she had a baby regularly every year. Instead we said, "That poor creature? Sure she has a child every fortnight." And of Tommy Anderson, who had been delicate as a boy, we did not say "His mother found him hard to rear," but, "Tommy Anderson? He went to bed when he was seven and didn't get up for fifteen years." We had a way of our own, too, of changing the very essence of words according to the mood of the speaker. Yards, pints, miles — these were set inelastic standards elsewhere. In Ballyderrig they could stand for big or small quantities. It all depended on your humour while speaking. When Jed Healy delayed overlong in Duffy's pub at night, he would excuse himself to his mother saying, "Aw, I was only having a few little oul' pints above in Duffy's," thereby making the pints harmless moderate little thimblefuls. Those selfsame pints could be turned into monstrous intemperance next day when his mother scolded Jed for his shortcomings. "You can't get up and go to the bog now! Last night you could stand above in Duffy's drinkin' great big pints!"

"How is Nellie getting on, Mrs. Lynn?" Gran inquired as we walked. "Did you hear from her lately?"

"I had a letter only last Saturday," Granny Lynn replied with satisfaction, a lamp of youth lighting up her voice, as it always did when she spoke of her beloved grandchild. "She's doin' real well."

"She has two children now, hasn't she?"

"Aye. A fine lump of a gossoon, an' the little girl they christened Maggie after meself. Judgin' from a likeness that came in the letther, the childher must take after her man, for I can't see a sign of a Lynn in them at all."

"Is he workin' regular?"

"As regular as the day, thank God. Earnin' fine money deliverin' milk to the women of London. He's crazy out about Nellie. Bought her a fur coat for the winter. Can you beat that, now? Our Nellie in a fur coat an' with a husband and childher an' a home of her own! Sure God is very good."

"He is indeed," Gran agreed. "And Nellie deserves it all. If ever a child earned her reward she did."

It always gave me a pang when people spoke of Nellie Mack.

There was a story for you!

Nellie was a good deal older than I, but I could remember well seeing her pass our door on her way to school in her white pinafore and with her hair in two plaits to her waist.

Her father, Jem Mack, was married to Granny Lynn's only daughter. He was a road-mender earning good regular wages and he lived in a little cottage on the Kildare Road. There were two children in the family, Nellie and an older boy. When Nellie was twelve her mother went into a decline.

While she was dying she was visited often by her sister-in-law, a widow called Mrs. Magee, from some place beyond Clane, with a grown-up daughter in service in Newbridge. I never liked her. She was a hard-eyed woman, red-haired and with thin legs, huge bony ankles and splay feet. She made out that her visits were inspired by friendship for the sick woman, but it seems that in reality she was making ready the way to step into her shoes. Not long after Mary Mack's death, the hard-faced widow cajoled Jem Mack into letting her come to keep house for him. He was a weak spineless creature, anyway, and no match for her wiles.

At that time, we had an old retired Excise Officer living in Ballyderrig. He was seventy-three years of age, and had been living in the hotel for donkeys' years. It would be hard to say what had induced Mr. Graham to pick on Ballyderrig as the scene of his waning years. We had no golf, no sea-breezes, no promenade, no society — none of the things which are supposed to influence retired civil servants in their choice of a final habitat. Gran always said it was the devil who sent him. I think she was right. If anyone ever had a look of being the devil's messenger, Graham had it. He was a tall unhealthy old man who looked as if a good puff of wind would blow him asunder. He had yellow-whited eyes set under shaggy brows that met over his beak of a nose. His mouth was horrible and always frightened me. Thin rubbery lips that stretched in a leer over yellow teeth. I heard my mother say of him that a man with a mouth like that should always wear a beard.

When Nellie Mack was a little over thirteen, she started going in to the hotel kitchen after school every day to help Mrs. Murphy who was housekeeper there. Nellie got a shilling a week and her tea, and an odd sixpence from old Mr. Graham for running messages. The child must have been grateful for this escape from her home which was an unhappy place since her aunt had taken possession. Not even the presence of Granny Lynn, whom her son's new housekeeper grudgingly permitted to retain her corner in the kitchen could shield Nellie from the harshness of that woman.

She had been working in the hotel for some time when suddenly all Ballyderrig was horrified to hear that fourteen-year-old Nellie Mack, of the plaits and white pinafore, was going to have a baby. The horror was changed to fury when it was learned that the father was old Mr. Graham. And all that terrified Nellie could sob when questioned was, "He promised me a bicycle. He promised me a bicycle!"

The men of Ballyderrig, headed by Nellie's father, would have lynched the old beast but that he got an easy way out. A few days after the story became known, he went out of his mind. I saw him myself being taken away to Carlow Asylum. He was strapped to the seat of Johnny Dunne's outside-car, with a peeler on each side of him. His mouth and chin were covered with foam.

The most shocking part of the whole terrible story was the indecent lack of charity of Nellie's aunt. That woman behaved with diabolical cruelty to the unfortunate child. She developed a complex of outraged virtue that found expression in blows and foul epithets. She refused to sit down at the same table as Nellie, and but for the girl's father, would have turned her out on the road.

Nurse Cassidy, who attended Nellie when the baby was born, told Gran that it turned her stomach to think of that night. Mrs. Magee became like a devil, and could not be kept out of the room where the little girl was in labour. She stood at the foot of the bed, gloating over Nellie's pains. At one moment, she became so overcome with devilish fury that she caught the semi-delirious girl by the plaits and beat her head against the wall.

With the help of Jem Mack, Nurse Cassidy got the inhuman wretch out of the room while the baby was actually being born. Afterwards, when the Nurse came into the kitchen with the cause of all the trouble in her arms, Mrs. Magee leaped away from her as if from the plague.

"Don't bring that thing near me!" she screamed. "Take it away! It's a devil out of hell!"

She need not have worried, for the baby was dead.

Soon after that, Nellie Mack was sent away to some convent for fallen women in Dublin. A week later, old Granny Lynn was also evicted. It was then Gran befriended her. She took her in and kept her until the old woman found a home for herself with Mrs. Sheehy, another lonely old-age pensioner who lived on the Monasterevan road.

When Nellie was eighteen she was allowed to leave the convent and to go to service to a woman in Belfast. While there she met a grand fellow, a milkman, who found so much to love in her that he forgot her story ten minutes after she told it to him. He married her when she was over twenty, and took her away to England.

What happened after to Mrs. Magee seemed like a judgment from God. Her inhuman treatment of Nellie was inspired chiefly by the fear that the scandal would spoil her own girl's chances.

A few months after Nellie's marriage, Mrs. Magee's daughter was involved in a scandal that, tolerant though we were, shook Ballyderrig to its foundations. She ran away with a travelling showman who left his wife and four children on the streets of Newbridge. Whatever our shortcomings, we had great respect for the sanctity of marriage, and we felt a girl would be better dead than to live with the guilt of breaking up a home on her.

Mrs. Walsh had her little girl beautifully laid out. The Confirmation dress which her sister had worn three years before had been put by for Lisheen and she now wore it in all its glory of blue satin ribbon and cutwork. A veil covered her bright dry hair and her hands, which, during her lifetime, her mother had kept bound with rags to prevent her eating the plaster, were locked on a blue rosary.

When we had offered our sympathy to Mrs. Walsh and had knelt for a moment beside Lisheen's bed, room was made for us at the fire and we proceeded to carry out the real object of our visit. To offer Job's brand of comfort was not our way in Ballyderrig. We went to a wake, not to increase the sorrow of the bereaved family by our tears, but to help them to forget their trouble in a flood of good stories. In our part of the country, you could get as good a night's entertainment at a wake as at a wedding.

Barney Holohan was there, and Lizzie Neale.

Barney was a saddler, a stunted wizened little man with a crippled leg. He lived with a drunken brother at the top of the town. 'Holohan Bros.' was what the sign over the door said, but the 'Bros.' might as well have been deleted, for Jim Holohan was never known to put a stitch in leather. A big hulking brute who would have made four of Barney, he drank and lazed his way through life on the fruits of his brother's labour. The devotion of the puny industrious creature to useless Jim was incredible. On Saturday nights, when Jim grew cantankerous in drink and stood howling for fight on the flagstones outside Duffy's, it was pathetic to see Barney come hopping down from the workshop, his canvas apron tucked up under his coat. With a woman's gentleness, he would coax and plead until he induced Jim to come home.

Barney had a cruel wit and was feared for it. If it were to save him from hanging, he could not resist giving a dig whenever he got the chance.

"I hear Sam Pringle is after your blood, Barney," Gran said, as soon as we had disposed of the weather and the crops and Sheila Clinton's engagement. "What did you do on the man at all?"

Barney twinkled wickedly.

"I only asked him a civil question, Mrs. Lacy."

"You an' your civil questions!" Lizzie Neale said. "Civility an' yourself never went to bed together, Barney Holohan. Go on an' tell us what you said to the man."

Barney put his hand in his pocket and took out his pipe and his knife and a square of twist. He proceeded to cut himself a fill of juicy black shavings.

"Well, you know he's courtin' Miss Regan's new shopgirl — the wan we christened 'Biddy Doyle'! She's the spittin' image of Doyle the tinker."

"Now you have it, Barney," whispered Granny Lynn in agreement. "High colour, yalla hair an' all. I don't care where she comes from, the Doyles had a hand in the makin' of her."

"The poor girl!" Gran expostulated. "I happen to know she comes of a well-connected family in Kilcullen. Though she *is* like the Doyles, to be sure."

Barney lifted a bit of griseach in the tongs and held it to his pipe. He puffed luxuriously before he continued.

"Here a month back my oul' ass strayed for a few days. Sam was passin' the door on his way to meet the mot. All I said to him was, 'Eh, Sam, will you ask that wan where's my little ass?' Where was the harm in that, I ask you?"

Even Lisheen's mother had a laugh at this.

"God forgive you, Barney Holohan!" said Gran when she had caught her breath. "That tongue of yours will be the end of you."

Barney proceeded to draw out Lizzie Neale, but he got no change out of her. Lizzie's tongue was a match for anyone's living. She had a contempt for softness. She was fond of boasting that though she had a husband and five children she had never been kissed in her life.

Other sympathizers dropped in and soon the little room

where Lisheen lay waking was crowded. In their efforts to cheer Mrs. Walsh, Barney and Lizzie tossed the ball of anecdote from one to another with occasionally one of the rest of us joining in. Mrs. Walsh seemed to appreciate their efforts for she shed no tears, and even joined in the laughter. But every now and then, I saw her eyes turn from the company to the little bed in the corner, and then for a long second the muscles of her face grew rigid and her eyes were heavy.

Granny Lynn was staying the night to sit up with the corpse. I was leaving for Wicklow in the half-eight train from Kildare next morning, so at nine o'clock Gran and myself knelt for a last quick prayer at Lisheen's bed. We said good-night to Mrs. Walsh and came home.

Since I was tired, that night did not seem different from any other night and I fell asleep quickly. But in the early grey morning something wakened me. I lay still for a minute. Beside me, Gran seemed to be breathing queerly . . . little jerky snuffling breaths through her nose. Could she be crying? I stirred and then sat up and leaned over her. No; I must have imagined it, for there was Gran breathing deeply and evenly as usual. She opened her eyes in the dim light.

"What ails you, alanna? Can't you sleep?"

I lay down again and, cuddling into her, I put my arm around her. Her gentle old hand closed on mine and then all at once I realized what I was going from. There was a great emptiness in me and a fear. And I knew that I did not want to go. That all I wanted in the world was to stay here in Derrymore House. To go on forever being nourished by Gran's love and wrapped around with all the familiar things that were part of me.

"Do I have to go, Gran?" I begged.

Gran's hand tightened on mine. She did not reply for a minute and when her voice came it was harsh and strange.

"Don't be a little oinseach," she said. "Of course you have to go to school. Didn't I promise your mother I'd make a teacher of you?"

"But I don't want to be a teacher, Gran."

"That's nonsense and you know it. Don't you want to make something of yourself? Don't you want to be able to make a decent living for yourself? You know there'll be little enough here for you when I'm gone."

"Couldn't I stay here and marry a farmer?"

"A nice-looking farmer's wife you'd make! A girl that couldn't boil a pot of pig's food to save her life. Have a bit of sense, child. You're not cut out for a farmer's wife, Delia, and that's sure and certain." She sat up in bed and looked at me quizzically. "You'd hand him up a poem instead of a clean shirt on Sunday morning."

In spite of the ache inside me, I had to join Gran in her laughter.

"That's better," she said. "Now we'll have no more whingeing and crying. You're getting a chance that many a girl would give her eyes for. Turn over there now and get a wink of sleep or we'll never be up in time for the train."

Well, there was no way out of it.

I turned over obediently and soon we were sleeping again. Never a word had been said by either of us of how we would miss each other. But we both understood and words were not necessary.

CHAPTER 13

THOSE first weeks in the convent were bewildering. Apart from the head-whirling effects of wrestling for the first time with French and algebra, there were a million new things to learn.

Mary Joe Heffernan was quick to watch for and avoid the pitfalls of unladylike behaviour into which I fell twenty times daily. Mary Joe had never liked me. She resented my having come to the same school as herself, and my discomfiture when I made a mistake gave her great satisfaction.

Mealtime was a nightmare. Instead of the happy company of Mike and Judy and Gran at the kitchen table in Derrymore House where we suited our own convenience in the matter of forks and fingers, I now had to sit at table with a crowd of strange girls who were all more or less conscious of the fact that they were young ladies at a boarding school, and they acted up to it. Indeed, it was in their interest to do so, for to relax even for a moment brought public humiliation. The nun on duty in the refectory prowled constantly up and down between the tables, keeping a sharp eye out for any evidence of the inadequate training in table manners we had received at home.

I had so much to unlearn. It was a crime, it seemed, to spear a potato from the dish in the centre of the table with your fork. Instead, you helped yourself daintily with your fingers. There was a new and incredibly complicated way of peeling them, too. The old way of holding the potato in your left hand and removing the peel with the help of a knife and the ball of your thumb had been much simpler. No lady, it seemed, ever mopped up the gravy on her plate with a blotter of bread stuck on the end of her fork. And it amounted to a mortal sin to take a bone in your fingers and pick it, no matter how sweet or how inaccessible to cutlery the scraps of meat that clung to it. To me, the mortal sin lay in wasting it.

I was unfortunate enough to antagonise from the start the nun who was on duty in the refectory that term.

On my second day there, we had stew at dinner. Not the rich oniony stew of Gran's making, but a watery concoction sparsely dotted with uninviting islands of hard potatoes, tough pieces of meat and stringy carrots. To make matters worse, the cook had been far too liberal with the salt. I could not make myself eat it.

Sister Liguori came behind me and stopped at my chair when she saw my untouched plate.

"What is this?" she demanded. "Why are you not eating your stew?" Consideration for her feelings prevented my telling her exactly why.

"I'm full up, Sister," I lied. Her face tightened at the inelegance of this statement. She was a dumpy square little woman with a long chin and a thin line of a mouth.

"Stand up," she said acidly. "Don't you know better than to remain seated when a nun addresses you? Nuns are the apple of God's eye." I was to learn that this was her favourite war-cry.

Obediently, I stood up, while the other girls stopped eating to enjoy the scene.

"To waste good food is a sin. It is also unmannerly to show a lack of appreciation by leaving the food that is prepared for you. Does it not make you ashamed to think that this plate of stew will now have to be thrown out to the hens?"

Salty stew for hens? Now, there was a queer thing to say! Was it possible that Sister Liguori really didn't know that salt was fatal to hens? Unfortunately for myself I proceeded to enlighten her.

Innocently — I swear it was in innocence and with no intention in the world of being impertinent, I said:

"But, sure that stew would poison the hens."

The gasp that went around the table and the look on Sister Liguori's face told me of the *faux pas* I had made. I rushed to explain.

"I didn't mean that, Sister! I only meant — " But my stammered explanations did nothing to repair the damage. From that day, Sister Liguori seemed to have decided that to make a lady of me was the duty for which God had sent her into the world and for which He had called her to the religious life. The poor nun did not succeed in her mission. But she did manage very effectively to make my life a hell while I remained in Wicklow.

She never let me alone. She believed me to be a surly, unmannerly, impertinent girl who might be saved from perdition only by constant surveillance and reprimands. In so far as she was concerned, I was certainly all this. As always when I believed myself unjustly treated, a devil rose up in me. Her constant nagging had the effect of wakening all my bad qualities and of making me show myself to her in the worst possible light.

Towards the middle of October I got a temporary respite from Sister Liguori's tongue, for I developed the itch. This meant that I was removed from all contact with the rest of the school. I was taken from the dormitory and put to sleep in the infirmary, a small dark room at the back of the cloakrooms. I walked apart from the others at recreation and my night study was done in the solitude of the infirmary instead of in the big study hall. At class and in the chapel I had a bench to myself and my meals were sent up to the infirmary on a tray.

I could hardly have been more completely quarantined had I been a leper.

This calamity occurring as it did during my very first term at school was, I now believe, largely responsible for my unsuccessful career there. It explains why I formed no friendships in Wicklow, for even when I was cured and allowed to rejoin the other girls, the majority of them were still inclined to withdraw from me. It was responsible for the inferiority complex I carried away from the place and which even Gran's wisdom and understanding could never completely cure.

I cannot say that I was devastated by my isolation. It brought me humiliations, of course . . . as when I saw Mary Joe Heffernan pick up an Irish grammar in the study-hall and drop it with a little shriek when she read my name on the fly-leaf. But these were minor things. To be bereft of the girls' company did not worry me, for the society of my contemporaries had always made me awkward and shy.

On the whole, I enjoyed my six weeks of quarantine. In the first place, they freed me from Sister Liguori's nagging. More important still, to be left without supervision in the infirmary at night meant that I could read insteady of studying. I made the most of this opportunity and devoured the moth-eaten old books in the infirmary press — bound volumes of *The Rosary* and *The Sacred Heart Messenger* and *Home Topics* and other dog-eared discards from the school library which had been stored there for the benefit of poor lepers like myself. Strictly speaking, I was not supposed to touch these books except during the two hours allotted us each week for reading — from seven to nine on Saturday nights. This regulation meant nothing to me, and I gladly committed the sin of disobedience several times daily.

All this idling meant, of course, that I dropped far behind the others of my class. The Intermediate Board reigned in those days. I had been placed in junior grade, and it was expected of me, as of the four others who were intended for the King's Scholarship, that I should pass with honours at the end of the year and thus qualify for the position of pupil-teacher in the National School attached to the convent. This appointment carried a small salary, the amount of which was deducted from our fees.

Only two of the nuns at Wicklow made a lasting impression on me. I remember Sister Liguori for her no doubt well-meant but very galling interest in my manners. Sister Conleth I remember for her kindness.

She was a middle-aged woman and just a little queer in her head. Twelve months before, when this queerness had manifested itself in an absent-mindedness which made her come down to Mass one morning without her veil, she had been deposed from her position as teacher of preparatory grade. I heard later that she made a complete recovery some time after I left Wicklow, and was allowed to take up her teaching once more.

We became friendly during my time in the infirmary.

Maybe we were drawn together by the realization that we were both outcasts. Sister Conleth filled her classless days by doing beautiful needlework. Altar-cloths, vestments for the foreign missions, missal markers and lovely little cloths for the arm-rests of *prie-dieux* — she covered them with the most exquisite embroidery. She often brought her work to the infirmary and sat there talking to me while she embroidered. Probably she would have got into trouble had this been known. But her queerness had made her sly, and she was clever in evading discovery. She could hear the rubber-heeled approach of Sister Paul, the infirmarian, from a mile away, and would gather her silks and stuffs together and glide away like a tall wraith in plenty of time.

She was an immensely tall woman. Painfully thin, with a dead-white face and pale lips and eyes. There was an austerity about her, a self-denial, which was the epitome of convent life. I loved to sit watching her work. On her black lap the coloured silks rioted in gorgeous prodigality. Reds and blues and purples as brave and loud as a trumpet call. Seen thus on the peaceful lap of one whose life had passed in sombre austerity, they provided a strange disturbing contrast. It fascinated me to see those bony parchment fingers thread the silk and draw a many-coloured trail through the milk-pure satin until gradually the design took shape — wheat-ears and grape-leaves and frequently the Latin letters, A.M.D.G.

She was embroidering a *prie-dieu* cover one day, and an odd thought came into my head as I watched a rainbow bird take form under her practised hand and slowly poise on a golden stalk.

"You're like Our Lord, Sister Conleth," I said.

In shocked amazement, Sister Conleth braked her needle half-way through a stitch.

"What a thing to say, child!" she expostulated. "And what makes you say it, anyway?"

"Well, didn't He — when He was small — find a dead bird on a garden-path and, by taking it in His hands, give it life? When I was looking at you now, I just thought that the transfer was only a dead bird till you gave life to it with your needle. And I said to myself, 'Sister Conleth is like Our Lord.'"

"That was a bad sacrilegious thought, child, and I'm ashamed of you. Never compare a poor human being to Our Lord." There was annoyance in her high thin voice.

All the same, I thought Sister Conleth was pleased. She held up her work and looked long and smilingly at the tiny silk-feathered body she had created and that seemed about to fly, quick-soaring as a hymn at Benediction, to the throne of God.

Gran was very put out when she heard I had the itch and, although she knew our letters were censored by the Mother Superior before we received them, she did not try to hide her concern and annoyance when writing to me.

"It's the queerest thing I ever heard of," she wrote. "I never knew of anyone to get the itch except from dirt, and there was no sign of it on you when you left here. I hope that doctor who's treating you knows his business. I've a good mind to send you a bottle and some ointment myself, for you know I've cured itch and wildfire many a time.

"There's little to tell you about Ballyderrig. There was an excursion to Kilkenny on All Souls' Day and I thought I'd run up to see your mother. It's younger she's getting, and there's no doubt she made the wise move in leaving Ballyderrig. The rest of them are keeping very well, thank God, and Peg has the makings of a great business woman in her already.

"Judy and Mike want to be remembered to you. Granny Lynn as well, and Willie Beckett and Miss Flood and all your friends here. We pulled the last of the Bramleys last week and Mike has them stored in hay in the loft against the time you come home. I sent a box of rusty coats to you by the railway. There's a few dead-sweets in it, too, but they're not as good as usual this year for the tree is nearly worn out. It doesn't owe us anything anyway for it was planted in my grandmother's time. Be sure to write and let me know if the box goes astray.

"I hope you're eating plenty. I'm tired asking you what they give you to eat. But maybe all the news will keep till you come home.

"We're thinking of killing a pig for Christmas. There's one of them getting very heavy and it'll run into fat if we don't get John Dooley out to butcher him.

"With fond love from all.

Gran."

We were allowed to write one letter each Sunday and although that week it was my mother's turn to hear from me, I wrote to Gran instead. It was of vital importance to me that they should not kill the pig until I got home, for a pig-killing in Derrymore House was as festive an occasion as the turf-cutting or the threshing.

"We are getting our Christmas holidays on the 13th of December," I wrote. "Please don't kill the pig until then. Thanks for the apples. They arrived alright, and they were lovely. The itch is nearly gone, and if I wasn't going home so soon, Sister Paul says she'd let me back to the dormitory, but it isn't worth while now till after the holidays."

I was home in the train with Mary Joe Heffernan. Although I had been mixing again with the rest of the school for over a week, Mary Joe was taking no chances. She did not sit beside me and was inclined to be a bit stand-offish. But I did not mind much for I had stolen *The Girl of the Limberlost* out of the infirmary press and I sat and read it. I had put a brown paper cover on it so that Mary Joe would not see the white tab stuck on the back which would have betrayed it as belonging to the school.

CHAPTER 14

ON THE Monday after I came home from Wicklow we killed the pig.

Talk of cooking and feasting! We had days and days of it, for in our house a pig-killing meant brawn and fried liver and roast stuffed heart, lardy cakes and fillets and griskin stew, and black and white pudding.

There was so much to be done that Gran sent for Mrs. Noone of the Glebe to come over to help us. Mrs. Noone was the only woman in Ballyderrig whom Gran considered her equal as a cook. In her youth she had been cook to some grand lady in Meath where they had late dinner every night and a footman to wait at table. It would have made your mouth run water to hear Mrs. Noone's stories of the dinners she cooked in that house. Seven and eight courses, and every course a meal in itself.

She was a tidy-figured little woman with a lot of fuzzy dark hair standing out around her pale face with its red-tipped nose. With what her husband earned as a shop-boy in Dunne's she had little enough outlet for her cooking skill, for they had a big family — five boys and one girl, Molly. That girl was the apple of Mrs. Noone's eye, and she set an impossibly high standard for her. This was hard on Molly, for she was constantly disappointing her mother and getting into trouble for it.

Take the case of the school photograph.

Occasionally a travelling photographer came to the town for a week or so. There were no cameras in Ballyderrig and he did good business during his stay. His best clients were the children of the Convent School. We were marshalled into groups and photographed, class by class. For threepence we could buy a copy of the photograph. What Mrs. Noone expected for the three-pence she gave reluctantly to Molly, it would be hard to say. Whatever it was, she did not get it. When poor Molly brought home the washy brown print her mother took one look at it, and then boxed the unfortunate child's ears because she had not turned out good-looking.

We were up early on the morning of the pig-killing, for a huge fire had to be lit in the washhouse to provide water for scalding the carcass.

At half-past ten Mrs. Noone arrived with a brown paper parcel under her arm. It held cap, apron and sleeves she had preserved from her hey-day in Meath.

Half-an-hour later John Dooley drove up to the door in his pony and trap with Britches Healy, his helper, sitting beside him.

"Here's The Child and Britches," said Judy when she sighted them. "We're all ready for them. The water is on the boil and the clean sacks are laid out for the scaldin'."

John Dooley was the youngest of a large family, and though he was over forty at this time his mother never spoke of him other than as 'The Child.' And so 'The Child' he was to all Ballyderrig. Not in his hearing, though, for John was different from the rest of us in that he resented being called out of his name. He was a bad-tempered man, dark, sullen and foreign-looking, with a dark, heavy face. His appearance earned him a second nickname from Barney Holohan. One Sunday in the Chapel, Barney scandalized us by giving a sudden loud snigger right in the middle of Father Dempsey's sermon. "I couldn't keep it in," he explained afterwards. "I was lookin' at the Eleventh Station and it came over me all of a sudden that there's a man in it who's the bloody image of the Child Dooley." And so 'The Child' became also 'The Eleventh Station Man.'

Dooley gave occasional employment to Britches Healy, who was as cheerful as his employer was dour. Britches' mother called him Jed but to the rest of us he was Britches. Until he was nine or ten and the schoolmaster, for shame's sake, gave him an old suit of his own, the boy's only attire was a cast-off riding breeches belonging to Dr. Mangan. His mother made a grand one-piece suit of it by gathering the waist around the child's neck and cutting away the pockets for armholes.

Britches was the most carefree individual in the world. He was on friendly terms with everyone and everything except regular work. The occasional jobs he got from John Dooley suited him down to the ground. Twopence for a packet of Woodbines and, now and then, the price of a pint, were all he asked in the way of money, for he could always scrounge a feed and his early dress experience had taught him that the usual sartorial standards are unnecessarily high.

The foolishness that made other men waste their lives in working day after day was something that Britches could never understand. He felt that only an idiot will slave for money to buy things he can just as easily do without. This was not mere theoretical guesswork on his part, for he had once given work a personal trial. That was when his uncle in America had sent for him and had put him to work in a bottling store. Six months of it had been enough. Britches came back home to us, a work-hater for life. He was home only a few weeks when Miss Lynch of the post-office was misguided enough to cajole him into accepting a job as temporary postman while Willie Beckett was up in Dublin getting his false teeth. Britches had only got as far as Glanaree Bridge when the sun and the way the fish were rising convinced him that delivering letters on such a day was a criminal misuse of time. He threw the letters into the canal and returned the empty mail-bag to Miss Lynch. And that, naturally, was the end of his mail carrying.

Britches fancied himself as a poet. (By the same token, Judy Ryan christened me 'Britches' when my poem won the prize.) Maybe this gift was fostered by his carefree and irresponsible attitude to life. Conversely, his idleness may have been due to his poetry, for it is possible he had some inkling of the rights once enjoyed by poets to the patronage of the drones. When Dr. Mangan married a city woman and brought her home to Ballyderrig, she was horrified at the primitive sanitary accommodation of the old house at the top of the town. She demanded and — such was the bridegroom's infatuation — got a proper water closet. The installation of the W. C. — the first Ballyderrig had ever known — was the talk of the place. Britches grew lyrical about it. In Duffy's bar he composed a poem that deserves to be included in the manuscript materials of Ballyderrig's history:

> "Water closets were made by man
>   For lords and ladies fair,
>   God help the poor
>   Who must endure
>   With only the open air."

I was squeamish about listening to the squealing of the pig while he was being killed, so I rode into the town to buy the salt, saltpetre and sugar that would be needed for the curing.

"Bring me back word of the prices at the Dead Market," Gran warned me. "I'm anxious to know if I lost by selling last week."

The Dead Market was always held on the Monday of the week preceding Christmas Week. It was in full swing when I reached the town, and even before I came to the top of the bridge I could feel that unusual hum of activity. I could hardly wheeel my bike through the higglers and women and creels of dead turkeys that crowded the market-place and overflowed onto the footpath at each side.

I was sorry to have missed the Live Market which had been held the previous Monday and at which Gran had sold her turkeys. I always found the Live Market an exhilarating affair because of the exciting high-pitched gobble kept up by the turkeys. Many of the women sold their birds at the Live Market, but more preferred to take a gamble on the price going up and they held on until the following week.

There was great good humour in the town.

The shopkeepers were pleased because the higglers' money would enable the women to settle their accounts. The women were happy because now at last they were to receive the reward of the exacting labours which turkey-raising entailed. For the birds were delicately-made creatures and difficult to rear. They had to be guarded more carefully than children against wettings and cold. Now at last they would get their money — twelve and fifteen and twenty pounds, some of them. They could pay their debts with their heads in the air and have enough left over for clothes and Christmas shopping. Their husbands, dressed in Sunday suits of shiny serge, had accompanied them into town just to make sure the money was not squandered. Most of the men had already had a pint or two and they wore a holiday look.

The children were highly delighted, too, for pennies flowed freely at the Dead Market. The stolid shy-eyed children from the far bog who, heavy-booted and trousered or frocked to below the calves, clung to their mothers' skirts, and the more daring town youngsters who dived in and out between the wheels of the creels — they would all come in for their share of the unaccustomed plenitude before the day was over.

I made slow progress for I knew everyone and kind enquiries for Gran and my mother and the rest of the family held me up at every step.

Anyway, it was difficult to detach oneself from the various entertainments that were part of the Market. The Fairy Broy was there with his bunch of song sheets. A grizzled little man as gnarled as one of the trees in the rath, the Fairy looked at least a hundred. But he had a voice that could lift the thatch off a house. He had his mouth open now and was letting his voice out in one of his ballads in a way that drowned every other noise. The Fairy was doing his best to entice an audience away from his rival, a fellow whom we had never seen before in Ballyderrig. The novelty of the stranger's act outweighed the Fairy's best vocal efforts. Presently he realized that he was fighting a losing battle. He closed his toothless white bearded mouth on an ear-splitting note and philosophically joined the crowd that had gathered around the newcomer.

The stranger was a Strong Man. A huge brawny fellow with a big stomach and thighs like the trunk of a tree. He had a small bullet head that was as bald as a baby's, and when he took off his coat and handed it to his assistant, a tired-looking wisp of a woman in a black shawl, he rolled up his shirt sleeves and flexed his muscles in a way that made us all gasp.

Our eyes nearly popped out of our heads at the feats that followed. He lifted enormous weights as if they were sods of turf. He lay down and laid a slab of stone on his chest and let the men hammer it to smithereens on his bare flesh without turning a hair.

I had to clear off when the woman started coming around with the cap because I only had the ten-shilling note for the messages. I felt mean and dishonest about not paying for the entertainment I had enjoyed, and when I had bought my goods and had plenty of ready change I came out looking for her. I was just in time to see the two of them disappear into Johnny Dunne's bar. I could not very well follow them there, so I let it go at that.

The pig was killed by the time I got home. The carcass was lying on the floor of the washhouse which was streaming with the water that had been used for the scalding. The pig was covered with clean sacks to keep in the steam and make scraping easier.

Johnny Dooley, Britches and Mike Brophy were in the kitchen having a meal of tea, bread-and-butter and blue duck eggs. An unusually frugal meal for Derrymore House, but it was merely intended as a stop-gap until the evening when they would be given a supper worthy of their labours, for the hardest part of the work was yet to come. Mrs. Noone stood at the far end of the table stirring salt in a basinful of the pig's blood for black pudding.

"How did the turkeys go?" Gran demanded when I came in.

"Ninepence ha'penny a pound, Gran. Mrs. Joe Flynn got tenpence for hers."

"Good," Gran commented with satisfaction. "They're down instead of up. I'm glad I got rid of mine last week."

When this meal was finished, the men went back to the washhouse to scrape the pig. When all his bristles were scraped away and he was pale and smooth and naked-looking they would hang him up and disembowel him. The boning and curing would be done next day when he was cold and the lard was set.

In the meantime there were the heart and liver and stomach to be brought into Gran and the intestines to be washed and left soaking in cold salted water to make casings for the puddings.

Gran and Mrs. Noone were in their element that evening. So were Judy and myself as we bustled around helping them. There were a hundred things to do. The heart to be cleaned and stuffed with potatoes and onions and sage and set to roast in the baker. The liver to be divided up, a portion for Mrs. Noone, one for Granny Lynn, one for Britches. Our own share of the liver to be sliced, rolled in flour and fried with bacon in the big iron pan. Oatmeal to be toasted for the black and white puddings, and the stomach to be scrubbed for Mrs. Noone to take home. She knew how to make a tasty dish of it by packing it with stuffing, stitching it up and roasting it.

Judy Ryan brought in an armful of early cabbage from the garden. Clusters of frost diamonds nestled in the wrinkles of its green leaves. And presently Mike Brophy came in with a bucket of potatoes which he had washed under the pump by churning them around in the icy water with a fork-handle.

When the potatoes and cabbage were cooked, Mrs. Noone made colcannon by mashing them together with plenty of butter, a naggin of milk and pepper and salt.

And at last they were ready.

There was a supper!

Pale green colcannon light and fluffy as bog-cotton and floating in good rich gravy. Slices of brown liver, crispy on the outside as new-baked crust, but inside all tender and blood-pitted and sweet. Juicy cuts of heart saturated with flavour from the savoury stuffing. And the stuffing itself! Soul of onion, breath of thyme and smoothness of potato. That stuffing caressed your palate and glided lovingly down your throat to find a resting place, not in your stomach but in your heart's core, warming its very cockles.

"Well, I'm glad to have that inside me shirt," Britches said at last, pushing back his plate. "An' now I'll be off for I'm goin' to ould Jimmy Doyle's wake."

"And is he dead then?" asked Gran, whose face wore the proud contented expression of the artist who has laboured to produce a masterpiece, and who has seen the results of his skill and inspiration favourably received by the critics.

"Did you not hear, ma'am? He dropped dead half-an-hour after comin' out of second Mass yesterday mornin'!"

"The Lord have mercy on him," said Gran, to which we all answered "Amen."

Sure enough when I was in the town that morning I had noticed the shutters on the shops. When anyone went from us in Ballyderrig, every shopkeeper put up one shutter as a mark of respect for the dead.

"It should be a powerful wake," Britches said.

"Why? Did The Roach make a good collection?" asked Mrs. Noone, referring to our custom of burying our poor by means of public subscription.

"He did that," John Dooley said morosely, speaking for the first time that evening. "He got a ten-shillin'-note out of me."

"It should be a powerful wake entirely," Britches persisted. "I was talkin' to Dinny Mulpeter in the town this mornin' an' he told me The Roach spent most of the money on a half-barrel of porter. An' I believe he could well do this, for what he spent on the coffin was harmless. Like cardboard, Dinny says it is. It'll be the mercy of God if poor ould Doyle doesn't fall through it on the way to the graveyard."

"No fear of that, Britches," Mike Brophy said. "It won't take a very strong coffin to carry poor ould Jimmy. He was light enough, God knows. Sure he was no bigger than a dog's diddy — an' that's a small piece of mate."

Next morning the men returned to cut down the pig and cure him. Mrs. Noone came, too, for the main part of the cooking was still to be done — lard to be rendered, puddings to be made and the brawn to be prepared and cooked and moulded.

About twelve o'clock, Britches came into the kitchen with a basin heaped with the fillets and spare ribs and griskins — those juicy sweet little trimmings from the sides which it would have been a crime to salt. Before setting about making a griskin and rib stew for the dinner, Gran put a good share of both on one side for Mrs. Noone.

Later the casings were brought in clean and wet and viscuous from their bath in salt water. We hung them to dry over the back of a chair near the fire. Judy hung the big pot on the crane to boil while Gran and Mrs. Noone and myself prepared the filling for the puddings. Toasted oatmeal, boiled chopped onions, chopped lard and plenty of pepper and salt, this was the filling for the white puddings. The same mixture with the addition of the pig's blood and a little milk was used for the black puddings.

When the intestines were dry the real work of pudding-making commenced. We took the half-yard lengths of pig-gut and tied it at one end with string. Then we blew it open with our mouths so as to get in the filling. This was eased down to the end until the gut was filled to a length of nine inches, care being taken to pack the mixture loosely to allow it room to swell. The end of the pudding was then made secure with string. An inch or so further up the gut was tied again and a second pudding was made in the same way. A snip of the scissors between the two separated them. When all the filling was used up, Mrs. Noone took one of Gran's sharp steel stocking needles and prodded the puddings here and there so that they would not burst in the boiling. Then into the pot with them to simmer and bubble for half-an-hour or so, after which they were lifted out and hung in the buttery to dry — fragrant promises of the treat that would accompany the breakfast rashers of ourselves and our neighbours for the next week.

When that was done we turned our attention to the brawn. Britches brought us in the feet and the head chopped in two.

"You scrub the feet, Delia," Gran said to me. There was her kindness again. She allotted me that easy job to save me having any part in the unpleasant work of cleaning the head.

The brains were taken out to be blanched and put by for the following morning, when they would be parboiled, coated in batter and fried as an extra tid-bit with our rashers and puddings. The ears had to be cleaned and singed and the nostrils rendered immaculate with a sharp knife — cleaning out the snoggles, Mrs. Noone called it.

In our house we liked our brawn salty, so Judy got down the big pickling crock. She rubbed the head and feet with a mixture of salt and saltpetre and put it in the crock to pickle until the next day, when it would be boiled with pepper and onions and spices until it was almost jelly. After this the meat would be lifted from the bones, cut small and packed with a little of the liquor into bowls to set firm. A plate would be put over each bowlful with an iron standing on each plate. When set, it cut into delicious transparent pink slices, spicy and meaty.

We had the stew for dinner. For supper we had the fillets, sliced and pounded and fried and lardy cakes.

There was never anything in the world like Gran's lardy cakes. Golden-brown and pancake thin, you spread butter on them just as they came from the griddle. If you were as toothless as the Fairy Broy you could enjoy those lardy cakes, for their mouth-watering flakes melted on your tongue.

"They are the easiest things in the world to bake," Gran often said to those who praised her lardy cakes. "Flour and sheet lard and a good pinch of salt. Roll them thin and bake them quick."

It would be a mistake to let the apparent simplicity of this recipe fool you into trying to bake lardy cakes like hers. Many additional ingredients would be needed to make lardy cakes taste like those I devoured in Derrymore House that night. For they would need to be baked by the kindly old hands that had given you every happiness you had ever known. They would need to be eaten under the wise loving eyes of one for whom you felt the perfect and abiding love. And, as you ate them, your heart would have to be filled with the peace and wellbeing which attend a completely happy home-coming.

We had been so busy all day that we had completely forgotten the wake. Mike Brophy remembered it when John Dooley and Britches stood up to go home.

"How did the wake go, Britches?" he asked. "For a man who's been up all night doin' away with a half-barrel of porther you're lookin' purty fair."

Britches spat contemptuously into the fire.

He struggled for words — or to suppress words.

"The curse of hell on the drop of porther that ever passed me lips last night," he said. "It's the back of me hands to the Roach Doyle from now on. He's the lousiest, mangiest, stingiest ould get that ever came out of the Bawn."

"Why? What happened?" asked Gran.

"You'll hardly credit this, Mrs. Lacy, but when meself

an' Lar Casey an' Luke Heavey an' a few of the lads went to the wake, that ould bags — savin' your presence — had the door locked. Aye, an' wouldn't open it!"

"That was a queer way to hold a wake," Mrs. Noone said.

"But wait till you hear. We looked in through the window an' there was the Dummy Foy an' himself an' they guzzlin' porther for dear life. Barrin' the corpse, not one but themselves there."

"Did you knock?"

"Did we knock, is it? Did we nearly kick the —" Realising that his description of the door and of what they nearly did to it might offend Gran's ears, Britches checked his tongue with obvious difficulty. "Yes, we knocked. But that ould feck-me-la didn't open the door and ask us in decent like any Christian. What does he do? He opens the window the dawshiest little bit an' says, 'Go home, lads. This is a private wake.' He shut it right in our faces an' back with himself an' the Dummy to the porther. An' the rest of us got sweet damall of it."

The recollection of his deprivation brought such bitterness to his usually sunny heart that Britches took his cap abruptly from behind the door, and off with him into the town to seek company where a man might express his grievances freely and untrammelled. But the rest of us thought it a good joke, for that was the first time we had heard of a private wake.

The Roach Doyle — that wretch whom I hated on Annabel Gorry's account — had added to our vocabulary, for thereafter whenever any selfish inhospitable gathering took place, the people of Ballyderrig referred to it scathingly as 'a private wake.'

CHAPTER 15

WHEN I went back to school early in January, Sister Conleth had been sent away to some other house of the Order in the hope that the change of air and scenery might do her good. But Sister Liguori was there, as critical as ever of my behaviour, and just as determined to make a lady of me if it killed both of us.

That term was not any pleasanter than the first. Apart from the galling surveillance of my mentor, I was harassed by my backwardness in class. I had fallen so far behind the others during my isolation in the infirmary that I found it impossible to catch up.

Anyway, studying never came easily to me. The bewildering rules and regulations attached to French made me wonder why the French people did not take to English instead. And algebra was to me what religious knowledge must have been to the Reddin boys.

But Gran's training stood to me in the domestic economy class, and I loved Mondays and Thursdays when we had two hours of needlework and cooking. And in the English class no one could beat me at memorizing verse. I had always had a feeling for poetry. I could get drunk on lovely sensitive words and the different rhythm patterns in which their masters chose to arrange them. Sometimes the pattern was so loud and bold and clear that it made me almost sick with excitement. Sometimes it was a delicate thing of fine lines and tender shadows that brought a deep sweet sadness on me. And then again it might be a queer intriguing unexpected arrangement that made me hungrily restless.

There was a grand selection of English verse for the Junior Grade course that year. We had Shelley and Pope. A few Shakespearian sonnets. Milton, too, and Tennyson's *Morte d'Arthur*. A little Browning and a lot of Byron. It was my first introduction to them and they went to my head.

That poetry book was to blame for much of the trouble that overtook me in class. It was the cause of my being kept in from recreation day after day to study my neglected French and work out arithmetic and algebra problems which I had left undone. It gained for me the reputation of being duller and lazier than I really was.

Each day we were given about ten lines of verse to memorize. This was the labour of love I tackled first thing each night when we sat down to preparation. The memorizing of the ten lines engaged me for less than as many minutes. Had I been a conscientious girl and mindful of what I owed to my teachers, to Gran and to the yet unborn school-children I was expected one day to teach, I would then have closed my poetry book, and have got on with my other studies.

But to close it was something I could not do. As well give a drunkard the key to a tidily-stocked cellar and expect him to leave after one quick nip of port.

I stayed in the cellar. For the two solid hours allotted us for preparation I stayed there. I wandered about examining every bottle and taking a drink here and a drink there. And one tasted better than another. The good mellow satisfying ale of Milton, the heady bubbling champagne of Shelley, the tingling Burgundy of Browning. Byron was rum and whiskey and other virile manly drinks that filled you with the reckless courage of the Corsair himself. And the Sonnets were liqueur brandy, every tantalizing drop amber-rich in fire and light and colour.

A letter from Gran brought me to my senses. She who never scolded wrote:

"The Mother Superior wrote to me saying you are not doing well at your lessons. I can't make this out at all for you are bright enough with that ten-and-sixpence you won and everything. What ails you, child? You know you'll have to make the most of your chance in Wicklow and pass the King's Scholarship. If you don't, I don't know what's to become of you, for you have no taste for business. And you'll never make a farmer's wife, so get that out of your head. Have sense, alanna, and work at your lessons. You know I'm only writing this for your own good.

"Fond love from Judy and Mike and myself.

Gran."

The letter shamed me far more than the daily punishments I received. I put my weakness resolutely from me and took to opening my poetry book at night only when all my other lessons had been prepared.

That term I had one big triumph and one outstanding humiliation.

During my last year in the Convent School at home we had done Pearse's *Iosagán*. It impressed me deeply and gave me inspiration for a little poem that sang in my head for a long time. The bound volumes of *The Irish Monthly* which I had found in the infirmary press contained a good deal of poetry. This gave me an idea. At Christmas I wrote out my little poem and sent it to the Reverend Editor.

Early in March, Mother Superior came down to the study-hall one night. She carried a copy of the March issue of *The Monthly* which had been forwarded from Derrymore House and which contained my poem. In front of the whole school she congratulated me on it. She even read out the poem.

I forget now how it went. Maybe the fact that I never received any payment for it made me feel that it could not have been too good and therefore was best forgotten. I only know that it tried to convey in verse that scene on the dusty country road where the bare-footed little ones have Mary's Son as their playfellow, while in the chapel near-by their parents also hold communion with Him.

The rest of the community were very nice to me about it. They came and shook hands with me and congratulated me. They were kindly women, full of simplicity and the love of God, and it delighted them that one of their sheep should have been sponsored by such a periodical as *The Irish Monthly*.

But if Sister Liguori felt anything of this she did not show it. Instead, she seemed to be devoured with anxiety lest the publication of my poor little poem should add the deadly sin of pride to my other faults. She was determined to kill in me any sign of this further aid to damnation, and I had to endure many sarcastic and cutting references to what she termed "overweening pride of intellect" and "the rock on which Lucifer perished." No doubt it was all intended for the eventual good of my soul, but its immediate effect on my behaviour was very bad. I became more sullen and impertinent than ever — which was tactless and foolish of me, for Sister Liguori had the making or marring of my school life in her hands that term.

It was this way.

March 25th, the Feast of the Annunciation, was always a day of great importance in Wicklow, for on that day worthy aspirants were admitted to the Sodality of the Children of Mary. I was one of the aspirants. To prove our worthiness we had to produce a sheet of paper bearing the signature of every nun in the school. If any nun knew you to have offended deeply, she withheld her signature and you lost your chance of joining the Sodality until the following year.

The inevitable happened. Sister Liguori refused me her signature and I was publicly branded as unworthy.

I cried bitterly about that. Not in Sister Liguori's presence, though, but in the dormitory at night. I was deeply disappointed. Not only because I was genuinely religious and regretted being kept out of Our Lady's own Sodality, but also because I would have enjoyed the privileges which the Children of Mary enjoyed. Would have liked being able to write E. de M. — Enfant de Marie — after my name. Would have loved wearing the Sodality uniform — the blue cape and the wide blue ribbon and silver medal. Would have enjoyed above all the distinction which initiates owned of taking precedence over all others in the refectory and in processions.

But it was easy to forget all the trials of my school life in the welcome that met me when I went home for the Easter holidays. In Derrymore House there was only content and a deep happiness to be with Gran once more.

Gran examined me anxiously for signs of a decline. She did this every time I came home from Wicklow, for nothing would convince her that I got enough to eat there.

"She looks thin enough on it, doesn't she, Judy?" she asked in concern.

"She did get a bit thin," Judy admitted. "But sure what harm's that? She could well afford to lose a bit — isn't she growin' anyway? You don't want her to be like Maria Doolin, do you now, ma'am?"

Gran was indignant that poor Maria should be mentioned in the same breath as myself. "There's not the least fear of her ever bein' like Maria," she said shortly.

To make up for the starvation fare she believed me to be getting in Wicklow, she stuffed me with food, and a half-pint of cream was poured over my stirabout every morning.

On Holy Thursday we yoked the pony and drove into the town together to visit the Altar of Repose and to bring a wedding present to Ned Reddin who was getting married on Easter Saturday.

The Reddins lived up the bog road a mile or so beyond our house.

"Will we call up to Reddins now or on the way back?" Gran asked when the pony brought us to the end of the boreen.

"On our way back, Gran," I said. I liked the Reddins, liked sitting with Mrs. Reddin in her little kitchen. I knew the visit would be cut short if Gran had the chapel on her mind and I wanted it to last as long as possible.

Obligingly, Gran turned the pony's head towards the town.

Oh, it was lovely to kneel there in the dim scented chapel. To feel the waves of devotion and fervour sweep over your soul at the foot of the candle-lit altar where masses of waxy Easter lilies stood like angel sentinels around the Host enthroned in the golden monstrance.

People kept coming and going, reverently soft-footed, but you knew nothing of them for faith made a flaming curtain about you and God.

Presently Gran's hand reached through the curtain, plucking gently at my sleeve.

"Come," she whispered.

I arose and followed her to the end of the seat where we genuflected in turn on both knees. We tip-toed down the chapel and, as we dipped our fingers in the holy water font we turned for a last look at the shining Glory on the altar.

I heard Gran whisper, "Good-bye, dear Lord Jesus."

We had some shopping to do in the town and dusk was falling as we drove over the bridge. At Mitchell's Forge, Gran pulled up the pony and I got down and lit the lamp of the trap.

When we reached the Reddins' cottage, the window was lit and the yellow light of the paraffin lamp streamed through the open door.

Ned heard us stopping.

"Good-night, Mrs. Lacy," he said. "Are you comin' in?"

"Just for a minute, Ned," Gran said.

"Let me lead the pony in for you, then," Ned said. "This is a terrible treacherous ould bridge and the wheel might go over it."

He caught the pony's bridle and led her over the structure of planks and sods that spanned the bog-stream which ran between the road and their gate.

Mrs. Reddin met us at the door. She was a small woman with a worn wrinkled face and harassed eyes. When she was silent, her mouth was fascinating to watch, for she kept her lips pursed together poutingly and some nervous affection made them jerk and relax, jerk and relax, steadily and unceasingly as if they were keeping time to her thoughts. Her white hair, which was so sparse in front that the scalp showed through it in pink stripes, bunched into amazing luxuriance at the back where it showed thick and grey and coarse, through her snood of black crocheted wool. Judy Ryan said that the bunch of hair which Mrs. Reddin wore in her snood was not her own hair at all but the tail of a cow.

She made us very welcome.

"Come on, Bids," she said, "an' get down the cups till I make a cup of tea for Mrs. Lacy and little Deelyeen."

Bids rose obediently from the creepy-stool beside the hearth while Mrs. Reddin, deaf to Gran's "Don't-bother-now-this-is-too-much-trouble-sure-you-shouldn't-put-your-self-out-for-us," proceeded to cut and butter a griddle cake.

Bids Smullen was Ned's intended bride. A nice-looking girl with brown wavy hair and a pale freckled face. There seemed to be great affection between Mrs. Reddin and herself, whom she addressed lovingly as 'Mother.' "Will I take the pink cups out of the press, Mother?" and "Will I turn the jam onto a saucer, Mother?"

"I can see you're getting a good daughter, Mrs. Reddin," Gran said.

Mrs. Reddin straightened herself from the fire where

she was bent over the teapot. With soft eyes she looked across the kitchen to where Bids stood with Ned before the dresser.

"Faith, she's all that, Mrs. Lacy," she said. "A good girl who goes to her duties regular an' hasn't a bad word to say of anyone. She can bake an' mend an' churn as well as any girl in Ireland. A decent girl, too. Don't let anyone tell you different. Bids is a decent girl, even if she *was* took advantage of."

Bids's face flamed while her mother-in-law spoke. But her blushes were for the praise and not because of Mrs. Reddin's charitably-worded reference to her one lapse. That was such an old story that the mention of it did not worry her now. And, anyway, Ned Reddin's love for her had so changed the world that she had almost come to believe some other girl, and not she, had figured in that little tragedy.

"It'll be grand for you to have Bids living with you," Gran said. "You need a woman to give you a hand around the house."

"God knows I do," Mrs. Reddin said feelingly. "I'm that fed up with men! Boil for them all day long. Mend an' make for them all night. The four of them under me feet here in the kitchen on a wet day when they wouldn't be out in the bog. An' not wan of them able or willin' to do a hand's turn in the house to help me. To tell you the God's honest truth, ma'am, many's the time I near drowned meself in a bog hole just to get away from them!"

"Ah, they're not that bad," Gran said. "Look at all the fine money they ever earned for you."

"Musha, that's true enough, too," Mrs. Reddin admitted.

"They're not bad lads. An' himself is the best in the world."

"How is he, then?" asked Gran.

"Above in bed, God help him. He's that bad with his joints he can't move hand or foot this two days. Open the room door, Ned, an' let your father speak to Mrs. Lacy."

Ned opened the door of the room off the kitchen and presently Mick Reddin's voice came down to us in friendly greeting.

"How are the two lads, Mrs. Reddin?" Gran asked when the tea and griddle-cake had been handed around.

A veil came down over Mrs. Reddin's eyes as it always did when any mention was made of Willie and Joe, her two eldest boys who were on the run.

"Real well, Mrs. Lacy, thanks. Real well." She changed the conversation quickly in case any word of hers should betray the whereabouts of her boys.

After the signing of the Treaty, Willie and Joe Reddin had elected to take the Republican side. They left down their slanes and disappeared with their rifles from Bally-derrig to continue the fight with those who would not be-lieve a half-loaf was better than no bread.

Presently it was time for us to go home. Gran came to the real object of our visit. She opened her bag and took out a pound-note which she handed to Bids.

"That's to buy a little something for yourself and Ned, Bids," she said. "And you have my best wishes with it." They were both delighted.

"It's too good of you altogether, Mrs. Lacy," Ned's mother protested. "Sure we never expected anything like that."

"Whisht, now," Gran said. "It's nothing — I only wish it was a hundred. I owe a lot more than that to your boys for all the grand fires I've ever had from their work."

"You paid us decent for it, ma'am," Ned said.

"I always said there isn't a man in Ireland who'd give an honester day's work for his money than one of your sons, Mrs. Reddin."

"An' they will again, Mrs. Lacy," the woman replied. "They will again, please God." And from the way her face lit up, you could see that she was envisioning a happy future day when Willie and Joe would be home with her once more and free to slice the slanes through the rich moist bog.

Ned, who was seeing Bids into the town, accepted a lift from us as far as Derrymore House. A better thought struck Gran as Ned and Bids got into the trap.

"Can't you two drop us at Derrymore?" she said. "Take the trap into the town. You can leave it into us on your way back, Ned." And so it was arranged.

The romance of Bids and Ned was an interesting one. It went back to the Black-and-Tan days when the Reddin lads were members of a district tribunal set up by "The Boys." The functions of the tribunal were many. They meted out justice to spies and informers in their own ranks. They arrested and punished the petty malefactors who took advantage of the troubled times to loot and rob in the hope that their depredations would be laid at the door of the I.R.A. They were the terror of the love-and-run Don Juans, for they were ruthless in seeking out reluctant lovers and in forcing them to marry the girls they had wronged.

There was a robbery in Newbridge one night. A public-house was broken into and spirits, cigarettes and money were stolen. From irrefutable evidence that came their way, the tribunal was able to pin the crime on Shaun Kelly, a good-looking rake of a lad who lived in a place called Brusilloch, a few miles our side of Newbridge. The Reddins were deputed to arrest him.

They dragged him out of his bed in the middle of the night and brought him as far as the Shift Carrolls, where they made Corny, the eldest son, get up and yoke a horse and trap. Corny was a little miserable fellow of twenty-five or so, and the cowardliest sod that ever lived. He was shaking with fear as he hastened to do the Reddins' bidding.

"Drive us down to Barnalea, Corny," Willie Reddin commanded, naming a deserted old mansion that stood halfway between us and Robertstown. "Drive us around by the Sand Pits, for we don't want to run into the Tans."

The reminder that they might meet up with a bunch of Black-and-Tans was all that was needed to complete Corny's demoralisation. He wept, begged and cajoled to be let off that drive. He even offered to make them a present of the horse and trap. But Willie Reddin was adamant. He pushed Corny into the trap and ordered him to take up the reins. The prisoner was blindfolded and pushed into the trap beside Corny, and then the three Reddin boys got in.

When they reached Barnalea, they dismissed Corny, with blood-curdling threats of what would happen to him if he divulged a word concerning that night's journey. Corny turned the horse's head towards home with great reluctance. He would willingly have gone before the tribunal himself rather than face that lonely drive home through roads which his terror infested with Black-and-Tans.

Shaun Kelly was found guilty of breaking and entering and robbing and told to clear out of the country. He obeyed with an alacrity that astonished his captors. Before the week was out he departed silently and without farewells of any kind for an unknown destination in England.

A couple of months later, the tribunal was faced with a knotty problem.

Bids Smullen's mother stopped Joe Reddin on the bog road one day and begged him to get her daughter married.

"Who is he?" asked Joe.

"He's a blackguard that hasn't come next nor near us this while back," Mrs. Smullen said. "It's Shaun Kelly from Brusilloch."

Well, there it was and nothing could be done about it. The culprit was safely out of reach of those who could have forced him to make reparation. And, irony of ironies, they themselves had effected his escape.

Shortly after, Bids Smullen went to stay with her married sister in Portarlington. She returned to us six months later, shyer and quieter in her manner, but otherwise unchanged.

That love of justice which animated all the Reddins may have been responsible for the way that Ned went out of his way to be nice to Bids. But whatever the initial motive there is no doubt that it was love made him decide to marry her.

You could nearly feel the love that was between them

as they sat opposite Gran and myself in the trap that
night.

"It will do us good to stretch our legs a bit," Gran said
when we came to our gate. "You can let us down here,
Ned." We collected our packages and got down.

She put her arm through mine as we walked up the
boreen. She was silent and I guessed she was thinking
of Bids and Ned. So she was, for presently she said:

"Everything comes right in God's own good time. Always remember that, alanna. He rights everything in
His own good time."

CHAPTER 16

"SAY a prayer for me, Gran," I said when we said good-bye after Easter.

"Will you listen to her?" she said laughingly. For all her laughing, I knew she was as near to tears as I was, for these partings were becoming more and more difficult for both of us. It was as if we realised that we ought to be making the very most of the time that was left to us. It was almost as if we knew how short that time was to be. "Will you listen to her? Amn't I always praying for you, you little oinseach?" And then, more soberly. "I won't pray for you to pass your examination, Delia. If the knowledge is not in your head, that would be asking a miracle of God. And He has so many big things to look after that it would be a sin to ask Him to work a miracle for a little thing like that. But I'll pray to Him to protect you and make you a good girl. There's the train now, alanna. Give me a kiss . . . there. No whingeing out of you now. It'll be no time till you're back home again."

I got into the carriage and looked at her dumbly for there was a sore hardness in my throat that would not let me speak. Wise kind mouth, brave chin, wrinkle-framed eyes that were misted over with the tears that she valiantly blinked back.

And then I could not see the face any more, for as the train drew out, the big scalding tears blinded me. It was five minutes before I could turn and speak to Mary Joe Heffernan who was travelling back with me.

After the first day's papers I knew I had lost the examination. A pass, maybe, but never honours.

When I came home for the summer holidays, one look at my face and Gran knew, too. She was disappointed, and she tried not to show it.

"What matter, alanna," she said. "What matter . . . sure that needn't keep you back. You can go on for the King's Scholarship just the same. You'll do better next year, please God."

I tried to tell her then what I knew in my heart — that she was wasting her money in trying to make a teacher of me and that I would never be able to pass the King's Scholarship. Not if I stayed in Wicklow for twenty years. But in the next breath she said something which kept my tongue tied.

"I'd die happy if I could see you a teacher, Delia. It's what I'm living for. You'll do your best next year, won't you?" And of course I had to promise.

When I was home a fortnight, my mother came down to stay for a week. She had the twins with her. It was only when she had gone back that Gran told me she had come to announce that she was thinking of getting married again and to arrange for Gran and myself to come to Kilkenny to meet her intended husband.

By this time, I had become so dissociated from my family that my reactions to the news were different to what they might possibly have been had I not come to live with Gran. At first I was incredulous. Then as I accepted the news and all it implied I was, I think, rather pleased. It was nice to think that my mother would have some one to look at her lovingly again. He had a good job in the Brewery and had, so Gran said, a good deal of money saved.

We went to Kilkenny the following Sunday. I liked my stepfather on sight. He was a grey-haired man of forty-seven. Not good-looking, but with a kind humorous face. It was plain that he was very much in love with my mother. It was also plain that she was very fond of him.

That was a pleasant Sunday. The whole family were there. Paddy and Joe seemed to be great friends with Mr. Dunphy, and although Peg seemed inclined to be jealous of him and to resent him, you could see that she, too, liked him even if it was against her will. They were to be married in October.

Weddings seemed to be in the air that year, for in August Molly Nolan got married.

I think my liking for the Nolans will always be slightly coloured by the fact that for five years I cherished an unrequited passion for Paddy, the eldest boy. When I was seven and he twenty-two, he came on me one day with my nose pressed to Donoghue's window, devouring with my eyes the jelly-babies, a particularly toothsome and long-lasting delicacy which Mrs. Donoghue had just introduced to the sweet-lovers of Ballyderrig.

"Hello," Paddy said to me.

I tore my eyes from the glutinous object of my lustful desires. "You get ten of them for a ha'penny," I breathed wistfully.

"Come and have twenty of them," was Paddy's noble reply.

For five years from that day I was his devoted slave. Then he married the daughter of a vet. in Portarlington and, resignedly, I transferred my affections to Willie Campbell, the son of the Protestant minister.

Grandmother liked the Nolans, who lived in Boherkill House, about two miles from Derrymore. It would have been hard to dislike this charming, happy-go-lucky family with their good looks and their free-handed generosity. At one time they had owned practically all the land around Ballyderrig. Wild spending, however, and the frequent illnesses of Mrs. Nolan played ducks and drakes with their fortune.

The people of Ballyderrig considered the Nolans' ways of getting rid of their money foolish to the point of lunacy. For instance, when Mrs. Nolan gave a dinner-party for Paddy's coming of age, we agreed we had never heard of anything so daft. We could understand a mother giving à "hooley" for her son's twenty-first birthday, but a *dinner-party* with special little rolls of bread ordered from Murphy's, the bakers in Kildare, seemed too ridiculous for words. He might have got over that in time if, soon after the famous party, the Nolans had not got in a supply of notepaper with "Bohercille House, Ballyderrig" printed on it. This unheard-of extravagance seemed to be begging for trouble and, though we were sincerely sorry, we were not surprised to learn one day that Johnny Dunne had foreclosed on almost all the Nolans' land.

We hated to see Johnny Dunne profiting by the Nolans' downfall. He was a crafty quick-eyed man who had started life as a higgler. By marrying a plain elderly woman with a fair fortune he had succeeded in opening a grocery and public-house in the town. He lent money to the needy farmers and allowed them to run up big bills on the security of their holdings. Then, when their need was greatest, he suddenly foreclosed. His house was furnished with the good mahogany tables and presses of widows to whom he had given credit.

He foreclosed on Tom Nolan while the man was still stunned by the death of the wife he adored. Mrs. Nolan was only forty-seven when she died, but she looked twenty years older, having borne twenty-two children, only five of whom lived to maturity. Sis, the eldest of the Nolans, was a quiet girl with a lovely smile and nicer manners than anyone in Ballyderrig. Then came Paddy, and after him Seamus and John. Molly was the youngest.

She was an exquisite girl. She had shining hair of red-gold which she wore wound around her head in a coronet. She had a flawless skin and eyes of that rare true violet shade. Molly Nolan was certainly the loveliest girl in the County Kildare.

The first news that greeted me when I came home that summer was that a match had been arranged between Molly Nolan and John Kehoe, a wealthy farmer.

I was horrified, for John Kehoe was fifty years of age and Molly only twenty-one or twenty-two. Arranged matches were common enough in Ballyderrig among the farmers. Nearly all their young girls were married to men old enough to be their grandfathers. Frequently the bridegrooms were from another part of the County, in which case the happy couple met only once or twice before the wedding. The marriage settlement was considered a far more important matter than the tastes and the affections of the girl, and I had heard of matches that were broken off at the last moment because of an argument over an extra heifer.

I was familiar, therefore, with these loveless marriages but I could not reconcile myself to the thought that lovely Molly Nolan was to be bartered away. She was too young and too lovely to be sold to John Kehoe for the financial help he would give her family. He was a generous man, and good to the poor. He never grudged the loan of a horse and creel to a poor family for the drawing home of their turf, and where the borrower was a widow he would lend one of his workmen as well. But, as a husband for fair-skinned, violet-eyed Molly Nolan, he seemed all wrong.

I tried to speak of this to Grandmother, but she brushed aside my scruples with a few brisk words.

"Rubbish!" she said. "The novelette-reading is filling your head with romantic notions. Molly Nolan is doing very well for herself to be marrying John Kehoe, and she with not a penny fortune to her name. Let me tell you, there's many a well-off girl that would like to be marrying into John Kehoe's snug place."

And then her face softened, and she said: "I don't hear anything about a wedding-party. I've seen Molly Nolan grow up from a child. She belongs to the decentest people in the county, and even if she has no mother to look after her, the Nolans are not going to be shamed by letting Molly go from them without a hooley. If I have to cook the food myself, there will be a send-off for Molly on the night she's married. I'll walk over to Boherkill and talk to Sis about it this very evening."

When supper was over, Grandmother put on her best

coat and hat and we set out together over the fields for Nolan's.

The entry to Boherkill was through heavy iron gates set in a stone wall along which virginia creeper was draped in flaming scarlet and gold. In the days of their prosperity, the Nolans had built greenhouses and arbours, summer-houses and little playhouses. These were neglected now and dilapidated. It was disheartening to see the weeds taking control of the lawn and flower beds. The tennis court had not been sown since the summer before and its grass was rank and high.

Grandmother looked around her and shook her head sadly.

" 'Tis a pity," said she, "that such nice people should be so shiftless. Wouldn't you think, even if they *did* lose their money, that they'd tidy up the place a bit?"

But I had a feeling that neither tidying nor money could ever again make Boherkill the gracious happy place it was when its lovely little extravagant mistress had reigned there, petted and adored by her husband. The heart seemed to have gone out of Boherkill with the death of Mrs. Nolan, and her passing had taken from the house and garden more than had Johnny Dunne's greedy hands.

Sis Nolan brought us into the long low drawing-room. I drew my breath at the loveliness of the quiet room where faded chintzes, polished woodwork, gleaming brasses and a few charming prints provided a perfect setting for Sis's gentle ways. I had never before sat in a room like this. In Grandmother's house the sitting-room was called "the parlour." It was a cold uncomfortable place, smelling of disuse, with horsehair furniture and enlargements of family photographs. And in my own home, the parlour was where we ate and studied and played and fought — a place of kick-dented furniture and ink-scarred wallpaper.

Sitting in the Nolans' drawing-room, I remembered hearing Grandmother say once that Mrs. Nolan should never have been a farmer's wife, and I suddenly understood and agreed. The woman who had created the restful beauty of this room should never have been expected to adjust herself to the practical hard-working ways of farmers' wives. Nature intended her to be the gracious consort of some diplomat, or the spoiled petted spouse of a great politician.

Grandmother did not waste words in coming to the point.

"I've known you a long time, Sis," she said, "and I always had great respect and liking for your poor mother, God rest her, so you'll know that anything I'm going to say to you is said in friendship." Without giving Sis a chance to reply, she went on: "Tell me, child, is it true that you're thinking of letting Molly go from you without giving her a send-off?"

The delicate colour mounted to Sis's cheeks.

"Well, it's this way, Mrs. Lacy," she said in her low gentle voice. "I haven't had the heart to bother about a party. I'm all against this marriage, for Mother always said made marriages were wrong. Her own match was a love match and she used to say that she'd like it to be that way with Molly and myself." She made a little fluttering movement with her hand. "I'll never marry — I would have entered at Kilcullen long ago only that Father and the boys need me here. But, I wanted Molly to have everything." Her voice rose a little. "Everything, Mrs. Lacy. Molly is so young and sweet and pretty. She deserves everything. Love and youth and laughter. She'll never get them with John Kehoe."

Grandmother sat up in her chair.

"How do you know she won't get them?" she said. "She'll get love from John Kehoe. I saw him looking at her when she was coming out of the Chapel last Sunday, and anyone could see he adores the ground she walks on. He's a good kind man, and he'll treat her like a little queen. As for youth and fun, she'll have all the youth and laughing she'll want when her children start growing up around her. Now, be sensible, Sis, and take the word of an old woman for it that a man's age doesn't matter a lot to his wife in the long run. It's the feeling he has in his heart for her that counts. And how old is John Kehoe, after all? Fifty? Sure that's the prime of life for a man — especially for a sober, quiet-living healthy man like John."

Grandmother talked on and on, and by degrees I could see the worry and strain begin to leave Sis's face.

"Perhaps you're right, Mrs. Lacy," she said at length. "I hadn't looked at it that way."

Grandmother sat down again and settled herself to discuss more important matters than romance.

"Now, about this wedding," she said. "Molly will have to go off like a Nolan. You'll have to give a good night for her."

"I don't know that I'll be able to manage a crowd, Mrs. Lacy," Sis said weakly. "You see, I'm not a very good cook."

"Isn't that why I came over to see you?" Gran retorted. "Here am I going mad with idleness all day long. I'll be only too delighted to do all the cooking that's to be done."

In the end it was settled, and Sis even became cheerful enough to take us upstairs to see Molly's trousseau.

They still talk about Molly Nolan's wedding in Ballyderrig. Few of the guests — and they came from as far as Dublin, mind you — ever ate the like of the food that was served that night. I, for one, shall never forget that wedding. Not merely because of the food and the fun, but because for a full fortnight before the wedding day, there was little done in our kitchen but cooking.

Grandmother boiled the hams and roasted the chickens and the great cuts of juicy beef. She spent nearly a whole week in preparing two jellied pigs' heads. This was an extra-special dish that was eaten only on great occasions. The heads were cleft in two and left for four days in a pickle of salt and spices. They were then simmered in the biggest of Grandmother's iron pots in water containing cloves and lemon rind. When the flesh was quite tender but unbroken, the heads were taken up and all the bones removed. This was a delicate operation that could only be performed by Grandmother herself, for care had to be taken to keep the shape of the heads intact. The tongues were chopped small and little scraps used to pad out the outer skin wherever the loss of fat in boiling had caused it to shrink. Finally, the halves were bound together with tape and the heads were pressed and glazed.

Wearing necklaces of parsley, they looked very lordly sitting on Grandmother's big blue-and-white dish, and sliced thinly and eaten with chicken and beef, they were the *pièce de résistance* of the Nolans' party.

With the exception of the wedding-cake which was a

present from Murphys, the Kildare bakers, in memory of the days when the Nolans were their best customers, Grandmother baked all the cakes.

White bread, brown bread, Indian meal bread and bran loaves. Short cakes, butter cakes and scones of all kinds. She made seedy cakes and Sunday cakes and prune cakes. And an enormous rich fruit cake with a whole glass of brandy in it. My arms ached from beating the dozen eggs that went into the cake, and from cleaning and preparing the pounds of currants and raisins and candied peel and nuts.

She made apple cakes and Carrigeen shapes and flummery and jellies, and Mike Brophy carried over to Nolans' a big basket of Grandmother's famous preserves — haw-and-apple jelly, sloe jelly, blackberry jam and damson jam and a half-dozen bottles of spicy mushroom ketchup to add piquancy to the cold meats.

Judy Ryan, who was noted for her 'green fingers,' was lent to the Nolans for a week to help Sis and the boys to get the garden into some kind of order. They weeded and mowed and raked, and at the end of the week the place was unrecognizable. Grandmother had a passion for geraniums. She had pots of them on every window sill in the house. She now denuded her windows of the precious brilliant plants and lent them to the Nolans, who dug holes in the flower-beds and sunk the pots to add temporary brilliant beauty where it could be most effective.

In our part of the country, wedding festivities lasted right through the day and during the whole night.

I lost many of my misgivings when I saw John Kehoe sitting at the head of the table beside his bride. Molly looked like an arum lily in her sheath of white satin. She was pale, and in her eyes lurked a shadow of fright. But John Kehoe's eyes rested on her with such obvious adoration that I felt prepared to forgive him his age if he would only go on feeling like that for white-and-gold Molly. He was a tall, broad-shouldered man and his light grey suit showed up the rich tan of his kind homely face and the blue of his honest eyes, that were so humble when he met the glance of his bride.

"It is a pity," I thought, "his head is so bald. If he had hair he wouldn't look half so old."

When the bride and bridegroom had departed on their honeymoon, the festivities proper commenced. The bulk of the guests began to arrive in cars, in traps and on bikes, for only close friends and relatives had attended the wedding breakfast.

Right through the night we danced to the music of fiddles and melodeons. Mrs. Byrne, the school-teacher's wife, played the piano, while we sang all the songs that had ever been composed. Some of the strangers there may have found disconcerting at first our custom of speaking, instead of singing, the last line of the last verse, just to show the song was finished, but they soon got into the way of it.

Though there was plenty of drink served no one became unruly or boisterous. Old Jim Mooney, to be sure, was inclined to be a little maudlin, and as the night went on, he evinced an increasing desire to recall his own wedding and the good looks and virtues of his wife who had died thirty years before. But none of us minded Jim, for he was a gentle old fellow, even if lachrymose in drink.

It seemed we had been enjoying ourselves for only a few hours when five o'clock wheezed out from the big clock in the hall, and the buff window blinds showed up grey and pale against the early morning light. "You're nearly dead with the sleep, child," Gran said, coming over to where I sat between the piano and the fireplace. "We'll leave Judy here to help them tidy up a bit, but let you and me be making off."

Sis came with us as far as the door. "I can never thank you enough, Mrs. Lacy," she said.

"Will you whist now, Sis alanna," Gran said. "Can't you say a prayer for me when you're a little nun beyond in Kilcullen?"

"God knows when that will be," Sis said ruefully. "Until Seamus brings in a wife to look after the place, they'll be needing me here."

When we turned the corner into the avenue, we almost bumped into two figures who, lost to the world in each other's arms, had not heard our approach. They were Seamus Nolan and Margaret Mary Lee. "Faith there'll be someone to take Sis's place in that house before long, or *I'm* greatly mistaken," Gran said when we had passed out of earshot.

CHAPTER 17

"YOU CAN take a couple of pots of this back to school with you next week," Gran said, scraping the last drop of sloe-and-apple jelly into the last thick tumbler. Amorous shafts of sunlight poured down from the high window of the buttery and threw themselves on the jelly-filled glasses, kindling them to a passion of lucent amethyst. I licked the rim of the wooden spoon so as not to lose the scraps of fast congealing jelly which clung to it. The house was filled with the hot rich smell of boiled sugar and fruit juice.

There was a step in the yard outside, a quick, high-heeled nervous step. Judy Ryan ran to the kitchen window and peered through the curtains.

"For God's sake look who's comin'," she said in an excited whisper. "It's Mrs. Timson-Ling!" Gran whipped off her apron and pulled down the flannelette-lined sleeves of her black bodice.

Our visitor came into the kitchen. A thin jerky woman of forty-five or so, with gold-rimmed glasses and a worn yellowish face. She was dressed in deep mourning. Black patent shoes, black silk stockings, a pleated dress of black crepe-de-chine. And yards of black crepe hung from her shiny straw toque.

Gran's face was full of commiseration when she saw the widow's weeds.

"Tess, alanna!" she said compassionately. "What in God's name happened?"

Mrs. Timson-Ling took out a black-bordered handkerchief and held it to her eyes for a moment.

"It's poor Fred, Mrs. Lacy," she said. "Two months to a day on Wednesday last he died on me."

"God comfort you child," said Gran, putting her arm about Tess Behan's shoulder. "That's a big cross, surely. Here, sit down and tell me about it."

We all sat down, the widow, Gran, Judy Ryan, and myself.

"I only came home yesterday, Mrs. Lacy," said Tess. "You're the first person I came to see for I knew you'd be sorry."

I listened with avid interest to the details of Mr. Timson-Ling's sudden illness and death.

It was a moving story. It appears that shortly after Fred's regiment had come back from India, he had been taken ill in the London boarding-house where they were staying. In three days he was dead.

He had a beautiful death.

"He died in my arms, Mrs. Lacy — just like a baby going to sleep. He was very resigned to go, although he hated leaving me. 'Don't forget me, Tess,' were the last words he said." At this recollection, the widow raised her handkerchief to her eyes again.

"Well, well . . . the poor lad!" Gran said sympathetically. "He was young enough to go. How old was he, Tess?"

"Only twenty-six, Mrs. Lacy. But in his ways as old as a man twice his age. I was a little older than him, you know." She took her handkerchief from her eyes and gave us a quick glance. The hypocritical incredulity which courtesy commanded us to express must have been convincing for, reassured, she continued — "not *very* much older, just a little. But Fred used to say I made him feel an old man. I was always so gay and light-hearted. Fred suffered from depression now and then — all clever men do — and I would chatter on like a child to cheer him up." The bereaved widow managed a wistfully reminiscent smile. "He used to call me his little chatterbox."

In spite of her sympathy, the corners of Gran's mouth twitched irrepressibly at this. To disguise her amusement she broke into voluble orders to Judy Ryan and myself concerning the tea. We were glad to escape into the buttery, for to us also there was something very ludicrous in the notion of blond young Fred bestowing baby-names on his sallow elderly wife.

Come to think of it, the marriage itself was ludicrous. Tess Behan was a Ballyderrig girl who deserved every credit for her rise in the world. She was a daughter of old Nick Behan of Glanaree who spent his life opening and shutting the lock gates for the heavy sluggish canal boats.

When Tess was sixteen she went up to Dublin to serve her time in a sweet shop. She was full of ambition. She attended night-school and when we next heard of her she was living in London where she had a good job in the Civil Service.

She came home on holidays every year, always dressed in the latest fashion, and each year her accent was less Ballyderrig and increasingly London.

There is no doubt she was a clever girl. Ladylike, too, and fit to pass herself anywhere. She was good to her father. When he got too stiff to open the lock gates and was capable of no exertion beyond driving into the town in his ass-and-cart to draw the pension, Tess sent him fifteen shillings every week of her life.

Gran liked her for this. She admired her too for having

bettered herself. She always went out of her way to be nice to Tess and she made much of her during her vacations.

The years went on and Tess Behan never married. It is not surprising that none of the Ballyderrig men ever approached her. Though she was a respectable girl and far from bad-looking, and though she was suspected of having a tidy sum saved, her accent and her ladylike ways frightened them off.

Then, during the last year of the War, when Tess was well over forty, she gave us a great surprise. She drove over the bridge and into the town one day on an outside car. Sitting with her was a good-looking fair-haired chap of half her age — her brand new husband. She was Tess Behan no longer but Mrs. Timson-Ling.

They spent their honeymoon in the cottage at Glanaree Bridge. No one in Ballyderrig had ever seen anything like the affection that existed between these two. With their arms lovingly entwined they strolled along the canal bank and up the bog road. And Willie Beckett even said that when he was doing his rounds one day he came upon them sitting in the ditch where Fred Timson-Ling was putting a daisy-chain around his wife's neck. None of us believed that, for Willie liked to embroider his stories. But we did see enough to convince us that Englishmen made very loving husbands. Thereafter, when a Ballyderrig woman demanded from her husband signs of affection over and above what he considered decent between married people the man would say indignantly, "Arrah, leave me alone, woman! Do you want to make a Timson-Ling out of me?"

Fred was a corporal in the British Army and when the

honeymoon was over he went off with his wife and his regiment to India. We did not see Tess Behan again until she came home in her widow's weeds.

On the Sunday after her return, she had Fred prayed for at Mass. We were genuinely sorry for her and when Father Dempsey read from the Altar, "Your prayers are requested for the happy repose of the soul of Frederick William Timson-Ling lately deceased," the congregation turned as one man to look with sympathy at the crepe-enveloped widow who knelt with her black-bordered handkerchief hiding her glasses.

That was in the latter end of August.

Early in September, I went back to school. I must have shown the misery I felt on leaving, for Gran looked at me in silence for a minute and then said gently, "I don't think you like that old school at all, alanna. Well, give it another try, and I'll ask God to direct me. And maybe we'll find another way for you to earn your living besides teaching. We'll talk about it at Christmas."

In the middle of October I had two letters by the one post. One was from Peg to say my mother and my stepfather had been married that day and had gone to Dublin for their honeymoon, and that Paddy, who was now a fully-fledged cabinet-maker, had come to work for Aunt Rose in her furniture shop. It gave me a queer feeling to think that from now on I would have to address my mother's letters to 'Mrs. Dunphy.'

The other letter was from Gran. It was mostly about Tess Behan.

"There was a great stir in the town last week," Gran wrote, "and I'm afraid poor Tess Behan will never show her face here again. The Guards went down to Glanaree looking for her to go to England. She was wanted over there to give evidence against Timson-Ling. The black-guard never died at all but deserted her to marry another one. It seems he made a habit of it, for Tess wasn't his first either. There was another wife giving evidence against him, too, the wife he married before he met Tess. God knows I'm sorry for the creature, and it's easy to see why she made up all that story about his dying. Still and all, she shouldn't have dragged her religion into it, getting that fly-boy prayed for from our Altar.

"I'll have a pleasant surprise for you for All Souls' Day.

"No more for now. Fond love from all here.

Your loving Gran."

Poor Tess Behan was neither wife, maid nor widow.

Incidentally, Gran prophesied aright for we never saw Tess in Ballyderrig again.

My interest in this piece of news overshadowed Gran's announcement of the pleasant surprise in store for me, and if my mind dwelled on it at all it was to wonder would it be sweets or a barmbrack, for I believed it concerned nothing more important than the parcel which Gran would be sending me for Hallow-e'en.

That is why the surprise was so overwhelming when it came.

On Hallow-e'en Night, I got into trouble at study-time. Sister Liguori was on duty. In taking a book from my desk I accidentally slammed the lid. For this offence which, Sister Liguori said, was merely another demonstration of my clumsiness, lack of consideration for others, and general uncouthness, I was made to stand out in the middle of the study-hall floor for twenty minutes.

By the time I was pardoned and allowed to return again

to my desk I was seething with resentment and bitterness. I was sitting there, not studying but — God forgive me — hating the woman, when I suddenly thought of a mean, a diabolical way to get my own back.

Only a fortnight before, Sister Liguori had caught me reading *The Way of an Eagle* at study-time. I had smuggled it back after the holidays. Incidentally, it was lent to me by Sarah Gorry. For punishment, I was forbidden to speak a single word at meal-time for a whole week. The book was confiscated and left on a shelf in the Oratory where it would meet my eyes — a mute reproach for my wickedness — during morning and night prayers. Its presence there was intended to inspire me with fervour and contrition. Instead, it proved a distraction, for every time my glance rested on it I fell to speculating on the conclusion of the passionate love scene so abruptly interrupted by Sister Liguori's intervention.

Since then, she had watched like a lynx for any signs that I was indulging in contraband literature during study-time. It was this very watchfulness which gave me my idea. . .

I waited until I felt sure that Sister Liguori's eye was full on me. Then, with every appearance of careful stealth, I opened my desk and extracted a book. I held the open book on my lap below the level of the desk and commenced to read it with what I hoped was the attitude and expression of one who gorges covertly on forbidden fruit.

The fish rose to that well-baited hook.

Out of the corner of my eye, I saw Sister Liguori sail towards me in her best I-have-you-now style. She came to a halt at my desk.

"Hand me that book, Delia Scully," she said in tones

which sounded as if she expected *The Decameron* or *Peregrine Pickle* — or whichever books corresponded in her innocent experience to these classics.

I stood up respectfully and with bland innocence I handed over the book. It was an Irish dictionary.

Incredulity was the chief expression on Sister Liguori's face. She made me empty my desk before her eyes. She looked on the seat and under the desk. She even made me stand out on the floor and walk about a few steps in case I might have hidden a book in my clothing. My trick was completely successful.

It must have been the triumphant sneer on my face which at last gave her an inkling of the truth. She looked me full in the eyes. Brazenly, I looked back into hers.

"Yes!" my glance shouted. "Yes, Sister Liguori! I thought out this mean disrespectful trick to fool you and annoy you and humiliate you. To pay you back for your sarcasm and nagging. To get even with you for the number of times you've made a scapegoat of me. For your unjust punishments and petty persecutions. To make you pay, not only for these things, but for other things as well. For Annabel Gorry and Nellie Mack and my little brother . . . for those five bewildering miserable years before my father's death . . . and for the heart-hunger and loneliness I've known since this place separated me from Gran! You are not to blame for these things, but I have made them a part of you because of the bitterness you have sown in me. To me you are the cause of the misery of all children who have ever suffered. You are the laws which seem senseless to us. The suffering which is pointless. The stupidity which lays rough hands on our young souls. You are intolerance and injustice and cruelty."

Naturally, I did not know that the screaming insolence of my eyes held all this. I had no analysed understanding of the complexities that peopled my heart, and at sixteen a girl has not learned to listen to and interpret the divers-tongued voices that clamour within her. Naturally, too, Sister Liguori could not interpret the babel of my hot defiant stare. But there was a recurrent word of esperanto there which she could not but hear and understand. The word was 'hatred.' She realised that I had plotted to humiliate her because I hated her.

That is a frightening thing — to realise you have made someone hate you.

A slow redness mounted in the nun's face. The congestion grew until brow and chin and cheeks glowed brick-red against the white of her coif. The flat wide line of her mouth trembled. Into her eyes came an aghast look, and I saw two tears form there, brim over and roll, heavy as drops of grease, onto her starched guimp.

She handed me back my dictionary.

"Here, child" — it was terrible to see the trembling of her lips as she spoke — "get on with your studies." Without another word she turned and walked heavily and slowly back to her high desk in the centre of the hall.

There was a faint sniggering ripple from the girls who sat near me. They had witnessed the scene and had enjoyed Sister Liguori's discomfiture, for she was not popular. There should have been gloating triumph for me in that snigger, in the nun's slow heavy walk and in those two tears.

I wish I had not seen those tears. They spoiled everything for me.

I sat down and opened my history, but I did not study.

For there was a queer weakness on me and a kind of sad emptiness. Now that I had paid off my score I felt drained and bereft. For a little while I sat there woodenly, staring dully at a page on which print merged into solid black lines before my eyes. And then a slow realization of the cheapness and unworthiness of that trick came to my mind — a mind which because of long and close association with Gran was in some respects developed and matured. I began to see something to which resentment had blinded me for more than a year: that Sister Liguori did not hate me. She had merely been doing her duty as she saw it, and the failure of her work was due as much to the imperfections of my nature as to the things I found irritating in hers.

Another realization came to me as I sat there. The realization that in playing my shabbily-clever trick on a woman who had given up the world for the service of God, I had been guilty of a sin amounting to sacrilege. Everything that was Catholic in me rose up to reproach me for my nun-baiting. A hotness flamed in my cheeks and spread from there over my whole body, mantling me in shame and frightened guilt.

I carried that load into supper with me and it burdened me during the hour of recreation which followed. I lay down with it that night and rose with it next morning. During the two Masses which we attended that day, since it was the Feast of All Souls, I could not pray because of the way the load lay on my soul.

After Mass, we filed into the study-hall to write the extra letters which were our privilege on feast-days. I took out my writing-pad to write to Gran.

"Dear Gran," I started, but there I stopped short. For the sight of the four letters which spelled all that was dear

to me in life filled me with a longing to tell her everything, to unburden myself onto her wisdom and understanding. But this was impossible for my letter had to be
handed up unsealed so that Mother Superior might censor
it before posting. And as with all that trouble inside me
I could not bring myself to write the usual trivialities, I
tore out the page and put away my pad.

The lid had not closed on the desk when Sister Joan
came into the study hall. A wave of hopeful expectancy
that was almost tangible swept through us as it always did
with Sister Joan's entry, for this sweet-faced little lay-sister
with her tripping walk was the school portress, and her
coming meant that there was a visitor for one of us.

She walked towards my desk but I had no great expectations, for my next-desk neighbour was a girl whose people
lived two miles from the school and who was always being
summoned to the parlour.

And then came the miraculous incredible words,

"Your Grandmother is in the parlour to see you, Miss
Scully."

A singing in my ears. A dazed standing-up. A sleep-
walking out of the room. And all at once a running,
stumbling, rushing up stairs, down corridors — until at last,
the parlour-door. And then — Gran! Her arms about
me, mine about hers, and I crying great tears and trying
to say words that would not come because of the tongue-
thickening, throat-aching, heart-pounding.

I frightened her and she shook me, not roughly, but
persistently, so that gradually, I calmed and became intelligible.

"Tell Gran, all about it, alanna," she said, holding my
poor swollen face between her kind warm palms. And

looking into her eyes, I could keep nothing back. It all came out. Haltingly, but it came out. My impertinence to Sister Liguori, my laziness, my unwillingness to become a teacher, my misery in being parted from her. And, finally, the shameful story of last night's meanness. I saw her eyes grow stern and grave at this and though I knew I deserved it, I shrank from the reproach which I expected her lips to utter.

But Gran did not reproach. She only said, "That was a sin for you and you must tell it in confession." And then, quietly and sorrowfully, "They must have treated you terrible bad here to drive you to doing a thing like that." She saw me with such kind eyes that my worst sins were not mine but the results of others' faults.

She rang the bell. When the lay-sister came, Gran said, "I wonder would the Mother Superior ever spare me a few minutes, Sister?" When Sister went for Mother Superior, Gran sent me over to the school to get myself a clean handkerchief. I was not to return to the parlour for half-an-hour.

When I came back, Gran and Mother Superior were having a great time discussing home-made remedies for coughs and colds. It was natural that they should get on well together for they were both big-souled women, wise and generous.

Mother Superior put out a hand and drew me to her side.

"Your grandmother tells me you are not happy with us, Delia," she said. "Do you want to leave us, then?"

"Whatever Gran says, Mother," I answered.

"Your grandmother had decided that since you don't

want to be a teacher, she will keep you at home at the end of this term. Now are you happy?"

Happy? I was so happy that I heard very little of the conversation that followed. But I heard Mother Superior say something about my being a bad mixer and inclined to be solitary. And I heard Gran say that she blamed herself for this.

"I did wrong to keep her so much in the company of an old woman," she said. "I should have made her mix more with boys and girls of her own age. I'll see that she will from now on."

Oh, Gran, that resolve was foolish of you. Did you not see that the harm — if harm it was — was already done and could never be remedied? That the richness I got from companionship with you had spoiled me forever? That the company of the very young would always seem insipid and useless to me?

She was leaving on the four o'clock train. Dinner was brought to both of us in the parlour and afterwards we walked together in the garden. I got all the Ballyderrig news.

In the middle of her good-bye to me, Gran's face suddenly grew very grave.

"I want you to pray for Joe and Willie Reddin," she said. "They were on their way home to see their mother last Saturday when they ran into a party of Staters. The two of them were killed. Pray for their poor mother, too. She needs everybody's prayer to help her to bear that cross."

There was only one thing that troubled me in the weeks

that followed. I was leaving Wicklow for good, but without my Child of Mary medal. I regretted it deeply.

Early in December, Mother Superior sent for me to tell me that, thanks to the earnest request of Sister Liguori, I was to be admitted to the Sodality on the 8th, the Feast of the Immaculate Conception.

And thus it was that the happiness of my home-coming that Christmas was perfect.

But there was one thing kept me in a state of wonderment from Wicklow to Kildare.

Sister Liguori had cried when saying good-bye to me.

CHAPTER 18

THE GLOOM which had hung over Ballyderrig for a month after the death of the Reddin boys had departed by the time I came home.

I found the countryside in a ferment of excitement over the Ball-Alley Dance.

The men had got together and had decided that a ball-alley would add to the amenities of the place. As a first step towards raising the necessary funds for its erection they settled on a dance for St. Stephen's Night.

Derrymore House had a big interest in that dance. Mike Brophy was on the Committee and Gran, who was recognized as the best cook in the district, was asked to cook the hams. Judy Ryan was in such a state of wild anticipation that she could not keep her mind on her work and she burned the sodabread for three days in succession.

Judy had got Mrs. Lawler of the town to make her a new dress for the dance. On my first night home she brought down the dress for my inspection and admiration. It was primrose yellow taffeta with a wide gathered skirt. The bodice which was cut with elbow-length sleeves and a low round neck was gathered at the waist. There was a wide folded sash of the taffeta which tied at the back and floated in two long streamers.

I loved the dress. I loved its gay colour and shining softness. I envied Judy when I thought of how she would look in it and how those streamers would float entrancingly out behind her as she danced.

"It's well for you, Judy," I said wistfully. "It must be grand to be going to a dance."

"Well, maybe if there's a dance this time next year your Gran will let you go," Judy said kindly.

Gran's voice spoke up suddenly from the corner of the settle, where she sat under the oil-lamp turning the heel of a stocking.

"She needn't wait till next year if she's that anxious to go," she said. "What's to prevent her going with yourself and Mike on St. Stephen's Night?"

"Oh, ma'am! do you mean that?" Judy was genuinely delighted at the treat in store for me.

"Why not?" said Gran. She scratched the back of her head with her free needle, a little nervous habit of hers when knitting and talking at the same time. "Isn't she nearly seventeen now? I'll go bail there'll be many a young one there not near her age. And isn't it time for her to get out and see a bit of the world and not be stuck forever in the house with an old woman? If she keeps it up much longer she'll be an old woman herself before she knows where she is."

I nearly crushed Gran's brittle little bones with the hug I gave her.

"I'd love it, Gran!" I said.

"It isn't as if you were going among a crowd of strange go-boys from God-knows-where," Gran said, justifying herself. "There'll be just decent respectable lads from around the place."

"I hear they're expecting a crowd from Monasterevan and Newbridge," Judy said.

"Well, that's all right," Gran said comfortably. "Sure you might say the Monasterevan and the Newbridge lads are the same breed as ourselves. Are they expecting the Kildare crowd?"

"I believe they're not, Mrs. Lacy. It seems there's a dance on the Curragh the same night and it's hardly likely that the Kildare fellas would come over here."

"That's better still," Gran said with satisfaction. "I don't know what's over the Kildare crowd, but I don't like them. You saw them all last summer. Coming into a quiet respectable town like this on a Sunday evening, kicking up ructions and drinking Duffy's bar dry." Gran gave an indignant little grunt. "And their ties flying, into the bargain," she said, as if this were the crowning offence. The newfangled fashion of going waistcoatless seemed to her indecent.

"Well, no matter who turns up, Mike and meself will be there to look after Delia. She can go with us and come back with us in the pony-and-trap."

An awful thought struck me.

"But, I've nothing to wear, Gran!" I said.

"What about the white voile dress you had last summer?"

"Wouldn't it be too short for me?"

"Go up and put it on till I see it."

I put on the dress. It *was* too short for me. And my shape had changed so much since the summer that the dress would not button down the back.

"H'mmm . . ." Gran said, inspecting me. "If I let you out in that, you'd be a nice-looking sight all right. If I'd time I'd go to Dublin. But Mr. Johnstone of Newbridge has grand little dresses at times. We'll drive over there to-morrow and see what he has."

We yoked the pony early next morning and drove to Newbridge over a road covered with a glistening white network of frost. The bog lay silent and winter-bound, and the turf-clamps which those who lived convenient to them had not bothered to draw home, stood lonely and white-roofed at the edge of the road.

Mr. Johnstone had the very frock for me.

I have never since had a frock which gave me such pleasure. It cost thirty-nine and elevenpence, and Gran did not grudge a penny of the money. It was really beautiful. Periwinkle blue satin with a small tight bodice that flowed at the waist into a wide skirt. On the skirt were two small gathered pockets edged with rosebuds, and rosebuds also edged the puff baby sleeves and the little round neck. Gran bought me a lace-edged handkerchief, a narrow blue velvet ribbon for my hair and a pair of flesh-coloured silk stockings — the first silk stockings I had ever possessed.

"Your black patent Sunday shoes are as good as new," Gran said. "They'll do you grand."

I should think they would do me! As we drove home through the quick-falling dusk, I held the parcel containing my new finery on my knee and envied no woman on earth.

The hams were duly cooked and on the day before Christmas Eve the Committee sent us out the pan-loaves for the sandwiches. There were dozens of them.

"We'll leave them till to-morrow," Gran said. "They'll be easier to cut then. We can spend the day making the sandwiches. Then we can wrap them in damp tablecloths and pack them in the big clothes-basket and Mike can drive in with them to the town."

We had just stood up from our tea that evening when Andy Flaherty came in with a black leatherette-covered box under his arm.

Shyly, he laid the box on the table.

"I thought you might like the loan of these to cut up the hams, Mrs. Lacy," he said, opening the box to display a set of bone-handled carvers. "I won them at Brackna Sports seven years ago."

The boy's pride when we admired these proofs of his former athletic prowess was heartbreakingly pathetic to watch. Pathetic, because while Andy Flaherty had once been the best runner and jumper in the county, he was now in the last stages of consumption and could barely hold himself erect. His poor ravaged face with its hollow temples, sunken flushed cheeks and drawn white lips, was a fever death mask that night. But it became happy and less feverish when Andy sat down with us and commenced to go back over the days when no athlete could beat him.

He remembered every detail of every triumph. The names of his competitors and what the judge had said to him and how the people had clapped and cheered when he went up for his prize. Tragically, each boastful little memory was prefaced with such remarks as "One time, when I was in my health," and, "I remember another time before I fell into bad health." As the days of his glory came vividly before him, Andy Flaherty was no longer there on our settle, straining against a wasted body and losing his lungs cough by cough. He was in a summer field somewhere, flying from the starter's pistol like an arrow from a bow, the wind rushing to meet him, his muscles glorying in the strength that carried him over the springy turf and his good sound lungs doing their work proudly and well.

Andy was not sad in himself. At least, his was not the heavy sadness of despair, for he was firmly convinced that all he needed to become strong and well again were a few months in Newcastle Sanatorium. His people shared this belief and for a long time now they had been trying to get him into the sanatorium.

He was in great good humour that night, for the longed-for letter of admission had come at last. He was leaving for Newcastle after Christmas.

"That's great news, Andy," Gran said, although she suspected that no sanatorium on earth could do anything for him.

"Isn't it now, Mrs. Lacy!" Andy rubbed his thin dry hands together. "I believe they've sun balconies and everything there. I hear the doctors in Newcastle can put new life into you and that they make a new man of you after a week."

Six weeks after Andy went to Newcastle his mother got a letter to say he was dying.

"We can't let him die off there among strangers," she said, and she went up to bring him home. He travelled by train with her as far as Kildare station. The creatures could not pay for an ambulance and a motor-car was not to be had.

Their cousin, Jack Dillon, who carried the mails between Ballyderrig and Kildare, met them at the station with his side car. He had two of Andy's brothers with him. I was standing on the bridge myself when the side car drove into the town. There was the poor dying lad propped up between his brothers. His head lolled on Paddy's shoulder. Kit, the other boy, held a check cap before Andy's mouth. I thought he was trying to shelter him from the raw February wind. I learned afterwards that Andy had his last haemorrhage just as they came over the bridge.

The dance was to be held in a building owned by Johnny Dunne and leased to us for such functions at ten shillings a time. It was a leaky-roofed barn called The Temple. Just why, it would be difficult to say. To enter The Temple you had to go through an iron gate, across a small yard full of pot-holes, in through a low, scalp-threatening doorway and up a flight of stairs which were a real death-trap in their dark dilapidation.

Honesty compels me to admit that such, actually, was The Temple. But for many a year it was transformed in my memory because of what happened to me there that night. I forgot its leaky-roof and damp-stained walls, and remembered only the lights and the music and the dancing. I remembered it as a bright glamorous place, blossoming with romance. I could not think of it otherwise, for it was the scene of my first love-affair.

After our two o'clock dinner on St. Stephen's Day, Mike Brophy went into the town to help the other members of the Committee to make their last-minute preparations for the Dance. The Temple had already been decorated with bunting. Swinging paraffin lamps had been borrowed from the shopkeepers and hung from hooks in the rafters. Long forms had been collected from the schools and arranged around the walls. But the floor had still to be got ready. Mike and his colleagues would spend the afternoon in hammering down nails and in walking dozens of packets of Lux into the worn floor-boards so as to give them a semblance of smoothness. Judy and myself were glad to see him leave for it meant that for five or six hours we would have the house to ourselves for our preparations. To give us extra privacy, Gran went upstairs to lie down.

We filled every kettle in the house with water and hung them on the crane. While they were heating, we pulled in the big tub from the wash-house and set it before the fire. We filled it to one-third of its depth with cold water from the pump, and when the kettles boiled we added the scalding water. Then Judy threw in a few handfuls of oatmeal for extra softness, and the bath was ready.

She made me have my bath first. I stood in the tub and soaped myself well with the scented soap which was used only on gala occasions. Then, while I held a towel in front of me, she dipped Johnny Doyle's three-quart can in the gratefully warm water and sluiced me well.

She would not accept a like service from me, but made me turn my back and get on with my dressing while she performed her ablutions. Gran was obsessed with a fear that I might catch cold and before going to bed the night before she had made sure my clean underclothing would be well aired by hanging it over the back of a chair near the fire. Having regard to the thinness of my frock, she insisted on my wearing a double supply.

When I had dried myself well, I reached for the under-clothing and put it on. A woollen vest and on top of that another. Then the stiffly-boned corset, lacings in back, steel-busks in front, which though I had neither hips nor waist to corset, Gran insisted on as being necessary for the good of my figure, the health of my kidneys and the com-fort of my spine. Next a pair of grey fleece-lined knickers with elastic at the knees, and over these a similar pair. My petticoat went on now. It was white longcloth with a flounce of lace and a fine drawstring at the neck. The accumulative effect was not so bulky as it sounds, for I was as thin as a whip.

I loved drawing on the silk stockings, and I never knew legs could curve and gleam so delightfully as mine did in their flesh-coloured hose. My slippers, then, and finally — since my dress was not going on until the last minute for fear of accidents — my school dressing-gown.

All this time, there had been a splashing from Judy and, after, a rubbing and a whistling such as ostlers practice. Her dressing took longer than mine, for she had more garments to don. Bust-bodices and camisoles and such things.

But at last we were both finished. We emptied the tub and mopped up the floor. And when Gran came down she found a neat tidy kitchen, a set tea-table and two girls who felt as sweet and as clean as the babies Nurse Cassidy handed over, all washed and powdered, to their mothers.

Presently Mike came in and when we had tea, he went into his little room to shave and put on a clean collar. When he came out, Judy and I were arrayed in all our finery. He was supposed to admire both of us, but he could not take his eyes off Judy. She certainly was as pretty and as wholesome-looking a girl as any man could wish to take to a dance.

I looked nice, too. My hair — which was thick and curly and light-brown in colour — had been washed in rainwater the day before, and it shone like silk. Gran had combed and arranged it for me, and she had tied that narrow band of blue velvet about my head.

She gave my hair a final pat and stood back to admire me.

"There . . ." she said. "You'll do. If I do any more titivating on you you'll be a real Queen of Sheba."

Then she noticed the way I was standing, with my chest hollowed, shoulders hunched and arms pressed to my side. I had discovered one drawback to my new dress, and that was the form-revealing qualities of the bodice. I was agonisingly embarrassed by the way it showed off my recently-developed figure. My hunched attitude was adopted in the hope of minimizing the effect of my dress.

"Here, alanna — what's wrong with you? Straighten yourself up." She gave me a gentle thump between my shoulder-blades.

Mike had gone out to yoke the pony and I could unburden myself freely.

"It's — it's the way the dress makes me stick out in front," I confessed.

Gran and Judy laughed heartily.

"You poor little oinseach," said Gran. "To listen to you talking anyone would think you were a fine woman. Sure, you're as flat as a griddle."

Judy looked with pitying amusement at my miserable little buds of breasts, and then glanced down complacently at her own luxuriant bosom.

"Are we going to-day or to-morrow?" demanded Mike from the door.

"Here, give me a kiss," said Gran. "Enjoy yourself, now, and mind you don't catch cold."

On with our coats and gloves and into the trap. Slowly down the boreen and, once on the road, a rolling, bowling, quick-stepping, with a rhythm in our hearts keeping time to the pony's hooves.

Good-bye, Gran. Good-night, darling Gran. I love my
new dress. I love the way my hair is done. I love to be
going to the dance. And it's all only part of my love
for you and of yours for me. Oh, Gran, I love you for
everything!

Mike paid for us at the door of The Temple. His
committee badge secured him free admission, and he paid
a half-crown each for Judy and myself.

Although it was still early, the dance was in full swing.
To reach the ladies' cloakroom which was merely a curtained alcove to the right of the wooden platform where
the orchestra was enthroned, we had to jostle our way
through the fox-trotting dancers. The tune they danced
to, I remember well, was *Just Like a Thief in the Night*.

Mrs. Healy was the cloakroom attendant. She took
our coats from us and hung them on the long nails which
Mike and his colleagues had hammered into the walls.
With the nails, a small black-framed mirror, a comb and
a galvanised bucket, the cloakroom possessed every convenience any lady could require.

Mike took Judy out to dance immediately. I felt shy
about going out into the dance-hall to join the girls who
sat hopefully waiting for partners on the benches around
the walls. I stood just inside the curtains and peeped
out. I had company in my isolation, for Ellie Doherty
was there too, peeping and watching. That was Ellie's
way at every dance. She would stand close to the cloakroom until she saw an intending partner making for her
across the room. If he was tall, she stood her ground and
thankfully accepted him. If he was short, she beat a hasty
retreat into the cloakroom.

Ellie's stature was the bane of her life. She was six feet three in height. The rest of her family had been dealt with equally generously in the matter of inches. That was why we called them the Long Dohertys.

I was standing with Granny Lynn at Mitchell's Forge one day when one of the Doherty boys passed. The amount of ground he covered with each stride filled me with renewed wonder.

"Hasn't he very long legs?" I marvelled when he had passed.

"Long legs?" echoed Granny. "Sure, every one of them Dohertys is split up to the shoulders!"

The foxtrot finished, and the orchestra — two fiddles, a melodeon and a piano — struck up *The Walls of Limerick*. Judy Ryan beckoned me out, and before I knew where I was I was dancing with Mickey O'Neill of Duffy's bar. Mickey was a grand little dancer and since Irish dancing held no terrors for me we got through the number beautifully.

The next dance was not so successful. It was a one-step and I was taken out by Tim Coffey, a very stout and elderly farmer.

Tim was representative of the farming community of Ballyderrig. He had never read a book in his life. He took no interest in politics nor in humanity. He lived and worked with one driving motive — to provide good food and clothes for himself and his family and to pile up money in the bank. In common with the other farmers around our place, Tim found his golden opportunity in the War. It would have suited him perfectly had the slaughter in the trenches gone on forever providing him

with his chance to make more and more money. Willie
Beckett's story about him was proof of this.

On the day the Armistice was signed, Willie met Tim
Coffey driving into the town.

"Did you hear the news, Tim?" Willie said, getting off
his bike.

"No, what's the latest?" Coffey inquired, reining up.

"The War's over," said Willie.

Tim spat over the side of the trap in disgust. "Bad luck
to you anyway, Willie Beckett!" he said. "You're never
but you have the bad story."

I did not enjoy dancing with Tim Coffey. For one
thing, there was a smell of stout and sweat off him. For
another, I did not like the way he squeezed me so closely
in to him that his waistcoat buttons hurt my breast. Most
of all I disliked his dancing which was nothing but a
stumbling rush about the room. I was knocked against
the other dancers. My toes were walked on, and several
times I would have stumbled and fallen but for that close
embrace.

When the ordeal was at last over, I sank onto the nearest bench, hot and exhausted and with my ribs aching
from the extra tight-squeeze which Tim had inflicted on
me before he released me.

I found myself sitting beside Sylvia Gorry. I admired
her dress and she admired mine. In the middle of our
mutual admiration, the band commenced to play again —
can I ever forget it? — a waltz called *What'll I Do?*

And then I heard a voice saying:

"May I have this one?"

I looked up and saw the boy who was to introduce me

into a new and unguessed world. A world of kisses and tremblings. Of rapture and sweet longings. And — though this came long after and he had nothing to do with it — a world of heart-hunger, and disappointment and pain.

We danced well together. As we danced, we introduced ourselves. His name was Frank Breslin and his father owned the chemist's shop in Monasterevan. He was in a training college for teachers.

What did he look like? I cannot remember very clearly. Dark, a little taller than myself, eighteen or nineteen, and a rather girlish mouth with the lower lip protruding a bit because he was a little undershot. It is strange that though his appearance has clouded over in my mind, the smell of the cigarettes he smoked remains with me to this day. Sometimes, when I am in company or in a crowd, someone starts smoking that brand of cigarettes. The smell reaches me — making me thrill as if it had all happened only yesterday — to the memory of that undershot mouth, and then I am filled with nostalgia for youth and young romance and Ballyderrig.

During that first dance, he was no more to me than a rather nice boy, fairly good-looking, and interesting because he was a stranger and took such an obvious interest in me. But as dance succeeded dance my pleased interest changed to something that was exciting but a little frightening too.

They were playing *Marcheta* and we were waltzing when I felt his arm tighten around me. Ever so slightly at first, but then more firmly until my whole body was conscious of it and of the way his hand was trembling. My hand trembled, too, and I felt a heady languor.

We stopped dancing. We had to. Blindly, we made our way to a bench and sat down. I could not meet his eyes, for I felt ashamed of the way my face was burning.

"Look at me a minute, Delia," he said. I looked at him.

"Were you ever kissed?"

I debated with myself for a minute before I answered. Should I tell a lie? Or should I confess the shameful truth of my pitiable inexperience, and have him think me a mere school-girl? I decided on the truth.

"No. Never."

"Will you — " his lips seemed dry and he had to wet them before he went on quickly, "Will you kiss me when we are going out to supper?"

I nodded dumbly.

He put his hand on mine which gripped the bench between us.

"I love you," he said, staring straight at the cloakroom and Ellie Doherty.

"I love you," I whispered, looking right at Mickey O'Neill.

I have never been able to say exactly how the night went between then and supper-time. I have a vague recollection of dancing with Mike Brophy and with Willie Beckett. And I remember Judy Ryan coming over and whispering to me, "Who's the lad you're after clicking?" And at last Tim Dolan, the M.C., was saying.

"Ladies and gentlemen, the supper is ready now."

At dances in Ballyderrig, we had to leave The Temple at supper-time and cross the yard to a little low building which had once served as the boys' school.

Frank Breslin crossed the room to me.

"Don't you want your coat?" he said. In dazed obedience I went into the cloakroom, hunted for my coat and put it on. I was sorry that it was so typically school-girlish — navy nap and belted at the back.

I rejoined him. "We'll wait here a minute," he said. We waited, and then went down the stairs and out into the yard. The others had gone into supper and the yard was deserted. He drew me away from the path of light that streamed from the doorway and into the shadows. And then he kissed me.

There is a wonder to be remembered all the days of a woman's life when the first kiss comes like that. When the boy is right and feels only the warm tenderness that does not raven to sully or despoil. Then there is nothing to affright or shame. Only a rich soft warmth of strange lips and a wild sweet music in the head. And then, as the pressure of the lips grows stronger, nothing but a new blood-tingling and intoxication. There is no dissatisfaction, no sense of hunger unappeased, for the body has no knowledge of further mysteries. The lips are all satisfaction and the rich innocent sweetness of the kiss is all fulfilment.

I broke away from his gently urgent arms.

"Shouldn't we go into supper?" I said unsteadily.

"Wait a minute," Frank said. "Can't I ride over to see you during the holidays?"

"Come over and have tea with us on Sunday," I said, and I told him where I lived.

We got home sometime around two o'clock. Gran, who had gone to bed after our departure, had got up again at one o'clock to re-kindle the fire and have the kettle boiling for us.

I was in a trance of love and Gran thought I was dazed with sleep.

"You can tell me all about the dance to-morrow, alanna," she said, handing me a cup of tea.

"She'll have plenty to tell you, ma'am," Judy said to tease me. "She clicked the nicest lad in the room."

"Who was he?" Gran asked quickly.

"Young Breslin from Monasterevan. His father has the chemist's shop over there."

Gran nodded her head in relieved satisfaction. "He's all right," she said. "A decent family. His mother comes from Allanwood way. She's a cousin of poor Mrs. Nolan's, God rest her."

Frank's antecedents were known to Gran and his standing therefore was all right.

We were both nearly asleep when a sudden thought struck me.

"Gran," I whispered, "I've asked him over to tea next Sunday. You don't mind, do you?"

"Who? What?" Gran asked startled from her drowsiness.

"Frank. I've asked him to tea on Sunday. Frank Breslin. Is it all right?"

"Of course it's all right, alanna. It'll be a bad day with us when we can't spare a visitor a cup of tea." She chuckled. "But I can see I'll have to start keeping a wicked dog any of these days."

This was her Ballyderrig way of saying that I was now definitely "out," and that from now on young men might be expected to come besieging the place in droves. I went to sleep feeling very grown-up and important.

CHAPTER 19

JUDY RYAN brought Gran and myself our breakfast in bed next morning. To look at her fresh and bright-eyed, as she carried in the black-japanned tray, no one would think she had been dancing till the small hours.

As we ate our rashers and eggs and drank our tea, I told Gran about Frank.

"So he kissed you, did he?" she said.

"Yes, Gran," I admitted. "Sure it was no harm for me to let him?"

Gran poured herself a second cup of tea.

"Does your own conscience say it was a sin for you? Do you feel any way ashamed about it?"

A sin in that singing glory? Shame in the thought of that strange sweet wonder? A flame leaped in me as it all came back to me, sending pins and needles through my breasts and making my throat contract so that I had to put down my cup hurriedly.

"Oh, no, Gran! Not ashamed."

"That's all right, then. You've been reared to know right from wrong, and you'll always know in your own heart when a kiss is a sin and when it isn't."

As we dressed she talked about my future.

"I've been thinking," she said, "that it mightn't be a bad idea for me to buy a little business in the town. I'm seventy now, and the running of a place like Derrymore is getting to be too much for me. Wouldn't it be nice now if we had a little business like Miss Regan's, say, with the two of us running it? Me looking after the grocery end and you behind the drapery counter?"

The prospect was pleasant. No separation. No impossible examinations. Only an indefinite continuance of our companionship among the people we knew and loved.

"It would be hard to leave Derrymore, though," I said.

"It would that," Gran conceded. "There's a hundred and fifty years of me and mine in this place. But sure we needn't do anything in a hurry. It's just a notion I had and we can give ourselves a year or two to think it over. In the meantime you can find plenty to do with yourself, helping Judy and me around the house."

That suited me perfectly. But since All Souls' Day I had had an idea for a further use to which I might put my time. Diffidently, I put it forward.

"I was thinking," I said, "that maybe I could earn money doing odds and ends of sewing. Not dressmaking, of course, like my mother," I hastened to add hurriedly. "But little things, like tablecloths and inside clothes and baby clothes."

"Now, that's a good idea!" Gran agreed with enthusiasm. "You've a grand pair of hands when it comes to bits of fancy sewing, and there's no reason in the world why you wouldn't use them. Not that there's much of a demand for such things in Ballyderrig. But I'm sure there's some who'd pay good money for a nice little hand-made set of baby-clothes or for a cloth or a cosy to give for a wedding present."

That is what I had thought myself.

"I'll mention it to Miss Regan when I go into the town," Gran promised. "She has a way of spreading things that is better than a notice in the *Leinster Leader*."

"And I might get something now and again for a poem," I said hopefully.

"Maybe," Gran said briefly. Though she never said so in actual words, I think she looked on my poetry-writing for what it was: a waste of time that could better be spent in bread-making or knitting. She was indulgent towards it, as a fond father will be indulgent towards a craze for stamp-collecting in his pampered son. An expensive hobby, but tolerable.

"Would your fella have any great objections to having his tea in the kitchen?" said Judy Ryan, putting her head in around the door. It was Sunday morning, and we were preparing for Frank's visit. "There's a crow's nest in the parlour chimney and the fire won't draw."

It was true. The smoke from the kindling and turf she had put in the parlour grate was pouring down into the room. The parlour was filled with layer upon layer of fine white smoke-veils.

Thus it was that Frank sat at the kitchen table with Mike and Judy and Gran and myself. There was nothing awkward about that meal, for he was a nice, natural lad. Anyway, no one could feel ill at ease in Gran's company.

But I could not help wondering at the strange flatness I felt now that he had come. I had been expecting that the bewildering elation I had known at the dance would return to me immediately I set eyes on him. Instead, I found myself looking at him as if he were a stranger, and discovering faults in his appearance that had passed unnoticed on St. Stephen's Night. I was disappointed to discover that his ears were so large and that he did not come up to Mike Brophy's shoulder.

But it was different when, his visit ended, I walked with

him as far as the end of the boreen. It was dusk, a grey still dusk.

He propped his bike against the gate and turned to kiss me good-bye. Then, of course, the rapture I had tasted returned — in part, at least. Kissing had lost its newness and the keen edge of wonder was gone.

It was very enjoyable, all the same. Just one thing spoiled it for me. Frank, under Gran's pressing, had eaten largely of her treacle scones and hot seedy cake. While he kissed me I was conscious of the little rumblings which these things set up in his tummy. And this embarrassed me acutely because I felt it must be embarrassing him, too.

It cannot have done so, because before he went, he found words to propose to me. At least, it can hardly be called a proposal in the ordinary sense. There was no talk of undying passion or of wishing to blend our future lives for good and for ill.

Frank said wistfully, "Look, Delia. All the chaps in College are engaged. Will you be engaged to me?"

I have never been one to let anyone off with an aching heart for the want of a promise. Obligingly, I agreed.

"What do you think of him, Gran?" I asked when we were in bed that night.

"He's a nice lad," Gran said noncommittantly. "But you'll get over many a one like him before you're twice married and once a widow." I had a sneaking suspicion myself that she might be right.

Still, it was very nice to dwell in this grand new world where boys looked at you with an exciting kind of intensity and where lips and glances held a new importance. And I was proud to be able to say to myself that I was engaged. I never said 'engaged to be married,' for marriage was something that did not enter my thoughts. If I visualized Frank in my future life at all, it was in an endless succession of dances in The Temple.

He came over to see me several times during the holidays. On one occasion, he brought me a one-and-three-penny bottle of 'Californian Poppy' which I strongly suspected him of having stolen from his father's shop. He wrote to me, too. By the same token, those letters earned me from Willie Beckett what was known in Ballyderrig as 'a queer gait of goin'.' Each letter as he brought it exposed me to all kinds of teasing remarks from Willie. "I suppose you'll be giving us the Big Night any day now, Delia?" and, "We'll all be going over to Monasterevan to buy our pills on the cheap one of these days, Mrs. Lacy." The letters were neither flowery nor lengthy. There was one, even briefer than usual, which gave me a great thrill. It said: "Dear Delia, you're a peach and I love you. Frank."

I should like to be able to say that out of these small beginnings grew a grand and lasting passion. But human nature is weak and the human heart is very fickle. Ironically, it was my nobility of character that lost me my lover.

Our correspondence continued when Frank went back to college. With the approach of Lent, I was seized by a fit of unusual religious fervour, and I decided that my love affair gave me a splendid opportunity to do some good work for Mother Church. Frank was a Protestant. It would be grand, I thought, if through his love for me he should be drawn into the true fold. I saw myself as an Instrument of Grace. Believing that a threat to break off our engagement would bring him to his knees, literally and emotionally, I wrote him a restrained, dignified note pointing out that since we were of different religions it would be better if we ceased to correspond. He must have agreed with me completely, for he never wrote again.

When the Easter holidays brought neither Frank nor his letter, I was at first bitterly hurt. Hurt love soon gave way to wounded pride. This did not last too long, either, and I was both relieved and disappointed to find that my heart was not broken and that life continued to be enjoyable in spite of the fact that I had been jilted.

Life was very enjoyable that spring. There was no threat of departure lurking like a dark shadow, and since I had tasted the bitterness of separation, my enjoyment of the quiet secure happiness I now possessed was all the keener. If, on looking back, spring seems to have come earlier that year with bluer heather and more golden sunshine, with a tenderer green and a greater wealth of cowslips and primroses and violets, it may be because that spring I knew perfect happiness.

CHAPTER 20

NO SNOW had fallen at Christmas, and Gran had shaken her head forebodingly. "Green Christmas, green graves," she said. "We'll have many a death this year. Wait and you'll see."

"You and your prophecies," I teased her jokingly, when the young year passed without bringing any deaths.

"Wait awhile," Grand said. "Wait awhile. The cat didn't eat the year yet."

We had the first death towards the end of May. I was standing at the end of the boreen when Willie Beckett came along the road on his bike.

"No letters today," he said. "Did you hear the news?"

"What is it, Willie?"

"Poor Father Dempsey died around six o'clock yesterday evening. He's to be brought to the chapel tonight."

"The Lord have mercy on him," I said, turning and running up the boreen to tell Gran.

She was in the yard, throwing pin-head oatenmeal to the chickens.

She emptied the last grains from her apron.

"Well, well," she said. "The poor man didn't last long after all, God rest him. I wonder who'll we get now."

We were not surprised to hear of Father Dempsey's death, for he had been ailing for some time. In latter years he had grown dropsical. He must have been glad to go, for as his flesh had grown burdensome, so had life.

"He'll be as well off in Heaven," I said.

"Indeed he will, alanna. Many a time I thought it a pity of him being stuck in a place like this and he such a refined educated man. Not one of us fit to converse with him but Dr. Mangan. And God knows it's little enough of his company Dr. Mangan gave him since he married that wife of his. He's that much in love with her he can hardly bear to do his rounds."

Father Dempsey had been eighteen years in Ballyderrig. There was truth in what Gran said. There was little understanding between him and his parishioners. We had nothing in common but our religion. His time with us must have been a time of loneliness and exile for him.

This, taken with his bad health, may have been the reason for the impatience and irritability which showed itself more and more in his manner and speech as the years went on.

His impatience intensified to harsh bitterness in the matter of De Valera's followers. God knows, we had few enough of these in our place during the early post-Treaty days. There may have been a few silent sympathizers, but the Reddin boys were the only ones who were definitely known to be Republicans. And against the three Reddins, Father Dempsey directed the full force of his clerical condemnation.

I suppose one could not blame him for this. He was an orderly man with a great respect for authority — possibly because he himself was a representative of the greatest Authority of all. His father had been a major in the British Army, and any nationalism he possessed was that of John Dillon. He was a great admirer of Dillon. At that recruiting-meeting long ago when the sergeant appealed to us: "Follow the example of your great leader, John Dillon!" Father Dempsey had approved.

And when a single voice had been raised in dissent —
strangely enough it was the voice of Sam Leadbeater, the
Quaker miller: "He's not our leader!" — Father Dempsey
had been so incensed that he made his housekeeper withdraw his custom from Leadbeater's Mill.

When the Bishops tried to restore peace by refusing
the Sacraments to the Republicans, Father Dempsey had
been their loudest spokesman. With his eye on where
Ned Reddin knelt with his mother and his wife, he de-
nounced the Republicans from the altar. He even said
that if Willie and Joe were killed he would not allow
their bodies into the Chapel. He said — and these, mark
you, were the very words he said: *I would not have my
church polluted by them.*

Though none of us were conscious of any partisanship
in the struggle that was going on, and though with the
exception of Gran and myself, few in Ballyderrig really
liked the Reddin boys, that shocked us.

"It was a queer hard thing for him to say," Gran said,
voicing the general feeling.

That is why Mick Reddin did not have his dead boys
brought to Ballyderrig Chapel. Although it is hardly
likely that Father Dempsey, in spite of his hard words,
would actually have refused sanctuary to the bodies, Mick
Reddin disdained to approach him. Before being carried
to their family burial ground near Newbridge, the Reddin
boys rested for the night in the Chapel of another parish.

Their father felt very bitter towards Father Dempsey.

Not so Mrs. Reddin. She was one of the first to reach
the chapel that night when Father Dempsey's body was
brought down from his house opposite the barracks.

The rosary was given out by Father Kenny, a priest from a neighbouring parish who had been ministering to us during Father Dempsey's last illness. When the last response had been said, we all went home, and Leesha Mooney, who was sacristan, closed and locked the chapel door.

At seven o'clock next morning, she came to unlock the door for early Mass. She put the key in the heavy door and pushed it back. She walked in as far as the holy water font to bless herself and say a prayer, as she always did. But her fingers never touched the water. Leesha's head spun around and a dreadful nausea wrenched her stomach. The chapel was filled with a frightful odour, for something terrible had happened during the night. The coffin that enclosed poor Father Dempsey's swollen dropsical body had burst and the floor around it was covered with awfulness.

Leesha dropped in a dead faint to the floor and was found there and carried out by Ber Carroll, when he arrived for morning Mass.

Not one in Ballyderrig that day commented on what had happened. But by the way frightened glance avoided frightened glance, each of us knew what the others were thinking.

CHAPTER 21

GRAN pulled up the pony in the yard. I went out to meet her and to carry in her parcels.

"Here you are, alanna," she said, handing me a bulky paper parcel. "Miss Regan got in the stuff for Mrs. Cullen's baby clothes at long last."

Mrs. Cullen had commissioned me to make her baby's layette, and for a fortnight I had been waiting for Miss Regan to get in the necessary materials. She had insisted on Miss Regan sending to Dublin for them, for nothing already in stock in any shop in Ballyderrig was, in her opinion good enough for that baby.

My fingers had been itching to get at the sewing of the layette, and I was delighted to get the materials.

I carried in the parcel and we opened it on the kitchen table, Gran and I. There were yards of the whitest French flannel for the long petticoats and little vests. A big length of fine white cambric for the day-gowns and of soft nun's veiling for the nightgowns. Rolls and rolls of narrow insertion and lace for trimmings and two pounds of silky white wool for the carrying shawl and jackets.

"That will be the well-dressed child and no mistake," said Gran, fingering and admiring the lovely stuffs. "As soon as the dinner is over you can start into it."

"You'll have to cut them out for me, Gran. The stuff is so lovely I'd be afraid to put a scissors near it."

"I'll cut them out for you, never fear," Gran promised. "Where's Judy? I brought home a paper of peppermint sweets for the two of you."

Judy was out in the wash-house boiling potatoes for the pigs. She came running at my call. We divided the blue sugar-bag of peppermints between us.

"What's the latest in the town, ma'am?"

"Oh, only that that crowd of blackguards from The Slip are up to their devilment again. If they'd mind their own business and leave decent people in peace, Ballyderrig would be better off."

Judy laughed uproariously. "Did they find out about Dr. Mangan yet?" she asked, her eyes twinkling wickedly.

Gran's eyes twinkled, too, but she managed to get a note of reproof into her voice when she spoke.

"Get along with you Judy Ryan! You ought to have more sense than to be inquiring after their depredations. And you know well I don't like you talking about their goings-on in front of the child here."

She need not have worried lest Judy enlighten 'the child' about the latest exploit of the 'blackguards from The Slip,' for I was fully conversant with their devilment. I understood, too, what lay behind Judy's query concerning Dr. Mangan. You could not live within five miles of Ballyderrig and be ignorant of it. The place was seething with interest in that topic and was anxiously awaiting a denouement. For weeks, the burning question in Ballyderrig had been: Did Dr. Mangan sleep with his wife, or did he not? 'The blackguards of The Slip' had undertaken to find out.

We had a clique of go-boys in Ballyderrig to whom nothing was sacred or private — not even the holy relations between man and wife. They neglected no opportunity that seemed to offer food for ribald mirth. They preyed particularly on those who were thoughtless enough to act in any way unbecoming to their age or station in life.

For this reason, the go-boys served one good purpose. The fear of attracting their attention kept many of us from committing foolishnesses. If we exposed ourselves to ridicule, the go-boys considered we were asking for it. And we got it.

They were the bane of faithless lovers who tried to indulge in a little double-crossing. A man, having made some plausible excuse to his fiancée that released him from her company for the evening, might be sitting in the ditch with another girl and believing himself safe from discovery, when suddenly he would find himself 'scrawed.' 'Scraws' — sizeable clods of grass and earth — would rain on him from all sides, and he would be forced to the reflection that fidelity is the better part of court-ship.

The go-boys also disapproved of bereaved husbands and wives who re-married too quickly. When the happy couple came driving back into the town after their honey-moon, they were met with a chorus of insulting booming noises from the very effective instruments which could be made by knocking the bottoms out of porter bottles.

The go-boys lived down The Slip, which was a row of small houses just below the chapel. Britches Healy was one of them, Soretoes Martin another. Then there were the Gub Ennis, Crab Gavin, Sounty Cross and Grouch Kelly. Though his crippled leg prevented him from taking any active part in their doings, there is no doubt that Barney Holohan was the brains and initiative of the gang.

It was Barney put them up to rain sods on the roof of

Mrs. Dinnehy's house when she married for the fourth time. Mrs. Dinnehy had buried three husbands and was a grandmother of fifty-eight when she took our breath away by marrying a young widower of twenty-eight.

She brought her bridegroom home to her cottage in the heart of The Commons. Since there was neither a house nor a road within miles of her, it is not surprising that she should have thought her privacy assured and have neglected to curtain the windows. When the go-boys stealthily approached with their scraws that night, there was nothing to impede their view of the nuptials. They tip-toed to the window and peeped in. What they saw was so good and so deserving to be bruited abroad without waste of time that they dropped their scraws and raced back with their story to Barney. The next day all Ballyderrig knew that Mrs. Dinnehy had been observed sitting on the side of the bed in a mauve night-dress, while her bridegroom knelt at her feet in a state of stupe-fied adoration and tickled her toes.

There was nothing incredible for us in this story, for Mrs. Dinnehy was known to be richly endowed with that rare and mysterious quality with which those few women who possess it can reduce men to a state of babbling idiocy. The outside world calls it strong sex appeal. In Ballyderrig we called it "The rale stuff."

When she was very young and in service with Miss Regan's mother, her fatal fascination had all the boys of Ballyderrig fighting for her hand. The contestants were finally eliminated to two. One was Dinny Lee, a little cobbler who was not much bigger than his own last. The other was Jack Moran, a big bruiser who worked in the grand bakery Ballyderrig then owned and from which, I often heard say, the whole Curragh was supplied with bread.

The rivals heatedly contended their rights in Duffy's bar. They cursed each other bell, book and candle-light, big Jack Moran towering over little Dinny Lee who squared back up to him as brave as you like. At last Jack lost his patience.

"Look!" he said, lifting up Dinny by the scruff of the neck. "Another word out of you about the girl an' I'll drown you in a pint!"

Brute force told and Jack Moran married the girl. They say that Dinny brooded long and bitterly on his wrongs and that sometimes his brooding drove him so frantic that he would dart up from his last and out with him, apron and all, into the street. Like an angry little hornet he would fly down to the house at the foot of the bridge where Jack Moran had brought his bride, and arriving there he would deliver a few furious kicks on the door. Then, his bitterness temporarily abated and his repressions eased, he would walk sanely and fairly happily back to his cobbling.

The tricks played by the go-boys were sometimes mean and rather cruel, as that year when Mary Regan earned their disapproval by blossoming forth in a biscuit-coloured costume with two pleats in the back, a pink satin blouse and a white straw hat such as a child might wear at her Confirmation. By these and other signs, Mary, who was sixty if she was a day, made evident to us that the slowing tempo of her bood had been unexpectedly quickened by the call of spring. In other words, that she was open to consider any suitors who might be forthcoming.

The go-boys felt that something should be done about

it. They tied a rope around the neck of Neddy Hackett's old puckawn and dragged him up to Miss Regan's shop door. Then they pushed him in — long horns, mud-caked coat and unbearable stench — and pulled the door to. It took six ninepenny bottles of Jeyes Fluid to rid the shop of that smell.

Poor Dr. Mangan was pushed into their hands by the long tongue of Nannie Dillon who worked in the doctor's house and who was keeping company with Soretoes Martin. There was no detail of the doctor's household that Nannie did not retail to her boy as they walked up the Kildare Road in the evenings. And Soretoes in turn carried the news to the go-boys, who found plenty of food for amusement in Nannie's accounts of Mrs. Mangan's queer city ways. Not only had she insisted on the water closet which inspired Britches Healy's poem, but she had also installed an up-to-date range in the kitchen. The three-legged pots which had been in use in the old rangeless regime she found indescribably quaint, and The Slip rang with the side-splitting laughter of the go-boys when they heard she had even turned the biggest of these pots into an ornament and had promoted it to the upstairs hall, where it held a palm.

The rest of Ballyderrig had no scruples about joining in the go-boys' laughter at the odd ways of Mrs. Mangan. She was not popular with us. An elegant, stand-offish woman with an unsmiling face and an unfriendly glance, we considered her cold and bloodless. We could not understand Dr. Mangan's infatuation, for he was a warm friendly man, jolly and human.

When Nannie Dillon disclosed to Soretoes that the doctor and his wife slept in separate rooms, the go-boys were frankly unbelieving. So were the rest of us. Such a state of affairs between a married couple had never been heard of in Ballyderrig. If they had been enemies, like George Hannon and his wife, we could have understood it. But it was plain that the Mangans were in love with each other — or, at least, that Dr. Mangan was in love, for we did not think it possible that his cold aloof wife was capable of being in love with anyone.

The story was hard to believe.

But Nannie stuck to her guns. No, she insisted, Mrs. Mangan slept in the front bedroom and the doctor slept in the back. Hadn't she every reason to know it? Didn't she have two beds to make every day and two rooms to sweep and polish instead of just one as she would have if her employers were normal human beings?

"I wouldn't be surprised at anything *she'd* do," Barney Holohan said, "for I don't believe the woman has e'er a drop of blood in her veins at all. But I don't like to wrong the doctor by thinking him such a poor bit of a man as at that." A sudden comforting suspicion struck him. "I'll tell you what it is, Nannie — they're coddin' you! I'll go bail the doctor goes sleep-walkin' durin' the night."

"But wouldn't I hear him?" said Nannie. "There's never a sound in the night."

"Indeed you wouldn't hear him. He could easily slip out of his room unknown to you."

Surmises were all right as far as they went, but what the go-boys wanted was irrefutable evidence. The three-legged pot which had been turned into an ornament gave Barney an idea. He coached Nannie well.

That night she took care to be the last up to bed. On her way up to her little room in the top of the house, she quietly shifted the three-legged pot from under the landing-window and placed it right outside Dr. Mangan's door where he would be sure to fall over it if he went sleep-walking.

Then she went to bed and lay waiting for developments. They were not long in coming. There was a clatter and a stumble and a cry of anguish. And — Judy nearly fell out of her bed in astonishment — the cry was uttered not in the manly baritone of Dr. Mangan, but in the ladylike soprano of his wife.

Sounty Cross, who delivered the milk at Dr. Mangan's, was the first to hear the news next morning. When its finer points and their significance penetrated his understanding he was frankly incredulous. So was the rest of Ballyderrig when he spread the news. But ample confirmation came when Mrs. Mangan came out to do her shopping at eleven o'clock. Her right shin was bandaged.

We liked her better after that. She had proved herself to be a creature of human flesh and blood and was not, as we had imagined, a refined iceberg.

Gran cut out the baby clothes for me and I spent the evening tacking them up. We were both going to the altar next morning for the Feast of Saints Peter and Paul, so we went to bed early.

I was in bed before her, for she had many prayers to say. Lately, she had increased her orations with the Thirty Days' Prayer which she was offering up that Mrs. Cullen's baby might come home safely. I lay there and watched the little figure that knelt by the bed, for it was lovely to watch Gran when she was speaking to God. There was so much there besides reverence. Such a brave confidence in the lift of the small withered chin. Such a trusting friendliness in the intimacy of her half-whispered words. When Gran knelt down to pray you could almost hear her saying: "Are You by Yourself, Lord? Can I come in for a minute or two? I'm afraid I'm no great shakes of a visitor for You. Look at the state of me! I didn't get a minute all day to titivate my soul. But I thought I'd drop in anyway — You always give me such a welcome. There's a few things I wanted to talk over with You — maybe You'll tell me what to do about them. A couple of friends of mine are in a bit of trouble and, if it isn't asking too much, I'd like You to help them. And then there's a few odds and ends of my own I wanted to chat about. Look — here's how it is . . ."

As I looked at her I thought that this, surely, must be the way God likes people to approach Him.

There was something about the way she knelt there, so small, so childlike and so trusting that made my heart contract suddenly and I put out my hand to her. Without taking her eyes from the Sacred Heart lamp and without interrupting for a moment the movement of her lips, she took my hand and held it between both of hers. I felt myself drawn at once into that warm intimacy and made a part of her great friendship with God.

She blessed herself and rose from her knees, murmuring as she always did when she had concluded her prayers, "Not my will, O Lord, but Thine be done," thereby signifying that if she had made any unreasonable or senseless requests she would not be offended if they were ignored, but would understand perfectly.

She stood looking at me for a moment, but without seeing me. It was obvious that her mind was occupied with some problem. Then with the quick little lift of her head that showed she had reached a decision, she walked over to the chest of drawers and, selecting a key from the bunch that hung at her waist, she unlocked the top drawer.

I sat up in bed as I saw her take out the long brown papier-mâché glove-box that held her treasures. I loved being allowed to examine the contents of that box, and it was a treat that rarely came my way.

Gran brought the box over to the bed and sat down. She held the box against her breast. She looked at me for a moment in grave silence so that I might realise the importance and solemnity of what she was about to say.

"Delia, child: I'm going to give you my mother's locket."

"Oh, Gran! But I thought — I thought . . ."

"Yes, I know. I always intended to have it buried with me. That and my wedding-ring and Alice's hair. But, I've changed my mind. I'm giving you the locket to keep and wear."

I could hardly speak. I felt grateful and humble and proud. I knew what that locket meant to Gran. It was a holy grail. It embodied the great love that had existed between her mother and herself.

"Listen to me, alanna." Still clutching the box, Gran smoothed my hair back with her free hand. "You know yourself that though your mother and myself love and respect one another, we don't — well — get on well together. Now, it was different between my mother and me. It's hard to put it into words, but I've often thought of it this way: when she was carrying me, it wasn't just her blood that went into the making of me. Her soul and her nature went into me as well. That was the kind of feeling that was always between us. A closeness and a love that wouldn't let us be happy when we weren't together. It's a hard thing for another person to try to understand — that grand warm closeness."

But *I* understand, Gran! Of course I understand. Wasn't it a closeness just like that that made me frightened when they talked of going to Kilkenny and made me miserable during my time in Wicklow? I know well what you mean, Gran!

But Gran was with her memories and she did not hear the way my heart was crying to her.

"Well . . . my mother went from me. I was married at the time and your mother was a little one of fourteen months. I did my best to shake the black sorrow off me and for comfort I said to myself, 'Sure, I have Sis. She'll be growing up and it will be the same all over again.' But it wasn't the same. And I didn't get that closeness from little Alice either, for God took her from me, early. Never to have the closeness between your mother and myself, that was always a great hardship on me. I often thought about it, and sometimes I used to think that maybe when I was carrying her I didn't give her all my mother gave me. But God knows it couldn't have been want of love, or a want of joy in getting her. My heart used to turn over with delight inside me when I'd feel her stirring under it. But it wasn't to be, I suppose. And when she grew up and I found the closeness wasn't there, I said to myself that it would have been too much to ask for, anyway. That a thing like that doesn't happen twice in a lifetime. And then you were born." She stopped short and the hand on my head ceased its stroking.

Gran, oh, Gran! please say it — say it just once! You know you've never said it. Yes, your kindness and understanding whispered it to me all the time, but you never said it in words. Just once, Gran — say that we have the closeness, you and I!

She said it.

"Between you and me I feel the closeness always, alanna. I might have borne you as my mother bore me. And that's why I want to give you my mother's locket. Here, take it out of the box yourself, for I want to go down to the kitchen for a drink of water."

Now that she had said it at last, she was shy, and she wanted to run away to hide her shyness. Now that I had heard it, I, too, was shy, and I was glad she had run away.

When she came back I was turning over the treasures in the box. It was a queer assortment. A green cut-glass bottle with a silver stopper at either end, one end for smelling salts and the other for perfume. A real mother-of-pearl rosary beads strung on silver which my father had given her the day he married my mother. A silver tea-infuser. An onyx watch-guard that belonged to my grandfather and his gold watch-chain — Paddy had his watch. Gran's own gold watch and chain, a coral necklace that had been brought back from Cork with the gilt tumblers in the kitchen, and a few odds and ends of brooches and rings. The locket was safely wrapped in cotton-wool in a silver snuff-box. Gran took it out herself and handed it to me.

"There it is for you now," she said, simply.

It was a little flat round locket, not much bigger than a shilling, with the entwined initials, M.K., engraved on the front. I opened the locket and looked at Gran as a baby. It was a little miniature painted on glass for which a travelling artist had charged Gran's mother twenty-five shillings.

"My mother always said he cheated her," said Gran, "for he made one of my eyes smaller than the other. I'll leave you the snuff-box, alanna. You can keep the locket in it when you're not wearing it." She returned the papier-mâché box to its drawer and came to bed.

I went to sleep with a sense of perfect completion, for I had been invested with the insignia of Gran's openly-professed love.

CHAPTER 22

"WHAT DO you think of it, Gran? Will Mrs. Cullen like it?"

I held up the long petticoat I had just completed for Mrs. Cullen's baby. It was the final garment of the layette and I had taken special pains with it. I was eager for praise and Gran did not disappoint me. She examined it inside and out, in detail and as a whole.

"It'll take the sight out of her eyes," she said at length. "She'll go daft entirely about it."

"There's no doubt you're the heart of the roll when it comes to stitching," Judy Ryan said generously. "That bit of work's a real credit to you."

I thought so, too, though modesty demanded some disclaimer.

"Och, I don't know. There's nothing much in it," I said, trying to appear off hand. But I doubt if my hypocrisy could have sounded very convincing, for I was bursting with pride. The petticoat really *was* beautiful and I knew it. No thick clumsy seams to form uncomfortable ridges under soft baby flesh. Where there was a joining, I had laid one edge of fine flannel over another, tacked them down and then secured them with a lattice of white silk feather-stitching. But for the feather-stitching, it would have been hard to know there was a seam at all.

I had not been content merely to neaten the tail in the usual way with a binding of silk braid or a hem. I worked out a complicated but lovely design of my own. I am certain that Beethoven did not get a greater thrill from the conception of his Moonlight Sonata than I experienced when the idea for that design came to me. It came in a moment of fine inspiration one morning before I got up. I was lying in bed, staring idly at the handful of pansies that stood in a wine-glass on Gran's altar, when I saw it all. With that frenzy of conception on me I could hardly dress quickly enough to put my idea into execution. Using a spool as a guide I traced out a series of scallops around the tail of the petticoat. At three-inch intervals I drew a pansy using two of the scallops as its top petals. I worked over the design in pale blue silk and cut away the surplus flannel around the scallops. I did the same with the tiny neck and armholes except that here a sixpenny-bit was my guide, since the scallops and pansies had to be so much smaller. And — this is surely rare in any work of genius — the finished result exceeded my expectations.

"Will you take it in to her yourself?" Gran wanted to know. "Or will Mike take it when he's going in this evening for the binding twine, and save you the journey?"

"I'd rather go myself, Gran. Maybe she'd pay me if I went myself." Mrs. Cullen had agreed to pay me twenty-five shillings for the making of the full layette. Not magnificent remuneration for work that had occupied me during all July and for a week of August. But it was a goodly sum to me and the value of the pleasure I had found in the work was beyond reckoning.

"Well, if you're bent on going in you may as well take her the remedy for after-pains. I promised it to her the last time I was in the town. She'll be needing to make it up soon — isn't she expecting around the fifteenth? And that's only ten days away."

"She told me she'd love the baby to come home on

Lady Day. Do you know what she's going to call it if its a girl, Gran?"

"What, alanna?"

"Mary Assumpta. She got the name in a book the nuns lent her."

"Mind you that now!" Gran said admiringly. "Trust a convert to have great devotion to Our Lady. It's only a bare twelve months since she turned Catholic to marry Ned Cullen, and here she is already talking about feast-days and naming her child after the Blessed Virgin."

"What about the remedy, Gran?" I was anxious to be off.

"Hand me The Book off the top of the dresser, Judy." 'The Book' was Gran's *Materia Medica*. It was a black-covered copy book into which she had written what she considered the most important of her recipes and pre-scriptions so that they might not be lost to posterity. She turned over the pages and found the remedy for after-pains.

"Copy it out on a sheet of note-paper," she told me. I had copied it so many times that I could almost have written it without reference to 'The Book.' Every mother in Ballyderrig had received a copy of it in her hour of need. Latterly I had begun to suspect that my penman-ship was being wasted and that few, if any, of those who thanked Gran so profusely for the remedy had recourse to it. They preferred — wisely, perhaps — to let Nature take her course. However, I sat down and wrote it out once more:

"Take nine single peony-seeds powdered, the same quantity of powder of borax and a little nutmeg; mix all these with a little white aniseed water in a spoon and give it to the woman, and a little aniseed water after it, as soon as she lies down."

It was not merely a mercenary wish to receive my wages that made me anxious to deliver the petticoat myself. I loved seeing the way Mrs. Cullen's face lit up when each little garment was brought to her. She had such a longing to hold her baby in her arms that she could not wait for the layette to be completed. As I finished each garment, I had to let her have it. It was as if she felt the coming of her baby was hastened with every little vest and gown and petticoat.

It was grand to work for such an appreciative employer as she. There was a great thrill for me in seeing her gloat over the baby-clothes I made. "For the child," she would exult, holding up a little gown. "Isn't it lovely? For the child!" And everyone in the house would be summoned to admire it — her husband, Tommy Cross, the shop-assistant, old Mrs. Murray who worked in the kitchen and Gub Ennis, the yard-man. I did not know then that her exultation was not due so much to the neatness of my sewing but to the fact that she saw her child clothed in those scraps of flannel and cambric.

I never knew the waiting-time to drag so slowly with a woman as it did with Mrs. Cullen. She had a hunger for that child which made every day of the nine months seem a year.

We all understood her impatience and sympathised with it. The bigotry of her father had already kept Mrs. Cullen waiting twenty-three years for her baby.

Matty Hetherington's hatred of Catholics was surprising in a man who made his living out of us. Ninety-five per cent of the customers who went into his shop for groceries and liquor and seeds and farming requirements belonged to the religion he hated. Come to think of it, it was not only the Catholic religion Matty hated. He hated everything and everyone. He must even have hated Bella, his only child, for otherwise he would never have forced her to waste twenty years of her life in looking after him when he knew she was eating her heart out for Ned Cullen.

I have called him 'Matty,' but in Ballyderrig he was never known as anything but The Feocadain. He had a shop-assistant from Clare once, and Matty's snorting ways irritated the boy to such an extent, that he christened him 'Feocadain' — which is the County Clare Irish for 'thistle.' We were quick to see the aptness of the nickname and it stuck to him.

Bella was twenty when she fell in love with Ned Cullen. Ned would not have her unless she turned, and The Feocadain would have been capable of horsewhipping her for the bare suggestion. The old man had a bad heart and the lovers had to content themselves with the hope of his early demise. It never occurred to Bella to defy her father and to become a Catholic and marry her man in spite of him. Nor did it occur to Ned to persuade her to do so. The Feocadain had a substantial fortune to bequeath. Both Bella and Ned were practical though in love and they decided that since a little patience would secure them the money, they would practise patience. It is not likely, however, that they anticipated having to be patient for over twenty years.

Theirs was the most astounding fidelity ever known. There was no covert courtship, no meetings on the sly to help keep alive their interest in each other. During those twenty years they had no conversation beyond good-morning and good-evening. They knew that if there were anything more The Feocadain would inevitably hear about it and Bella would be thrown into the street without a penny. Each could have made a good match ten times over while they waited for the old man to die, but they remained as faithful as if the world held no other man or woman.

When The Feocadain's long-threatening final heart-attack came at last, Bella lost no time in getting herself instructed by the nuns. She was received into the Church and in less than a year after The Feocadain's death she married Ned Cullen.

She did not look a day over thirty on the morning they married, for she had kept herself young for Ned. She took more care of her hair and skin than any actress. I remember her sending out to Gran for her cure for freckles: 'Four spoonfuls of May dew gathered from corn, and one spoonful of oil of tartar. Let it dry on the face.' And often when she brought me into the kitchen for a cup of tea, I marvelled at the care she took to avoid scorching her skin when making toast. She would sit sideways at the fire holding the long-handled fork in her left hand. With her right hand she held a plate between her face and the heat of the fire. The care she took of her hair was astounding. She had all the children of Ballyderrig gathering elder-blossom for her in May, for she knew how to brew a rinse from them that kept hair from fading. And Mrs. Murray told us she used a whole penny box of vaseline to massage her scalp every night so as to keep that lovely dark hair thick and silky.

All Ballyderrig wished them well, and we were genuinely delighted when we heard Bella was going to have a baby. Gran and myself took a special interest in that baby. The stitching I had done for it gave me almost proprietary claims. And Mrs. Cullen consulted Gran so often about symptoms and signs that Gran began to feel that she, too, had a claim in it.

In spite of Mrs. Cullen's exultation that the baby was coming to her, that pregnancy was not a happy one, for from the start Bella had notions. Most pregnant women have delusions of one kind or another. Some torture themselves with unfounded jealousy of their husbands. Others develop an exaggerated sense of injury. And there are others — and these are the ones to be pitied with a great pity — whose minds become a hell of worry lest the child they carry will not be born normal and perfect. Poor Bella was one of these. She got it into her head that her age would militate against the baby in some way. The notion grew in her and became an obsession.

When she was about four months pregnant, Gran called to see her one day and found her in a state bordering on hysteria. She had allowed over-anxiousness to take such a hold on her that she was convinced her child was going to be deformed.

Gran scolded her soundly.

"You're going the right way about harming the child with all this foolishness, Bella," she said. "Look at Mrs. Rice who had her first child when she was forty-three, and where would you see a finer lad?"

But it was not only what she believed to be the disadvantage of her age that sent those spectres to drive poor Bella frantic with their grimacing. Her fears had an additional source.

She moistened her lips. "What about" — she was almost afraid to say the name — "What about *Trant*, Mrs. Lacy?"

Ah, yes . . . Trant. He was someone, God help him, to chill the heart of any woman who was expecting to bring a child into the world. Particularly if the woman happened to be, as Bella Cullen was, his cousin. Trant had been born without legs. He lived about four miles from Ballyderrig on the Robertstown side and he often drove into the town in a little pony-and-cart that had a specially constructed seat. Usually he sat in the cart and had his messages and drinks brought out to him. But he could move from the cart if he wished for he had surprising power and dexterity in his long muscular arms. I remember seeing him pull up outside Duffy's one day. His pony had cast a shoe and he called young Tommy Neale to take her to the smith. "Are you comin' too, sir?" Tommy asked. "No, I'm staying here to have a drink," Trant said. He edged the pony alongside a near-by car and, using his arms as crutches, he shifted himself from one cart to the other in far less time than it would have taken an able-bodied person.

You could not have blamed Bella for feeling worried when she thought of Trant, but Gran did not give in to her.

"I'm surprised at you even to think of such a thing, Bella Cullen," she said. "You're a Catholic now, and you ought to have more trust in God and Our Lady. Besides, what has poor Trant's affliction to do with the little child you're carrying? What makes you think that your being a distant cousin of his could have any effect on the shape of your child? The Paynes and the Burrells and the Campbells are related to him, too, and I never saw anything but fine splendid children with them. No, Bella. You'll have to put these thoughts out of your head. They're bad for you and they're bad for your child. Pay a little visit to the Chapel every day and look your fill at the grand little Baby in Our Lady's arms. Tell yourself that your child will be just as perfect, and I'll go bail that's just what he'll be."

Gran succeeded in driving away Bella's fears for the time being. She fought them hard herself. But she never succeeded in vanquishing them completely. Though she laughed and rejoiced, and made plans for her baby, the fears were always lurking somewhere near, waiting to pounce on her the moment she was off-guard.

I did not get my twenty-five shillings after all. Nor did I get what I wanted even more badly — Mrs. Cullen's praise for the lovely petticoat.

Mrs. Murray met me at the kitchen door with a grave face.

"She's took bad," she said, "and it's over a week before her time. Dr. Mangan is above with her now. But what in God's name are we going to do at all? Nurse Cassidy is away in Allanwood and won't be back till the mornin'. Himself is gone up to the post office to see if they can send over a nurse from Kildare."

Muttering something about having to rush upstairs to give Mary Menehan a hand, Mrs. Murray took the petticoat from me and left me.

Mary Menehan was the handy woman who usually attended Nurse Cassidy at her work. She and Mrs. Murray did the best they could to carry out Dr. Mangan's instructions pending the arrival of the nurse from Kildare. She came in a car at seven o'clock but by then it was too late, for both Mrs. Cullen and her baby were dead.

Gran said afterwards that if either herself or Nurse Cassidy had been there, Bella Cullen would never have died, and she was probably right.

There was no real reason for her death, for she got over the birth perfectly.

What happened was this.

Everything went normally up to a point. Bella Cullen was valiant. Mrs. Murray said she never complained once. The baby was born, a beautiful perfect little girl. It seemed all right. Its lungs functioned properly, for it responded to slapping and it cried lustily. Bella Cullen heard that cry and it pulled her back from the between-world where a woman goes for a little space after her baby is born.

But something seems to have gone wrong with the child's little heart after it had been beating ten minutes, for the next thing Mrs. Menehan knew was that she was holding a dead baby in her arms.

"Where's the child?" Bella demanded weakly from the bed. "Give me the child."

The two old women looked at each other in consternation. Mightn't the shock of hearing that her child was dead prove fatal to the mother at this point?

"Should we tell her?" whispered Mary Menehan. She had a very loud whisper, which was unfortunate, for Bella heard that question. To her it could mean only one thing. She had heard her baby crying, therefore it had been born alive. There was something they hesitated to tell her, therefore she had given birth to a monster.

"Oh, God! Trant!" cried Bella, and died.

Gran wrung her hands in helpless rage against the stupidity of Mary Menehan and Mrs. Murray. "Bella need never have died," she said, "if only those two had a bit of wit. All they had to do was to wrap the baby in a shawl and put it into her arms for a minute or two. Then they could have made up some excuse about having to wash it and have taken it out of the room. In an hour she would have rallied around enough to stand the shock of hearing it was dead. God help us all, I often heard tell that ignorance kills more people than hemlock."

When they laid Bella out, they dressed the baby in some of the little things I had made and put her on her mother's breast. Under the lace edging of the gown you could see the pansies on the petticoat. It nearly broke my heart to think that Mrs. Cullen never knew about the pansies.

"Green Christmas, green graves" — what did I tell you?" said Gran. "I wonder who'll be next?"

CHAPTER 23

I WAS awakened in the night by the smell of something burning. I sat up and leaned over Gran.

"Gran. Gran, love." She opened her eyes and was alert immediately. "I think there's something burning, Gran."

She sniffed. "So there is, alanna. Mother of God! would it be the haggard?" The last of the wheat had been brought home that day and it was stacked in the haggard waiting to be threshed. Then we heard the kitchen door open and, a second later, Mike Brophy's step on the stone floor. With my heart thumping, I ran to the bed-room door and shouted down.

"What's wrong, Mike? Is the haggard burning?"

"No. The haggard's all right, but Loughlin's house is afire. If you go to the back window you'll see it. I'm goin' over there now to see if I can give a hand."

I ran into the back room and looked through the window. A second later I was joined by Gran who had pulled the quilt off the bed and wrapped herself in it, for she had had a cold since the day of Mrs. Cullen's funeral. Although the Loughlin's place was a good quarter of a mile from ours back in over the fields, we could see the blaze clearly, for the house stood on a hill.

"Well, the poor creatures!" said Gran feelingly. "Aren't they unlucky? It's been one misfortune after another with them. And now a fire to crown it. Well, they'll get the insurance money anyway — that's one consolation."

"Yes, but what'll they do for some place to sleep in the meantime?" I said.

"They'll come here, of course," Gran retorted. "Aren't we their nearest neighbours? And haven't we lashings of room? After all there's only Acky Joe and the two girls and Herself. I'd better go over and invite Mrs. Loughlin myself." She made for the door.

"Couldn't I go with you, Gran? Maybe you shouldn't go out with that cold on you, and the dew on the grass and all."

"Have wit, child. It would be a queer thing if I let a little bit of a cold keep me from doing my duty by my neighbour and she in trouble. How do you think 'twould look if I sent a messenger on such an errand? No, I'll go over myself and invite her. You can come with me."

We dressed hurriedly. I was dressed before Gran and while she was finishing I went across the passage to rouse Judy Ryan who would have slept through an earthquake.

"Gran says you're to get up and light the fire, Judy," I said, when I had succeeded in making her understand what was happening. "She wants you to air clean clothes for the settle-bed and for the two beds in the back room. We're going over for the Loughlins."

It was a silvered night with the moon spending itself in radiant prodigality on trees and hedges and on cornfields that lay naked and desolate after their rape. We talked of the Loughlins as we went.

Things had not been going well with them since the death of old Larry Loughlin, eight years before. The truth of the matter was that Mrs. Loughlin was not capable of managing a farm. She had been a servant in the house when Larry, who was an old man even at that time, had taken it into his head to marry her. She had never taken easily to her new station in life and she continued to look on her husband as her employer. She even continued to address him as "Masther." "Here's your clean shirt for you, Masther," and, "I'll have the dinner ready in a minute, Masther." When they came to Mass on Sunday, she always walked respectfully a few paces behind him. It was only when he died that she began to realise she was mistress of the place. Her subservience changed to arrogance, and no newly-crowned queen was ever so insistent on her rights as the Widow Loughlin. She reserved all authority for herself and gave Acky Joe no say in things at all. This had a disastrous effect on the farm, for Mrs. Loughlin was not born to oversee and manage.

"It's the pity of the world she doesn't give that boy a chance," Gran said. "She's making a laughing-stock out of him and ruining the farm into the bargain. That boy would be worth his weight in gold to her if she let him have his say."

We got our feet wet crossing the stream. I was worried about Gran's cold but she made little of my fears.

"What matter, alanna. It'll be easy for us to dry ourselves when we get back, and I'll make up a black currant jam drink for the two of us."

All Ballyderrig was gathered around the fire when we got there. When the outbreak had been discovered, Acky Joe's first act had been to cycle into town and get Leesha Mooney to ring the chapel bell. Men, women and children — they were all there to help and gape and sympathise. Two lines of men had been formed. One stretched to the pump and the other to the stream. There were plenty of buckets for every man who hurried in answer to the S.O.S. of the chapel bell had had the prevision to bring one. The buckets were passed from hand to hand with eye-confusing rapidity, but the flames had already made such headway that all the water in the canal would not have checked their greed. The men had to content themselves with concentrating their efforts to keep the fire from spreading to the harvest in the haggard.

With water-soaked handkerchiefs tied around their mouths and dripping sacks on their hands, a few of the most foolhardy dashed in and out of the burning house in an effort to salvage some of the furniture, but soon even this was impossible and the Loughlins had to look on while the hungry fire devoured their home and belongings.

That was a strange exciting scene for our quiet little place. The hot yellow light of the flames made water of the moonlight, and their leaping did something disquieting and almost evil to the ring of eager faces. The burning house was an altar. The people were a congregation so intent on their worship that they could hardly bear to stand at a safe distance from the heat and flying sparks, but kept pressing nearer and nearer. The sweating, grunting men swung their buckets as if they were incense-burners and the hissing of the water blended with the roaring and spluttering in a maddening litany. Over the paddock and haggard a cloud of sacrificial smoke formed and spread slowly south to the bog, and, as if exhorting the congregation to greater fervour, Acky Joe ran from one group to another, giving orders and making suggestions.

To see Acky Joe in authority was the most surprising

aspect of the affair. The emergency which had caused
his mother to lose all her airs and return to frightened
humility, had made a man of Acky Joe. Old Larry
Loughlin himself could not have taken charge with
greater self-confidence than the boy.

A little apart from the ring of on-lookers, Mrs. Loughlin
sat on the grass amid the scattered remnants of her pos-
sessions. Always an unbalanced woman, the fire had
made her hysterical, and it was taking all the efforts of
her two daughters and a bunch of sympathetic women to
soothe her. Gran made her way to her side.

"This is a terrible cross, Mrs. Loughlin," she said, "and
God knows I'm sorry for you. But sure there's nobody
hurt, anyway, and houses can always be built again."

"Ah, but the poor Masther's furniture, Mrs. Lacy!"
the woman blubbered, beating her hand frenziedly on
the grass. "All his lovely furniture in there and not one
doin' a thing to save it."

"Sure they did all they could, Mrs. Loughlin," Gran
comforted her. "No one but a madman would go near
the house now." At this moment part of the roof crashed
in and the crowd leaped back to escape the shower of
sparks and cinders. "Look at that now! Who could go
in there?"

"What's to become of me at all, at all?" Mrs. Loughlin
wailed. "Here I am without a roof over my head and
without a bed to lie on."

"Isn't that what brought me?" Gran said. "We've
plenty of beds over in Derrymore, and you can have them
with a heart and a half. You're kindly welcome to make
your home with us until you're settled again."

Mrs. Loughlin's face brightened at this friendly offer.

"We couldn't do that on you, Mrs. Lacy, ma'am," she demurred half-heartedly.

"Not another word now," Gran said briskly. "And there's no reason in the world for you to sit here all night catching cold. Let the girls and yourself come back with me now. You can have a nice cup of tea when you get into your beds. Acky Joe can follow us over later on."

Gran's tone did not admit further argument. Mrs. Loughlin welcomed the voice of authority. It comforted her to have decisions made for her and her path made clear. "God bless you, Mrs. Lacy," she said. "You're a real friend." Kitty and Mary Brigid helped their mother to her feet and we set out across the fields.

It was almost dawn when we reached Derrymore House, and Gran was shaking all over with cold and fatigue. But she refused to lie down until she had seen her guests made snug and comfortable in the beds Judy had prepared for them. At last she got into her own bed. When I brought her up a black-currant drink and a hot iron for her feet, she was thankful for the iron but could not take the drink.

"Drink it yourself, alanna," she said. "I'm too tired to hold it. Get into bed quick and warm me." I was asleep as soon as my head touched the pillow.

When I awoke next morning Gran was sleeping, but her breathing frightened me. It was harsh and loud and there were two rouge-like spots of colour in her cheeks. When she wakened I brought her a cup of tea. She drank it thirstily but she would eat nothing. I had never seen Gran ill before and I was frightened.

"Shouldn't I go in for Doctor Mangan, Gran?" I said. It was hard to keep my lips from trembling.

"No, Delia, alanna. It's just that old cold. I'll lie here for an hour or two and I'll be all right by dinner-time. Did the Loughlins get their breakfast?"

By evening her breathing had become so much worse that I went for the doctor without consulting her. When Dr. Mangan had seen her he told me to wire for my mother.

I do not often try to remember what happened after that, because when I do something confusing always happens to my brain. A crowd of people rush into it bewildering me and upsetting me. The people of Bally-derrig, my mother and Paddy and Joe and the priest. Not one of them ever stays quiet long enough for me to ask: What were *you* doing in Derrymore House when my Gran was sick? But they whirl and spin and make sorrowful faces at me and dart away again. I hear voices too, and the voices are worse than the faces for they whisper and jabber one after another, never finishing what they are saying but running one sentence into another until I am nearly driven mad. There they are at it now! Listen to them. . . and the doctor says she can't not my will O Lord but Thine she put up a great fight after look at the child she's nearly daft with always a real good neighbour breathing's getting very infant Jesus meek she's sinking fast Hail Mary full of quick the Crucifix the habit's in the black Sacred Heart I place all my my all my all my all.

Gran went to Heaven on the twenty-third of September, nineteen hundred and twenty-eight.

CHAPTER 24

DID YOU nearly get tired waiting for me, Gran? I wanted to get here earlier, but there were so many to say good-bye to since I came down from Kilkenny this morning that the day kind of flew on me.

Willie Beckett was good to give me the key of the house. I'm glad he bought Derrymore and that it will be himself and Miss Flood who will be living here and not strangers. He bought all the downstairs furniture too, Gran — the only thing my mother kept was Mary Kelly's photograph out of the parlour. It was nearly like old times to come into the kitchen and see the settle-bed and everything there just the same as ever. But it was lonesome to come up here to the bedroom and find it bare. Judy got our bed, and my mother took the rest of the furniture to Kilkenny — she says when I have a home of my own she'll give it all to me and the photographs as well.

I knew I'd find you here, Gran. Let me look at you, love.

Gran . . . darling.

No, I'm not crying . . . honest, Gran. It's only that I'm so glad to see you. You know how it has been with me these two months, don't you? A hundred times a day I say: 'I must tell that to Gran,' and 'Gran will laugh when she hears this,' and then when I go to look for you, you're — oh, Gran, the nights were terrible at first! I still make a seat for you. It's not so bad for you — you have the closeness still, for your mother is there, but I haven't —

I'm sorry, Gran. I didn't mean to talk like that. I promise I'll stop now. I'll try to be good. Look — I'm

all right again. We'll stand over here at the window together. We'll look out at the bog and I'll tell you all I
did to-day. I had my dinner with Mrs. Kehoe. She
talked a lot about you, Gran, and the grand things you
cooked for her wedding. Judy was in great form. She
says she likes being in service with Molly Nolan, but that
there'll never be anyone like yourself. John Kehoe is
giving Mike and Judy the gate-lodge when they get married after Christmas. Isn't that grand for them? It will
be nice and handy for Mike — only half-an-hour's walk
across the fields to Tim Coffey's place where he's working
now. Mrs. Kehoe was saying it's a pity I won't be here
to make her baby clothes for her. She's expecting for
Easter, Gran, and you should see the way John looks at
her and treats her. He's that careful of her he won't let
her wet a finger.

Look at the way the wind is tossing the trees about,
Gran. You always said the bog wind in November would
shave a pig. I felt it myself coming up the boreen. The
Johnny-McGoreys are done and there's hardly a haw left.
I don't suppose they'll have haws in Spain, will they,
Gran?

Isn't it funny to think of me going out to a job in Spain,
Gran, and I never farther than Kilkenny in my life?
You'll never believe me when I tell you who got the job
for me. Sister Liguori! She wrote to me after you —
after That happened. A lovely letter, Gran. It was sent
on to Kilkenny to me. She asked me to go down to Wicklow to see her. To tell you the truth, I wasn't on for
going, but my mother made me go — she said it would
take me out of myself. Sister was very nice to me, Gran,
which just shows you, doesn't it? But then I suppose

most people turn out to be nice once we get near enough
to them.

She asked me what I was going to do with myself now
that you were . . . you were . . . now that I wasn't living
in Ballyderrig any more. I told her the way things were,
how Derrymore had to be sold up to pay the bank and
how I had no taste for the business in Kilkenny. And
then she asked me if I'd like a job looking after three
children in Spain. I thought it might be as well to make
a clean break, Gran love, for since I can't be in Ballyderrig I might as well be in Australia. My mother and
Mr. Dunphy thought it would be nice for me, too. And
it won't be the same as if I were going to a real Spanish
house. The children won't be real foreigners to me for
Señora Basterra is a Wicklow girl herself and it seems she
met her husband when she was a governess in Madrid.
So I'm going to be a kind of a teacher after all, Gran.
Are you glad of that, love?

I said good-bye to them all in the town. I had to laugh
at Mickey O'Neill. He said I'd be coming home to marry
a Ballyderrig lad yet. "Court abroad, Deelyeen," he said,
"but marry at home." Miss Regan gave me a bag of
peppermints and Sarah Gorry gave me a book for a keepsake.

I had my tea at Leadbeater's. Miss Hope made sultana
pancakes for me and her father gave me a book about
Spain. I showed Miss Hope the locket and she thought
it was lovely. But I didn't tell her anything about the
closeness, Gran love. That was just for you and me,
wasn't it?

I left poor Mike below at the bottom of the boreen.
He got a loan of John Kehoe's pony and trap and he's

going to drive me to the station. Maybe I shouldn't keep him waiting any longer. Maybe I'd better be going.

Oh, Gran, Gran! Yes, I know I'm crying again, but I can't help it. There's something still to be said, love, and I'm not able to say it. I think I could say it if I'd my arms around you. Let me Gran — just for a minute. Like this —

Ah! you've frightened her now. She's gone. Nothing in the room but shadows and loneliness. You've frightened yourself, too. Down the stairs with you, quickly, quickly — don't forget to lock the door — And now down the boreen. Cry, cry — There's no need for you to say anything at all. The bog-wind is saying it all for you:

Good-bye, Ballyderrig. Good-bye, turf-banks and fields. Good-bye Granny Lynn and Miss Hope and Sarah and all of you. Good-bye, Gran.